I0665718

THE ABSOLUTION
OF ZERO

Meleisa Betts

Neighborhood Publishing

Copyright © 2013 by Meleisa Betts

ISBN: 978-0-615-75498-3

LCCN-2013900890

Printed in the United States of America

LIBRARY OF CONGRESS CATALOGING-IN
PUBLISHING DATA

Betts, Meleisa

The Absolution of Zero, Meleisa Betts, p. cm.

ISBN: 978-0-615-75498-3

LCCN-2013900890

Cover Design by SS Media and Meleisa Betts

"THERE ARE ONLY TWO KINDS
OF PEOPLE: THOSE WHO WILL DO
ANYTHING AT ALL TO GET WHAT
THEY WANT, AND EVERYBODY
ELSE."

David Englander, from the movie
Man on a Ledge.

{Chapter One}

This was my second visit to this place, an office building that looked as though it was built during the Depression Era in the 1920s. I had other things that I would rather be doing, like getting a pedicure, but the reality was that this meeting would accomplish something more than keeping a nail appointment.

My treatment by a psychologist had been ordered by the Department of Mental Health to determine my mental state or, more specifically, my competency to give a deposition in a pending court case. I am alleged to have been involved in or to have some knowledge of situations that I had no recollection of. It was as if I had amnesia concerning these events. I was not accused of anything; yet, I had been ordered not to leave the country as I was a person of interest in this case.

I was there to meet with a psychologist, Karen Oppenheim, who was charged with examining me. Karen was a blond, Jewish woman of average height and weight. She was in her mid-forties, and I guessed she was divorced since I saw pictures on her desk, during my first session, of two girls, both with brown hair and in their late teens, but none of a man. I wanted to ask her questions about that, but, right then, there were other, more important things, namely keeping myself free and clear.

Karen's office was on the fourth floor of the building in Suite 422. As you look around the office, it wouldn't be hard to picture some corrupt under the table deal with some wealthy racketeer and a shady detective. The ceiling was high and the light fixtures were antiquated. The building had a faint odor of old cedar. Nothing about it suggested that it had been renovated; rather, it was made functional and kept in decent condition. For the government, it served the purpose in that there was no need to spend extra tax dollars for something that was more trouble to the government than it was worth.

As I understood it, the government was in place to serve the community, but it was, also, a business. The more money they made in fines, the more they could keep by not spending it on fancy buildings or new police cars. This building was clearly a cost-cutting measure.

The first meeting between Karen and I set the stage for our future sessions. There was no way she could have prepared for what I had to say. I know my revelations hit her like an emotional avalanche.

My name is Angiel Royal. I think that my upbringing is precisely the reason why I find myself in the care of a mental health therapist. Some of the events of my life read like tall tales, yet it is the only life that I have known. I've lived a simple and a complex life mixed with the ridiculous and the sublime. In my mind, sometimes, there was a blurred or even invisible line and a series of enigmatic scenes that were like looking at clouds. Somewhere, in the town of my origin, lies my reason for being under a therapist's observation and care. For what that "treatment" is worth, I have nothing to lose.

I don't know where this life story will eventually lead, of course, but this is where it all began. I was born in a small town called Neverwills, Alabama. Neverwills was a place, at that time, where, if you sneezed, you could drive right through it. When people commented about passing through Neverwills, they would refer to it being so far in the country woods of Alabama that it was in the "sticks". When I was young, about the most exciting things I can remember are when someone got shot, got into a fight, or got pregnant, or when the state fair was in town. Regardless of this lack of surface excitement, Neverwills was a city of contradictions. One would think that such a small town, with squashing bugs being a game of sport for children, would be a quiet and unassuming place to grow up, but Neverwills was full of juicy intrigue. A great deal of that intrigue was centered on the Royal clan, my family, which was the epicenter of the soap opera known as Neverwills.

The Royal family was the preeminent family of the population of Neverwills, or, at least, I would like to think so. My father owned a lumber business and employed probably one third of the male population of the city. He was the King of Neverwills in my mind as his power over the population was clear and widespread. My father could do whatever he pleased in the city, and his influence extended to the female persuasion. It wasn't quite as clear to me as a child, but I later discovered that his reach into Neverwills' womankind was extensive.

My mother was his polar opposite, quiet and reserved. She was a stereotypical housewife, who took care of the kids. However, she assisted my father in his business to a degree, and I was spoiled to a great degree. My family was the envy of other families because of the things that my father could afford. I am sure that having virtually anything that I could imagine could have led to my perceptions of people with wealth being so much more desirable than the average Joe or Jane, yet I had no other reference point. I didn't know what it was like to want, so I could not relate to being poor. I can remember that I didn't look down on others, but I did feel as though I was "special."

One of my first memories as a child was having this thick, long, and kinky mane of hair. My mother used to straighten it with a hot comb, heated by the gas flame burners. Although it was necessary to do the hair straightening, it was uncomfortable because the heat from the stove made it seem as though it was two hundred degrees in that kitchen. First, my mother washed my hair thoroughly. She scrubbed and rubbed until my scalp was clean as could be and, sometimes, until it felt raw.

I vaguely remember sitting on the front porch outside until it dried. I hated to get it done because it hurt like hell each and every time. The only real benefit to me physically was the pleasurable sensation that my brain felt whenever someone touched my head. When Mother finished my hair, it was long and beautiful, at least, for a little while, anyways.

However, I can clearly remember my first grade teacher, Ms. Carmenza. She was a pretty lady, REALLY pretty, with an olive complexion and beautiful, bone straight brown hair. She would always ask me to ask my mother if it was okay for her to comb and style my hair.

I told my mother what Ms. Carmenza asked me, and Mother said yes to that seemingly innocent request. Ms. Carmenza would take me into the bathroom, and she would comb my hair and place it into a ponytail. She would tell me that I had such beautiful hair. When she finished working her magic, or so, I thought, my hair looked pretty. She would give me a little kiss, which eventually progressed to a sweet kiss on my little red lips. I didn't exactly know what was happening at the time, but I knew that the warm and soothing feeling that I felt as Ms. Carmenza stroked and combed my hair — plus, the payoff of the kiss — stirred something inside me.

To a child, that was an innocent act, and, to a mother,

at that time, there was little to contemplate, less the kiss portion of the story, which I never revealed. Yet, as I look back on the incidents, I seem to have blocked out much of what happened. I have asked myself if something sexual may have happened that made me block that memory, like the way the brain protects itself from trauma, but, try as I might, I get nothing more than a sweet memory. In fact, there seem to be blocks of things that I have only a wispy recollection of, but even will-o-the-wisps are no more tangible than fairies or the Boogie Man.

Something happened to Ms. Carmenza because she left in the middle of the school year, and we had a substitute teacher for the rest of the year. I never knew what happened to her, but I would long for her touch on my hair and for her moist kiss on my lips. In looking back, that may have been inappropriate, but I could not imagine anything that sweet being an evil thing.

My mother had tried to do her best with me, I know she did, but, with being a housewife, cooking, cleaning, and making sure all the other kids were okay, too, she did the best she could with my needs. The one thing that I knew for certain was that there was a huge difference in how I felt when Ms. Carmenza attended to my kinky strands. The feeling was as opposite as getting a hug from your distant uncle, as was my feeling with Mama versus the rush that you feel on Christmas morning, which was what I experienced with Ms. Carmenza.

Every day, when I got home from school, I would run to my room and get my match stems, which were my favorite toys, out of their special hiding place. I had every toy that a child could ever desire, but the matchsticks had that certain "something". They were little, inane pieces of burnt wood, that, for no apparent reason that I could understand at that time, I had an obsession over. But looking back, it could have had everything to do with my personality trait of trying to get or make something out of literally nothing or, maybe, even a darker tendency to destroy things by burning them to a crisp. Whatever the reason, I kept them in a secret place because I knew that my father, who was a stern disciplinarian, didn't want me in my room playing with them.

After creating a sufficient collection of the burned sticks, I would play with the matches for hours at a time. I'm sure that, to some, it would appear ridiculous that I was using what most people would consider garbage in order to amuse myself.

Even though she could smell the sulfur aroma coming from my room and my clothes, Mama never said anything to me at all about this, and I don't even know if she really cared about what I was secretly doing, as long as I was quiet and happy.

At that time, my father was smoking cigars, and Mama was smoking cigarettes, so there was always a ready supply of the inexpensive objects of my affection. It wasn't just the fire aspect of matches but, also, what my imagination could use the singed little wooden sticks for. My parents used the hardwood matches that came in a square box. Whenever they threw one away, I would run and get it to add to my already incinerated collection.

In my overactive and inventive mind, I would recreate them as men or women. The ones that burned to the quick at the round top were men with very little hair. The ones that burned a little and were quickly extinguished were women with long hair. For some reason, I would always imagine them to be beautiful. Although all the matches smelled of sulfur, I imagined that the smell was attributed only to the male matchsticks; while, the female sticks emitted the fragrance of a sweet perfume. The ones that had burned really low were the children, and the boxes that contained the matches were the cars. Sometimes, I would put them together as if they were a family, and the boxes would serve as the family's vehicle.

Then, I would separate the mother and father matchsticks, and the father would be placed on top of the mother, so they could have sex. How I knew that part of the equation eludes me. As far as I can recollect, the older kids must have said something about that; in fact, I can vaguely remember an argument by two boys where one of them said, "Yeah, fuck, just like your mamma and daddy do. That's how you got here, stupid."

I would play with my "toys" from the moment that I got off of the school bus at 3:15 in the afternoon until Daddy came home at around five or six P.M. My mother would have his food on the table like clockwork. I can hear Daddy's voice shouting, "Where's Angiel? Is she back there with them damn matches?" Even today, in my mind, I can hear him screaming, "Angiel, get your ass out that room!"

I would reluctantly put the matchsticks away. I hid them as well as I could from my father, given the circumstances. I knew that, when I wasn't inside the house, he was trying to find them, but, try as he might, he never could. I was not going to stop playing with the matches, as they were like an addiction to me, something I was compelled to keep doing. Nowadays, psychologists call it Obsessive-Compulsive Disorder, but I was not going to give them up on my own.

My parents eventually bought me Barbie and Ken dolls and an action figure named Big Jim for my birthdays and Christmas. I would take them into my inner sanctuary and invariably pretended they were having sex like the match families. Yes, I did have a working knowledge, as I stated before, of what sex was at the age of seven, but I was a little fuzzy about the mechanics. Eventually, I was able to stray away, to a degree, from the match stems, and I turned my attention to the little dolls. Big Jim ended up breaking his rubberized plastic legs, so I unceremoniously buried him in the backyard. They all, eventually, ended up losing a body part or two, so I just buried them, too. Maybe this ritual meant something because I refused to just throw them in the trash. I had to entomb them, as though they were actually flesh and blood that was being returned to their origins. The only thing that was added to each ritual was that the doll's remains would be burned, which went to my belief that I was always compelled to use the matches. The odd thing that I have yet to fathom is why.

A few years passed, and my mind went from fancying items such as matchsticks to movie projectors, pianos, and whatever else drew my attention. Eventually, I would receive whatever it was that was the object of my desire, usually sooner rather than later. I had everything that a girl could want. I didn't really realize how fortunate I was at the time. However, this act by my parents of fulfilling my every whim may have set the stage for my life. In fact, I am sure that it had a great influence.

I kept to myself most of the time as a child. I was always interested in what I could do or create. I was a bit weird. I have to admit that. I loved television almost as much as my dolls and, of course, my matchsticks.

We had one television, and it had only two channels that could be received in our area. Whenever one channel became fuzzy, regardless of the weather conditions, one of us would have to go outside and turn the antenna. If we woke Daddy up during the commotion, we had to turn the television off. It didn't matter if we were in the middle of a good movie or a dull commercial. If he had to tell us to turn the television off more than once, we were in big trouble. A whipping with his belt would have been the order of the moment. There was no such thing as a "time out" at the time, just a good, old-fashioned ass beating.

I seemed to be obsessed with obsessions. Later, music became my compulsive focus. I cannot remember one instance when I didn't have music playing in my room. I had a big stereo set with a record player, a radio, and an eight track player. Often, I would forget and leave it on whenever I went outside. By that time, I had become more sociable. I liked to go outside to watch my brothers, Blaine and Carlton, wash their motorcycles or play basketball with their friends. There were always a lot of people playing ball or just goofing off. It was a lot more fun than my previous hermetic lifestyle.

One day, I had forgotten to turn off my stereo when I left to go to do something, the details of what it was I can't remember. The one thing I do recall vividly was that Daddy had warned me before not to leave it playing while I was not in the house. When I came back inside, Daddy had gotten a knife and cut the cord to my stereo! But, when he cut the cord, he had dropped the end that was connected to the power outlet, so the frayed wires started a fire that engulfed the curtains in my room. That was what he said was the reason.

Daddy managed to put the blaze out before the

whole house caught on fire. He took the cord and plug out of the outlet and kept it to keep me from taping the wires back together and using the stereo once more. I was so sad. I went to tell Mama, and she just shook her head.

I can only guess that that incident was the moment that internalized that fire can change things forever. For some unknown reason, the scene of the fire and the memory of my father hacking my stereo cord into pieces made me crave my box of matches like a drunk who loved alcohol. I didn't want candy or a soda or any of the toys and dolls that I had. I just wanted to go to my room and burn matchsticks, watch the flame go out, and smell the sulfur that came from the extinguished head.

That night, I was awakened from my sleep by my mother. She said that I was having a nightmare. My mother said that I was screaming, "The man in the woods! The man in the woods!"

{Chapter 2}

In the fourth grade, I had a teacher named Mrs. Darlington. Every day, I would gaze at her because I had fallen in love. I was as in love with Ms. Darlington as any eight-year-old could be with a woman who was probably twenty years older than me. I made it a point to do whatever it took to be in her presence. If it meant cleaning erasers or asking her questions, whatever it took, I did it. In my childishly, love-struck mind, it didn't really matter that society said that girls should like boys. If I could have found a way to have married the already married Mrs. Darlington, I would have. I was an eight-year-old girl who was fully aware that I was in love with a woman! The paradox is that I can recall that I wanted to become her husband and screw the daylights out of her, but I wanted to be a woman doing it. I guess that makes as much sense as anything else in my life up to this point.

Mrs. Darlington was gorgeous. She had luminous bluish-gray eyes that seemed too beautiful to be real, long brunette hair, a flawless complexion, and lips that were constantly thick with red lipstick. I, also, knew that there were complete female opposites of my fascination with Mrs. Darlington.

While in the sixth grade, I was playing outside during my physical education class. I was far away from the rest of the class. I guess I was too far away from my teacher. This teacher, for whom I didn't have a Mrs. Darlington-type affinity, sent another student to tell me to come closer to the rest of the class because I had wandered into an area where a child had allegedly been kidnapped years ago. The fact that I can't remember her name speaks volumes as to how unappealing and nondescript she was. She looked like she could have been named Miss Crabapple, so I will use that as her name.

"Miss Crabapple said that you are too far and that you need to come closer."

"Tell that ugly, fat bitch that I said to go to hell. She can just kiss my ass. Fuck her and you, too," I said, glaring at the girl.

I really didn't mean that, not the go to hell part, but I did mean the ugly, fat bitch part. I don't really know why she ran and told the teacher exactly what I said, other than to get me into trouble. I don't know exactly why I had that outburst, but it came out of me as if from nowhere. I was called to the principal's office because of that statement and rightfully so.

The teacher and the principal, Mr. Scott, who was a fat, balding drunk who literally reeked of bourbon every day, called my mother and told her what I had said as I sat in a wooden chair in his stale, cigar-reeking office. She had to come to the school with me the next day, or I would be suspended.

When I got home, I told my mother what happened, but, of course, I conveniently left off the profanity. I tried to sound as angelic as possible to coincide with my name because that was the way that my mother tended to view me. She agreed that what was said was between two children, that it should have stayed that way, and that the girl didn't have to go back to the teacher with that comment. She, also, agreed that it was clear that the girl was trying to get me into trouble, but, in order to prevent me from being suspended, my mother agreed to allow the principal to keep me after school for one hour, which would last for two months. I thought that was harsh at the time, but my mother had few options since I was guilty.

It wasn't quite clear to me then, but, in looking back on that time, I was formulating my opinion that it wasn't just about the women and my desire for females. It was more than just the superficial; it was the kindness in them, as was manifested in my mother, that I was most attracted to and looked for. In my pre-adolescent mind, Mr. Scott was just a vile, disgusting male figurehead, who may have, in part, impacted some of my opinions of men. The teacher known as Miss Crabapple, besides being unattractive, seemed to view me as more of an inconvenient nuisance than a student. So, my affinity for her was about the same as my feelings for Mr. Scott. In short, I wasn't just attracted to all women but to the ones who were kind and compassionate, as well as attractive and nurturing. I didn't always follow that paradigm in later life, but, for the most part, I did.

While driving home from school after the meeting with the principal, I looked over at Mama and began to cry and plead, "Mama, please don't tell Daddy!"

I tried to look as innocent and pathetic as I could

muster.

"I won't, baby, but you must not use those types of words anymore."

She looked at me with sympathy, so I knew that I had gotten to her.

"I won't, Mama. I promise," I sniffed, trying to look doe-eyed and sincere, but I knew that I had meant everything that I'd said and done.

I, also, knew that Daddy would beat the hell out of me regardless of what my mother said. Because she knew that was the case, she didn't say a word to him about my brush with suspension, and I was so glad. I think, in many ways, my mother was my model of what was worthy and noble about womanhood. She was quiet but strong, soft, beautiful, and feminine. Through her, I realized, not only what I wanted, but what I didn't want in either friends or relationships. I wanted someone who would keep my confidence and best interest at heart and shun those who tried to harm or use me.

If only if I had paid closer attention to the lessons that she had tried to teach me, I may have saved myself some future heartache. Instead, I chose the other aspect of my personality, which would be pivotal in my life: my ability to manipulate the minds of people using whatever tactics that worked, be it sensuality, threats, the allure of wealth, or just downright intimidation. That was my superpower — to use anything at all to get everything that I wanted. I think it's time to find out why.

As I entered the office, I encountered the receptionist, who was gorgeous. Her raven hair was pulled back into a ponytail and a side-swept bang cascaded across her face from left to right. An oversized pair of glasses completed the ensemble, which accentuated pouty lips kissed with pink gloss. She smiled before she addressed me.

"Hello, Ms. Royal. Please sign in, and Dr. Oppenheim will see you shortly." It was not lost on me that the receptionist remembered my name.

After I signed the ledger, I looked up at her. She was still making eye contact, as though she was communicating something. I could see that there was a connection of some sort. I didn't acknowledge the obvious, but I simply smiled at her and sat down in one of the ancient, mahogany colored chairs in the waiting area.

There is a tremendously erroneous myth about the ability of a person to will or talk themselves out of their sexual orientation. Some religious figures talk about the "demon" of homosexuality. The reality is that the choice of whether or not one chooses to gravitate toward men or women is inherent. It is a feeling, desire, or affinity that is inborn. I knew very early in my life that I found women fascinating. I have always loved the softness of women, how they have a fragrance that is vastly different than that of men, even when they are musky with the scent of effort and perspiration. It was no more of a choice for me to like women than it was for me to decide whether or not I would be born with a penis or a vagina. Who would choose a sexual orientation that would cause instant vilification by society? I would be an absolute idiot to make such a choice given the social ramifications. I didn't know what my sexual orientation was at age seven, eight, or nine years old. But I could tell, as early as I could remember, that I was most happy in the presence of women.

I was escorted to the psychiatrist's office by the receptionist. After entering the office, I sat down in the mahogany chair, which was an item that I figured I had better get accustomed to. After about eight minutes or so, Dr. Oppenheim or Karen, which she had requested that I call her in our previous session, entered the room. Karen arrived in the room with my file in hand, and, after she had read over her previous notes for a short time, she began.

"So, let's resume our conversation from the point where we ended the previous session. You were discussing your sexuality at that time. You said that you pretty much knew that you were a lesbian by the time you were about eight or nine years old, right? Why do you think that is an important point of discussion, Angiel?" Karen asked.

"I didn't know that much about it, but I do know that I loved women in more than a casual way. At that time, in the early seventies, there was no talk of lesbians. They were called 'bull daggers', 'dikes', and many other names, and those names described the rough, manly looking women who had their own girlfriends. I can't remember more than one or two women who were clearly 'out' during that time in Neverwills. Of course, I wouldn't identify with them in that regard either. The fact that I liked females was just, you know, like a natural thing to me," I said.

"I understand completely. Just like how I knew that I liked boys. I didn't know how to have sex at eight or nine, but I knew that my sexuality pointed in the direction of males. I can see that clearly," Karen said.

"See, one of the problems is that, most of the time,

no one is one hundred percent of anything. I remember reading in *The Kinsey Reports* on sexuality that they said something like that. Sort of like on a scale of zero to one hundred, a man or woman, depending on what you are measuring, is either absolutely or degrees of something on that scale," I said.

"I don't quite follow you. I read the books, but I don't recall that. Please elaborate," Karen said.

I replied, "Okay. Say the scale is measuring homosexuality on a one hundred point scale. A man or woman who is completely heterosexual is a zero, meaning that they have no desires or inclinations toward the same sex. The thought of being with someone of their same sex is sickening to them. On the other end of the scale is the one hundred percent homosexual man or woman who has nothing but same-sex desires. Many women who are completely homosexual have never ever been penetrated by a penis and find that act revolting. They are lesbian "virgins" forever. The one hundred percent homosexual man is the same. They have never been with or desired women. The thought of kissing a woman or having sex with her is enough to make them gag. All of their sexuality is geared toward men.

Then, you have degrees of how much someone is or isn't in terms of sexuality. For example, I am probably eighty percent homosexual since I have slept with men and find qualities in them that are appealing. Don't get that statement confused, though. Just because I'm not repulsed by them, doesn't mean that I have to have them. I crave women, and that is the difference. Another example is that a man who is ninety percent heterosexual could find himself attracted to a transsexual who looks like a woman. That ten percent of him that would have sex with a man who lives life as a woman is why he isn't considered one hundred percent heterosexual. That's just what I believe, that the majority of normal people are not 100% in either direction. That's not to call homosexual people abnormal; it's just that I don't believe that 100% homosexuality is the norm, even in the gay community. Does that make sense to you?" I asked.

"Your rationale makes perfect sense in an anecdotal way, although conventional psychiatry does not make such distinctions. I guess that, in an extreme case, if no men were around, I could be physically attracted to a woman who looked very much like a man and have sex with her, but she would have to look like George Clooney," Karen joked. We both laughed at that comment for about a minute.

Then, I resumed.

"See, I hear people use terms like bisexuality for anyone who can have sex with either gender. Personally, I think that it is complete bullshit. It's like the comedian Richard Pryor once said, 'Either you suck dicks, or you don't.' That's the truth. I am a lesbian who doesn't mind having sex with men on occasion, but I am still a homosexual. I'm not split down the middle fifty-fifty, and I believe that most people aren't. There are probably a few people in the world who are split in their sexuality, if you go by my sliding scale theory. In the vast majority of cases, the person is either heterosexual or homosexual from birth. The question is whether or not they are completely one way or another, and then how close to that one hundred percent figure are they," I said.

"Your summary of your theory is very well thought out and makes more sense than a lot of the theories that my contemporaries have subscribed to," Karen said.

"I'm just keeping it real and truthful, Karen. I am a lesbian. I was born this way. I didn't choose this feeling. It more or less chose me. I'm not ashamed of it because my sexuality is just a part of who I am. Why lie about it or sugarcoat things? I am a homosexual who likes women, not a bisexual, or any other label that could mislead someone," I said. "The only thing that makes me different than a lot of lesbians is that, even though I have sex with men in very conventional ways, for some reason, I like to be the 'man' with women."

"Of course, that statement requires elaboration," Karen said.

"Okay, it's like this. I know this will be somewhat confusing, but I like masculine men, and I have done everything that a normal heterosexual woman would: sex, blow jobs, whatever, but not anal sex. That's where I draw the line. With women, it's the opposite. I will give oral sex, but I don't care to get it. I will use strap-on dildos to screw women like men screw them, but I cannot stand for that to be done to me by another woman. It should make sense that, if I could have sex with a penis being inside of me, then I could and would like the same from a woman, but I am the aggressor and not the receiver with women, ever."

"Okay. Thank you for the lesson on sexuality, Dr. Royal, but now it's time to continue," Karen quipped.

Something happened that caused a dark cloud to come over me. It took years for me to come to terms with it and to quantify it. Actually, I say that I have come to terms with it, but that isn't true since it is something that is dogging me, and it keeps me from being happy.

Even though I had everything that a girl could ask for in terms of material trappings, for the most part, my social interactions were more introverted than gregariously extroverted, which I longed for them to be. I would become less so later in life, but, at that time, darkness persisted and sad times prevailed, even to the point that at ten years of age, I tried to kill myself, and, again, for reasons that escaped me. Fortunately, for me, I was not skilled in the art of self-poisoning. I took twenty antibiotic capsules in order to perform the deed. I had no idea that all I did was prevent myself from catching a cold or bolster my defenses against infection. There was something that happened to me back in my early years that had really fucked up my psyche, but, as I said, I can't, for some reason, recall what that was.

My mother had to get permission from Daddy whenever she wanted to drive the prized family car, a Cadillac. She wanted to use it to drive me to my school one morning in order to speak to my teachers about my behavior. She believed that they might shed some light on my destructive behavior, but they would have had to have found some magic key or some golden incantation to help me.

Usually, she wasn't allowed to drive it. The majority of the time, only Daddy drove it, while she sat in the passenger's seat, almost like it was a ritual of dominance of sorts. He would hide the keys to the car in his office, so she couldn't sneak and drive his prized automobile without him knowing. I never completely understood their dynamic, but I believe that Daddy knew that my mother was beautiful, and he wanted to control her movement, at the house and in general. He figured that a woman's place was the age-old belief of cooking, cleaning, and having babies. The latter he made sure of because, as I stated, there were six of us, at least, to my knowledge.

I'm sure that my father's opinions of women, also, shaped my view of men somewhat. This belief, if my assumptions are correct on how he viewed women, seemed in opposition to what I felt as a female. The contradiction was that he, as well as many other men that had lived for thousands of years, shared the image in their psyche, of a woman being barefoot and pregnant, despite the fact that he/they were running around cavorting with other women.

My father was certainly guilty of this double standard

as he cheated on my mother with a harem of women, while his workers were in the woods doing their jobs. Sometimes, he would be sleeping with those very employees' wives, while they were toiling and sweating away in the forest. It was more than okay for him to have both his slice of the proverbial cake and slices of fifteen or more men's cakes, too. He would have been incensed to the point of physical violence if my mother had done to him what he had done to her.

All of the people involved with the incident, meaning me, my mother, and my teachers, met at the principal's office that day. I apologized to the teachers, although, inside of my mind, I knew that those words were as thin as paper. My mother met with my teachers in a separate meeting away from me in order to ask about my demeanor in class. She listened as they told of my acting out, as well as how good of a student I could be at times. My mother sat and listened, nodded a few times, said thank you to the principal and Ms. Crabtree, and that was that.

It was all over. My mother and the teachers knew no more of my psyche and had no more of an answer than they did before. The best part, as far as I was concerned, was that my mother did all of this in secret, and Daddy never knew a word of it. To this day, I probably value trust and confidentiality in my relationships more than any other attribute because of my mother. In looking back, if one of them had suggested that I go to a psychiatrist or therapist, then maybe my life may have been a lot different.

I visited my grandmother every weekend. I loved my grandma. Her name was Eliza. Well, to be more accurate her name was Elizabeth, but she was called Eliza for short. I often wondered why she had an outhouse, a wood stove, and a fireplace when indoor plumbing was prevalent everywhere. Maybe, it was because she was simple country folk. That explanation was more than enough for me. My older sister, Rebecca, lived with Grandma Eliza at the time. When I was a little older, maybe about ten or so, I asked my mother why Rebecca lived with Grandma.

Mama, then, gave me a vague reason which was, "Rebecca doesn't remember this, because she was young at the time, but, eight or nine years ago, she asked me if she could live with your Grandma. She kept saying that she was tired of the man in the woods messing with her."

I don't know anything about a man in the woods, but there was an urban myth about a thing or man that people called "Shack Sally" who snatched kids. Nobody could give a definitive description of Shack Sally. He ranged from man to animal-like. So, if in fact he or it existed, maybe, he was either a hillbilly or some incarnation of Bigfoot. Whatever the reason, Rebecca was terrified to live at our home.

During that time my father wasn't doing as well financially because he had lost some business. My oldest sisters and brothers didn't have it as well as me for some reason, but Rebecca was the exception. She had her own humongous playhouse on the side of Grandma's house. It was filled with toys and a big blue bicycle. The playhouse was bigger than a bedroom in some houses which seemed to be a curious combination, given the Stone Age surroundings of my grandmother's. Still, no one ever spoke about the oddity of the "man in the woods" comments that Rebecca had made or the fact that she was living with our grandmother. This was my family's version of the "white elephant in the room."

Visiting my grandmother for a sleepover was like taking a trip back to the 1800s. Our breakfast ritual was to have yellow grits in the morning. She cooked all of our food under a fire, even in the sweltering heat of the dog days of summer.

We took baths in a small bowl, which took the place of the large tubs we were accustomed to. We were not terribly inconvenienced by doing so. We got our drinking water and bathing water from a pump in the backyard. The water was always surprisingly good and cold, even during those dog days in August. I used to wonder why Daddy didn't help Grandma fix her house up since his financial position eventually improved and since Rebecca lived with her.

One day, I asked my mother, "Why won't Daddy help Grandma? She is living in that old house and taking care of Rebecca."

Mama replied, "I asked your daddy to help my mother, and he flatly said that he wouldn't. I told him, if you can't help my mother with anything, then you will not be helping your parents."

I know that she meant that at the time that she had said it, but she did not have the heart to treat anyone badly. In her mind, though, it was right for right and wrong for wrong, which equaled fair treatment. She said that she meant just what she had said even though I was not so sure, given her disposition. Sadly, neither of the relatives on either side received any help from our family as per that edict. I learned from her that even the softest and kindest of people have to take a hard line in life or they will be constantly pushed around and mistreated. Through her, I deduced that those people who would not stand up for themselves would eventually become victims. Although I knew this was not the nature of her indirect message, I would use that information in the future to manipulate those who wouldn't fight back.

Grandma Eliza passed away when I was ten years old. Two months after she had passed away, I saw her spirit sitting on my mother's bed looking at me. I believe she appeared because, earlier that evening, I had snuck over to my brother-in-law's party that was going on next door to us and secretly drank three big swallows of some strong beer. I knew that I had no business doing that being a child, although a precocious one. Honestly, in looking back, that alcohol could have factored into my vision, but I doubt that very seriously since I would see things while not having had anything at all. I had been having such visions for as long as I could remember. I could have been hallucinating like a schizophrenic does, but I will swear that I was as lucid as anyone when I had those visions.

At Grandma Eliza's funeral, I didn't sit in the front. Rather, I sat at the back of the church because I didn't want to see her. I was hurt, but that wasn't the reason that I chose to sit in back. I was scared of dead people. I have been scared every since I was old enough to know what it meant to pass away. Probably, because at that point, I understood that what I was seeing were earthbound spirits. I never slept with the lights off. Even today, I have to have a certain amount of light in my bedroom at night. The only time I sleep with the lights off is when someone is staying the night with me and sleeping in the same bed, and, even then, I prefer a little light.

My mother told me that when I was born, there was a "veil" over my face, which was a thin membrane. There is a belief by spiritualists that when a child is born with a veil that he or she has "the shining". The shining is the ability to see spirits, and I have seen many since childhood. Some of the spirits will, occasionally, make themselves apparent to me in the daylight, but they, usually, occur when the lights in the room are either dimmed to near dark or when there is total darkness. It is frightening to me to turn out the lights in a room because the cavalcade of spirits will begin to cascade back and forth through the room.

My mother's uncle had a stroke. He was in Selma, Alabama when it happened, so Mama drove to the hospital and brought him to our home. I only knew him as Uncle Sun.

As soon as Daddy got home and found my uncle there, I heard him say to my mother, "He can't stay here."

My mother had to put Uncle Sun in a nursing home in Neverwills. She reiterated to Daddy as before that "If none of my people can stay here, none of your people can stay here." Since her uncle, who really needed help, was turned away, then everyone, whether immediate family or distant, would be turned away, also. She was just a person that believed in treating people the same, regardless of status.

I guess this was why my Grandfather James, my daddy's father, never lived with us after his wife, Grandma Martha, passed away. Eventually, he became much too old to continue caring for himself. He had to live with his other sons at one time or another but never with us. This proved to me that my father had hardened my mother with his stance against my mother's relatives, and she did what I never expected. I supported her because she was right in giving back to my father what he gave, even though it may have affected Grandfather James. The difference was that he had somewhere to go, unlike my uncle. I never had the close relationship that I wish I could have had with

Grandfather James. Unfortunately, I was too young to remember the details behind Grandmother Martha's passing, yet I can remember her being very sick. As I mentally fast-forward to the time when I was about seventeen years of age, Grandfather James had begun to come by to see Daddy a lot, each time with one of his other sons. Whenever he came by to visit us, and, after a little while of sitting on the porch, he would always say, "Angiel, come on and take me for a ride."

I would always say, "Okay, Granddaddy." I was driving a car at the tender age of fourteen.

"You are kidding me, right? How was a fourteen-year-old driving a car in a city?" Karen asked, looking down at me over the top of her glasses.

"I did, and it was known in the city, even to the sheriff," I said proudly.

The thing is that I never did stop by whichever uncle's house Granddaddy was living with at the time to pick him up and take him for a ride. I would gladly take him for a ride when he visited our home. I could have easily stopped by wherever he was living at the time, but, for no reason that I can fathom, I never did. Some days, I passed right by Uncle Will's, where he spent the majority of his later years, and Uncle Will and my grandfather would be sitting right out on the front porch of the house, as big as the sun, and I would blow my horn and keep on motoring down the road. I have lived with that regret every day of my life for some odd reason, be it from guilt, remorse, or for some reason that I will never know. But as I reflect on that particular part of my past, it was at that time in my life, where I was focused on women in almost every aspect of my awareness and waking thoughts. Still, if I am being honest about it, I just never wanted to do much of anything that didn't serve my purposes. At that time, my mind was focused on women.

My obsession with all things female was at the point where I probably shortchanged the male figures in my life, particularly Grandfather James. At times such as now, I ponder how these relationships, or lack of them, have shaped my sensibilities and affected my karma, if they have at all. The thing that I am convinced of is that my father's self-centeredness was absorbed by my subconscious. That may have caused all of us to miss out on some of my oldest family members spending their golden years with us and the stories that they may have held.

Without a doubt, my self-centeredness during most of

my life was a direct reflection on what I had seen in my father.

{Chapter 3}

I can remember back when I was an attractive, adolescent girl of thirteen when these two crazy-assed boys, one a white boy and the other a black boy, came racing down the sidewalk. They plowed right over me as if I wasn't standing there at all. The result of the collision was that my entire chin was skinned and raw for months until it finally healed.

That incident didn't help my opinion of boys, who I thought were generally stupid and stinky like any pubescent girl would or should. I knew that it was dictated by society for me to like boys, but my subconscious was drawing the inference. "You see, those boys will only be trouble and pain. A sweet and soft woman would never hurt you that way." I was not anti-males at that point by a long shot, but it was starting to become clearer to me, more than at any other time, that I vastly preferred women.

However, there would be no real outlet for my desires for women until a little later, a year later to be precise. At that particular time, I could only fantasize about females until an opportunity to act on my desires came to fruition.

It was around that same point in time when I became aware that my daddy had illicit (but what was widely known among the local people) relationships within a family that had seven sisters, the Littlefield girls. I guess you could call my daddy a true womanizer since, eventually, he had gotten twenty or more women in Neverwills, who were stupid enough, to sleep with him. They all were just a bunch of money-grubbing whores, plain and simple. I guess I chose to go with the stupid whore assessment because it made me feel a lot better, but I do have to admit that my father did have the qualities most women desired. He was tall, dark, handsome, and financially well off.

At the time, he was dating Jenny Littlefield, the oldest of the very attractive Littlefield women. She had a nice, thickly built figure, large breasts, and raven hair that was long and shiny. She had no shortage of males or, I would even expect, female admirers in Neverwills. Jenny didn't like my mother one bit, and she made it known to all who would listen. This was the dynamic that I could never figure out because Jenny was the adulterer and not the victim.

It should be noted that all the women in that family were absolutely gorgeous and the men were handsome as hell. Their mother was a little, white-as-a-sheet woman, and their father was as tall, dark, and handsome as my dad was tall, dark, and handsome. Outside of the fact that my mother was not pale as bleached flour as was the matriarch of the Littlefield clan, there were several similarities between our two warring factions. In my mind, none of the animosity, as well as the relationships, made any sense. Eventually, even I would play a role in that very contradiction.

Jenny's husband, Grizzly, worked for my dad as a saw man in my father's lumber company. Jenny controlled virtually everything that Grizzly did. She told him when to eat, sleep, work, fuck, and everything in between. Grizzly surely knew that Jenny was sleeping with my daddy, but, apparently, a job was more important than self-esteem. It had to just tear him up on the inside, knowing that his boss was screwing his wife, but he needed a paycheck. All the husbands of the sisters knew about their wives sleeping with my dad, and none of them did a damn thing about stopping it. He had them all too paralyzed to act against him, because, if they pissed him off, they could easily be found homeless and trying to find a way to fill the empty bellies of their wives and children. It was a cold-blooded catch-22 situation, which they were more or less stuck into accepting. I guess the lesson I learned was to press the advantage that I held over a situation to get what I wanted. I most certainly have used that tactic several times in business, as well as in my personal life.

Jenny coerced her two youngest nieces, Sandra and Delilah, to attack me and beat me up after school, maybe out of spite and hatred over my mother, but it was supposedly over a boy. I had heard they were going to fight me the night before through my friend Becky. She told me what she'd heard, so I was prepared for them with a knife that I had hidden in my book bag the night before. I was dating a guy named Robbie at the time, and Sandra had made a claim for as her boyfriend. He was the first male I had actually decided to "go with" at the age of thirteen. I still knew that I really desired girls, but, paradoxically, I was in love with Robbie as much as my budding, but sexually conflicted thirteen-year-old mind could comprehend loving a male. In retrospect, Sandra Littlefield was also in love with him. In actuality, she may have truly been in love with Robbie, whereas I was going through the motions of doing what I was supposed to do as dictated by society. I wanted girls, but I knew that I was supposed to like boys as the social mandate required.

That next day, Sandra and her sister Delilah were standing at the bus stop waiting for me. Delilah had gone over to Robbie's motorcycle, which was parked outside of the school, and taken his helmet off of the handlebar. She had it in her hand. It was clear that she was going to use it on me. They were waiting to assault me, and that was clear, too. All the while, they were talking big shit about how they were going to mess me up. I had my hand inside my little green bag that hung from my shoulder. My fingers were wrapped around my red knife, ready to inflict some major hurt on those two heifers. I had gotten the knife out of my mother's drawer the night before. She had won it at the fair that came to town once a year. No one ever questioned what an odd as hell prize it was because winning was winning. I told Mother nothing about what Becky had told me.

When Sandra and Delilah started talking about what they were planning to do to me, I just stood there, eyeing the both of them. Sandra, suddenly, pushed me. Then, I pulled out the knife and stuck it in her right arm. The bitch started crying and bleeding. A split second later, I felt a blow to my head. Delilah had hit me with the motorcycle helmet. She had used it as a weapon, just as I had surmised.

I fell to the concrete pavement. Delilah, then, jumped on top of me and pulled my hair. All I could hear was her screaming, "You stabbed my sister!"

What seemed like seconds later, Mr. Joe, my favorite bus driver, and another bus driver snatched Delilah off of me. They came to my rescue like knights in shining armor. Mr. Joe put me on the bus and then retrieved his baseball bat from out of the bus and put an end to the lopsided affair once and for all. You see, the Littlefield family was known in all of the surrounding areas for jumping on and outnumbering people. They jumped on people in groups. They kicked people's doors down. They beat asses and didn't call names. The women in that family were such fighters that they were known for later whipping their husbands' asses.

This was a new day for me because they'd really beat my ass, even though I had stabbed Sandra. However, the truth was that only God, my mother, and my cousin Diane knew that when Delilah hit me on the head with that helmet, I had lost my bladder and peed on myself. It was a good thing that no one could see it because my green nylon pants camouflaged the stain of the accident. The incident happened in front of virtually the whole population of our small hamlet. It stood to reason that the entire town knew about it. The news spread like wildfire all over Neverwills, Alabama. People were so happy to see me when we went to town. Although, for the sake of self-consciousness, I didn't come back to town until after the plug of hair I had lost during the fight had grown back on the top of my head. I wore a cap for months.

Everybody said, "We are so glad you beat that girl. They are bullies, but you showed 'em." I didn't say anything whenever people congratulated me. I knew that they were basing their judgment on who won or lost on the stabbing. They didn't know about my loss of bladder control or the plug of hair that took nearly two months to grow back. They didn't see the bruises all over my body that those bitches had managed to inflict. Even to this day, I have these headaches all the time because of that vicious blow to my head.

Even though I was not the aggressor and was only

defending myself like anyone else would, I was the one who was kicked out of school for the remainder of the school year. Those evil little demons, Delilah and Sandra, were allowed to stay in school.

My mother demanded and got the keys to the Cadillac from my father. He didn't say one damn word because he knew that this mess was because of Jenny Littlefield. The next day, my mother drove me to another school in another county called Fitchburg High. I went to school every day at Fitchburg, and my mother drove me in my father's precious Cadillac. My mother told me that, if someone asked me why I was there, I was not to say a word. I didn't say one word about why I was going to school there, not that anyone ever asked me. I so enjoyed the kids there. I wouldn't know any of them if I saw them today, but they were all so sweet.

At the end of the school year, I tried to re-enroll in my former high school. I was told by those bastards that masqueraded as Marion County High officials that they could not accept my grades from another school because I had been expelled from Neverwills High School. They claimed that I was not eligible to be in any school for the rest of that year. Because of this ass-backwards decision, I had to go to summer school to make up my grades. The

Littlefield sisters were probably screwing the principal for him to come up with that decision. Although that was just another example of my wild imagination at work, I'm sure it was possible given their slutty nature.

They sure as hell were screwing the hell out of the deputy sheriff of the county. This was widely attested to and accepted among the people of the town. His name was Luther Roy, Sr., and they made no bones about screwing him at all. In fact, he pompously came to our house the afternoon right after the incident happened to try and serve me a warrant. It wasn't hard to figure out that the Littlefield bitches were behind this.

My oldest brother Sol stood up to him and said, "You go tell them heifers that, if they take out a warrant against Angiel, we will take one out against Sandra and Delilah!"

Sol stood tall on the steps of our house like he was the sheriff. He was six feet one and about two hundred pounds, so he looked the part of an intimidator.

Luther quickly jumped into his sheriff's car and blazed down to Harvey Drive. I, then, imagined him telling Jenny what Sol had barked at him. My daddy was sitting right there in the garage as all of this unfolded. He never once opened his mouth, probably because he had a somewhat twisted conflict of interest, seeing as how he was shoving his penis up into Jenny on a regular basis. Despite all of the fuss and hoopla, we never heard anything else concerning the warrant.

My mother later told my daddy, "You better tell your whores that they can have your sorry ass, but they better not mess with my children, or I will get them all!" She basically told him he had better get his women under control or she would do it for him. He did control them better after that statement because he knew that my mother was not playing around.

I have little doubt that these incidents, with all of the conflicted emotions and subtexts, have made an indelible impression on my consciousness and even my subconscious mind. It may have even warped my perception of life and sexuality in some abstract way. Oh, well, if that is the case, then I can only do the best I can with what I'm left with. For the most part, for whatever reason, I tended to do the worst of things at times.

"You had a lot of incredible activity going on in just a few years of life. There were all of these monumental crushes on women, and your father was an unabashed womanizer and apparently the kingpin of your city. It seems like you were thirteen going on thirty with all of this activity going on in your life. You needed therapy back then because it is clear that you were living in chaos," Karen said.

"I'm just at the beginning of that chaos that you referred to. There is a hell of a lot left to this story. Really, you've just heard the tame stuff. I haven't even told you the R and X-rated stories yet," I said.

"Go on, I'm listening," Karen said as she turned yet another page.

She wrote several entries in my file before I said another word. I could only imagine what was in that file.

As I grew into my teenage sexuality, I developed friends that, at first, I liked to indulge in innocuous activities with such as kissing and what people called "hunching", and some other people referred to as "dry humping". At the age of fourteen, I fell in love with this pretty girl who had moved to Neverwills from Indiana. Her name was Claire. She was the granddaughter of a town resident named Sam Morton. My daddy was, also, involved sexually with Mr. Morton's wife. He had all the women in Neverwills under his spell. Sam knew it, but he just resigned himself to it as did all of the other men in town.

Claire was so beautiful that I had to get the word to her in some way in order to gauge her interest. I persuaded my best friend Wesley to tell Claire how I felt about her, and he did.

One day, Wesley wrote a note and passed it to Claire during lunch. "Angiel likes you." The note bluntly stated. She wrote back to him. "I know that she likes me," which was just as succinct. Then, Wesley wrote back to her. "No, she likes you like a guy likes a girl". I watched her reactions closely during all of these interactions.

After lunch, she went back inside of the schoolroom and sat at her desk without looking at either of us. After a minute or so of doing nothing more than staring straight ahead like a zombie, she finally reacted.

Without warning, she began to laugh, and she couldn't stop laughing it seemed. She was amused by my proposal, and she couldn't wait for the end of class to blab it to her gossipy cousin, Patricia. Once she did this, that note became THE topic at the school. It spread like wildfire that I was a bull dike, the socially accepted term which meant that I was the "male" version of a lesbian. Hell, I didn't care because my declaration must have worked. Claire, eventually, warmed up and started liking me. The fact that

I was fourteen and driving a Chevrolet El Camino didn't hurt my chances at all.

"I still find it fascinating that you were driving around town in a car and no one cared or spoke out about it," Karen said incredulously.

"Well, that's the truth. I have no reason to lie to you about it," I said.

This is the way that my relationship with Claire began:

One afternoon, after school, I invited Patricia and Claire over to my house. They accepted without any jokes or reservations.

I asked Claire, "Can I kiss you?"

I was looking at her with shy puppy dog eyes in order to look unassuming.

She answered with an emphatic, "NO!"

Claire was looking straight ahead as if she was in the classroom, arms folded.

However, to my surprise Patricia encouraged Claire to kiss me, so she finally relented. Claire's lips were soft and moist, but it was clear to me that she had not kissed much, if any at all. However, I could feel that Claire was enjoying her first lesbian kiss immensely. I held her at the small of her back, as would a man, and allowed my tongue to dance with hers. We kissed for, at least, a minute until she, suddenly, broke away from me, saying that she was upset and that she wanted to go home.

They left, but I called her that night, and we talked for hours. Eventually, we could not go a day without talking to or being with each other. We started riding together in my El Camino. We, sometimes, talked on the phone all night. We kissed, hunched, and just generally enjoyed each other. Neither one of us knew about oral sex at that time, but we knew that we had a strong physical attraction to each other.

"Let's pause for clarity just so I am not misunderstanding. You were riding in your own car and not your father's vehicle, right?" Karen asked.

"My El Camino. Yes, I had my own vehicle. I know that you are wondering how in the hell did a fourteen-year-old manage that, but I'll get to that. Trust me," I said with a sly smile.

"Pardon the interruption then. You may proceed," Karen said.

Mrs. Morton, Sam's wife, got wind of our relationship, and she shipped Claire back to Indiana posthaste. I cried over the loss of my beloved Claire, and so did she over me. We were madly in love with each other by that time. To be quite honest, in retrospect, she may have been my first true love. Even today, we still communicate, despite the fact that it has been more than twenty-eight years. It's been about six years since I last saw her. She's as pretty now as she was back at that time. From what I understand from people who know her, she is still a beautiful lady with long straight hair, a gorgeous complexion, pretty teeth, and a nice body, all qualities that men, as well as some women like me, covet.

A few months before the age of eighteen, I had actual consensual heterosexual intercourse for the second time.

"I must ask you to interrupt your story once more, but what do you mean?" Karen asked.

"Something happened when I was about fifteen that I have trouble talking about, but, in time, I will speak about it. Once I explain that event in detail, you will understand completely what that statement means," I said.

That first time was with a young black man named Lance, who I met just messing around town. He was a member of the infamous Littlefield family. He and I had sex because of a rumor I had heard. The scuttlebutt was that Lance had a big penis, and I had to find out for myself if this was true. He damn sure did, just as advertised! We had sex in my car in the parking lots of several places, some private and some public. This is an example of the paradox which is me. I like women, but I had no problem seducing a man, in this case, because of his allegedly big dick of all reasons.

I rationalized that I only did it to get back at his family who thought that they were so much more than my family, but, of course, there was much more to it than that, given the revelations of my ambiguous sexuality. Besides, they had been tormenting my mother by screwing my father, so I thought it was only right to return the favor. How in the hell they figured that they were above us in stature was beyond me. We were the "It" family in Neverwills, at least, as far as my perception went. My reasons may have been fucked up, but that was my rationale or, more accurately, the excuse that I told myself.

Somewhere in the midst of my encounter with Lance, I pretty much came to the conclusion that, although sex with a man was not disgusting, it was something I could take or leave, like eating a bologna sandwich versus having a nice steak dinner at Bone's. No pun intended.

Three years after that experience, at the age of twenty-one, I moved to West Palm Beach, Florida. I would drive back home, at least, once a month. On one of those weekend trips, I happened to begin having some rather risqué and racy conversations with, of all people, Sonya Littlefield. Just as I said, I am a paradox.

Sonya was Jenny Littlefield's sister and Sandra Littlefield's aunt. Sonya was the prettiest of them all by far. She had sandy colored hair, beautiful teeth, smooth skin, and the body to go with it. She had a soft, sweet voice. Sonya was drop-dead gorgeous!!!

At this point in time, my sexual desires were geared toward women. I had virtually excluded men, but it was still difficult to label myself as a total lesbian at that point since I was involved with men to a small degree. Still, I was probably more on the lesbian side of the fence than anything. Again, I did not find men and the act of intercourse disgusting. Rather, I found women beautiful, and I enjoyed the emotional kinship that we shared. Sonya and I started screwing around every time I drove home to visit my mother. The wild card in this situation was the fact that Sonya was married!

The point to this was not that I had experienced both a heterosexual and a homosexual relationship. The point was that, within a three year period, those relationships were between a male and a female within a family which, because of my past with them, I should have been at war with. Given what they had done to hurt both me and my mother, I should have been trying to kill the Littlefields, instead of having sex with them.

Incredibly, defying all reason and logic, I even had a sexual tryst with Sandra Littlefield, the same Sandra who had jumped me along with her sister Delilah back when we were thirteen. The same Sandra who I had stabbed in her arm with a knife! On the outside looking in, a person would say that I was pretty fucked up to do that, but I just wanted what I wanted and did exactly what I wanted to do.

Sandra and I ended up in my car, just like Sonya and I, kissing, fondling, and dry humping. I cannot explain this intense series of events with the Littlefield family, except to hypothesize that hate and love are strong emotions. Both are passionate responses in their intensity and just, maybe, there was a lot of sexual tension between our families. Whatever the case, I seemed to be screwing a lot with a family which should have been my mortal enemies, like the Hatfields and the McCoys. It made no logical sense whatsoever, but, again, I did as I damn well pleased.

The sanctity of marriage was an arbitrary concept in my hometown of Neverwills. The Littlefield women took their vows of chastity and faithfulness as no more than a formality, as did my father. As a subtext to it all, I wanted to get back at the Littlefield family. First, through Lance, and three years later, through Sonya and Sandra, for having caused my mother so much pain.

Ironically, Sonya had, also, been intimately involved with my father at one time. So, in this regard, my father and I had crossed paths sexually. The hamlet of Neverwills, with its one traffic light and small population, was like an orgy in the wildest parts of San Francisco.

It was difficult to describe my situation at any point in my life, but it was particularly difficult at this time. While I was screwing with Sonya, I, also, had a boyfriend in West Palm Beach, Florida. His name was Andrew Bollinger. He was a well-to-do and very much older gentleman. He was far more infatuated with me than I was with him, obviously; yet, our relationship was not sexually oriented in the least. That he liked the way I looked was the probable reason that we were together.

As long as he kept me financially satiated, that was enough for me at that time. I am sure that most of my many relationships with men stemmed from financial reasons, but my dealings with women were predominantly based on desire or, to a degree, control. To that end, Sonya and I would meet practically every other weekend and be intimate in the back seat of Andrew Bollinger's Rolls Royce. He trustingly let me drive it home to Neverwills, not knowing that I was using it to parade in front of the hometown folks. I thought that, because I was driving a one hundred thousand dollar vehicle, I was the baddest bitch on Earth and, if not Earth, then, for sure, in my hometown!

Sonya screwed up royally in 1990 at my brother-in-law's funeral. I had told her that my parents could never know about us, and she agreed to keep her mouth shut. She came up to me with her stupid, oblivious–to-the-truth husband while we all were standing outside. While we conversed, she tried to hold my arm and hug me, which to me seemed to, without a doubt, telegraph the nature of our relationship to whomever had any amount of common sense. I walked away from her and stood under a huge oak tree and tried to act unemotional because I knew that my mother had seen what had happened. I tried to appear as if I didn't know her and that this was our first conversation, but anyone with an ounce of perception could see that

Sonya's body language suggested a whole lot more.

The next day, Mama asked me, "Baby, are you friends with that woman Sonya Littlefield?"

I said, "No!"

It was almost a defiant shout rather than a rational reaction. My protesting probably gave me away more than anything in my mother's eyes.

This was the first and only lie, to my recollection, that I had ever told my mother. I never volunteered the truth about Sonya — that we were probably more intimate than she and her husband ever were.

My mother, then, said something that blew me away. She said, "Well, Sonya's husband told your daddy that you were friends with her and that you come by and pick up Sonya, at least, four or five times a week."

I said in a loud voice, "MAMA, SHE IS LYING!"

I thought about my mistake seconds after it left my mouth. My mother hadn't said anything about Sonya saying anything. It was her husband who had said that to my father. That slip of the tongue probably confirmed everything my mother had suspected.

Mama didn't say anything to me whatsoever. She simply stared at me with cold eyes that had the look of someone with the sadness of betrayal; I truly believe she knew that I was lying, but she never asked me again. Her look told the sadness of a thousand nights of crying over being cheated on by my father with her mortal enemies, and, here I was, her child being the traitor, a Judas, a Benedict Arnold. After that incident, I completely cut my ties with Sonya forever. When she called, I never answered. I never dialed her number again in my life.

"I have a question for you. How did you justify all of this sexual activity with whomever and wherever you pleased?" Karen asked, with a hint of "I know the answer already" to the tone of her voice.

"Hell, I wanted to do what I wanted to do. I guess, maybe, it's because I was so spoiled and self-centered that I didn't care about who got hurt, as long as, it wasn't me," I said this with a wide-eyed, mock crazy person expression.

"I see. So let me ask you— what is the end result that you hope to receive from our therapy sessions?" Karen asked.

"I'm hoping that I can understand why I did and still do the things that I do. There is something…a….a… like a black hole in my memory." That was my only response.

Meleisa Betts

"What? What kind of black hole are you referring to?" Karen asked as she sat taller in her seat.

"I'll get to that, but, first, let me get back to my story," I stated.

One afternoon, someone called my mother on the phone and told her something she obviously didn't like, as evidenced by the scowl on her face. She hung up and went to her drawer, got her little .22 revolver and said, "Come on, baby."

She knew how to get into Daddy's office to get the keys to his precious Cadillac. It was very clear that Daddy wasn't very good at hiding things.

On many occasions, my mother had snuck into the office and gotten those keys to the car. Then, we would just joyride around Neverwills. She knew that one of Daddy's women would probably tell him if they saw her, but she really didn't care.

Once we got into town, Mama parked the car in front of Leland Motors, the local car lot. She had me by one hand, and the pistol in the other, while we crossed the street. She wasn't looking in any direction but straight ahead. I was looking right at her all the while. We almost got hit by a car while crossing the street because she was so focused on her target.

The sound of the horn blowing from the car that almost hit us alerted Daddy and Jenny Littlefield. They were together in the car lot, talking with a salesman. They ran away before Mama could get all the way across the street. For good measure, my mother took her pistol out of her purse and pointed it in their direction as they ran away like the wind.

The phone call that she had received was from someone alerting Mama that Daddy was getting ready to buy Jenny Littlefield a new car. That plan was put on hold forever as the transaction never happened. To this day, I believe that Aunt Gertie, my father's sister, called my mother with the information. She and my mother were extremely close. My mother loved Aunt Gertie, whose real name was actually Gertruse Anne.

Aunt Gertie would come by the house, and she would curse with every word that came out of her mouth. She would have Mama laughing, and so would I.

I listened to their conversations and learned a lot of intimate details about the affairs. I wasn't leaving Mama's side for anybody, and she never tried to make me, so the information was readily accessible. I never kept any secrets from her other than the Sonya Littlefield affair, and she never kept any from me, at least as far as I had ever known. I learned a good lesson from Mama and her informant, Aunt Gertie. It was important to have eyes in high and low places.

"So, let's recap. You were a hot little mama back then who was self-centered and cared about nothing but satisfying your own needs, wants, and whims," Karen surmised.

"That little bullshit is nothing. You're about to hear some real deep things about me. Some are things that only me and my family know. Hell! I may as well tell you the whole story since I've gone this far. This is the point in my story where it gets really graphic, and you will understand some of those things that I had put off discussing until now. Let me warn you that these stories are not for the weak minded, so you better be sure that you're ready for it," I said with a quasi-joking/serious tone.

"You aren't scaring me with those threats, madam. I would like to see if these secret stories are as poignant as you claim. Go ahead. Let's see what you have to shock me with!" Karen joked.

"Be careful what you ask for," I warned.

At some point in my life, I should start heeding my own advice.

{Chapter 4}

When I was fifteen, I received another brand spanking new car, a 1979 Monte Carlo. I was getting a new car every six months. If I wasn't blowing a motor, I was running into something. I was the only child in Neverwills, especially at the high school, driving a brand new car or one of the very few driving a car at all. The fact that I could even drive at all should have been questioned. Remember, I was allowed to drive at the ripe old age of fourteen! I managed this feat because my daddy, as I had stated before, was powerful in the town of Neverwills, Alabama.

He was best friends with the county lawman, Sheriff Melvin Morrison. Sheriff Morrison was sort of like an Andy Taylor kind of small town sheriff. Although, Andy would have arrested me for sure, if I had been driving my fourteen-to-fifteen year-old ass around Mayberry without a driver's license. These kinds of things contributed to my feeling that I was the most special girl on Earth and that everything that I wanted I should rightfully get. I can see that those instances were reflected in my every interaction with either sex.

Of course, this was not my new first car. The first was the El Camino that I had received the previous year. The El Camino was sharp as a tack until Daddy started using it every day to feed the cows that we owned. As a gift and a substitute for the battle worn El Camino, Daddy bought me the Monte Carlo. My classmates would scratch it up with pens and nails out of pure spite and jealousy. Because of this, I only had a couple of friends. They were Becky, who had alerted me about the Littlefield girls' ambush, and Wesley. Wesley was my best friend, but, somehow, I managed to bend that relationship into something that served a purpose for me, both then and, eventually, in the future. And, because of my relationship with Wesley, I endured one of the most traumatic events of my twisted existence.

I started going out platonically and hanging out with Wesley more and more during that year. We were best buddies and partners, who were more like a brother and sister than anything. I loved my best friend, and he loved me. It was clear to me, at least, that it was a friendship-based relationship. Although I don't know how Wesley viewed it, he knew that I liked girls, so that part of the equation was not a factor in our friendship.

Wesley and I would hang out during the week at a dance club over in Jasper, Alabama. At the club, I danced for hours. All of the club patrons would just stand back and watch me. I loved to dance as much as I loved to be seen and admired. I had aspirations of being a professional dancer at some point in the future, so I tried to copy every dance that I saw, from *American Bandstand* to *Soul Train*.

At the time, I could remember always seeing this guy who was not attractive at all. He was small in build and had cross-eyes. He would always ask me for a dance, and I would always say no.

The night before I went to the club on this particular occasion, I'd had a vision of Grandma Eliza. She was shaking her head at me as if she was telling me no or not to do something. I screamed, and Mama came into the room. I told her of my vision. Mama said that it was a sign from her. There was something that I shouldn't do, or she was warning me about something that may happen in the near future. If only I had paid closer attention, I could have avoided the catastrophe that was to occur the next day.

Prior to this particular night, the only person who I ever danced with at the club was Wesley. On this particular night, Wesley didn't want to go to the club. He had started dating some girl, and he was spending a lot of time with her, talking on the phone. So, I went to the club by myself that night. I danced with several attractive guys, but, then again, I never danced with any man who was not up to my standards. That same unattractive guy, who had asked me to dance a thousand times previously and who I had rejected several times more that night, kept watching me for hours.

After leaving the club for the night and while I was on my way to my car, the same guy who I kept rejecting was waiting for me in the parking lot. The parking lot was dark, and there was not a star in the sky or even a streetlight in the distance.

He flashed a long knife in my face and said menacingly, "Get in the damn car, bitch!"

His crossed eyes blazed, and they were gray, which made him look like a werewolf.

I got into the back seat of the Monte Carlo. He started

my car and began to drive down the club exit, but he was having a hard time. It was obvious that he couldn't drive.

He looked back at me, cowering in the back seat and threatened in those exact cryptically chilling words, "Bitch, I'm going to kill you! Your mother and father will never see you again!"

He took me down a dusty road that was not far from the club. It was an endless path that seemingly led to nowhere. That monster slammed the car into park so violently that it lurched forward. He opened the driver's side door, slammed it, and opened the passenger door, and leaped into the back in one motion.

He held the knife to my throat and shouted, "TAKE OFF YOUR FUCKING CLOTHES!"

He, then, held my head down forcefully, grabbing my hair with the hand that held the knife as he unzipped and pulled down my pants with the other. In seconds, he had unzipped and pulled down his jeans. I tried to put up a fight, but he was much stronger than me. He tore off my panties and raped me repeatedly and relentlessly, and it seemed to be happening in slow motion, like a movie.

He would rape me, have an orgasm, and, within minutes, he was back on top of me for another assault.

After about three hours of being raped and tortured, he dragged me out of the car and over to a barbed wire fence, which was about twenty feet away from where he had stopped my car. He, then, pushed my head through an opening in the fence, which was only slightly larger than the diameter of my head. I was bleeding so much that my face looked like a crimson dam overflowing. My vision was blurred by the blood. I was close to losing consciousness.

He, then, hit me so hard in the mouth with his fist that I just knew that all my teeth had been knocked out. I couldn't feel them or anything else for that matter, because my face, mouth, and body were numb. Finally, I began talking to him through my bloodied, mussed lips, trying to appear as though I was going along with the assault.

I pleaded, "Let's just go to your place."

He looked at me with a surprised but agreeable change in his expression. He no longer looked as intense as before, yet he was still in a violent state.

Even though I looked like I needed to be in a hospital emergency ward, I did this to try to survive. He told me that he was going to take me to his house, tie me up, and rape me until he decided to kill me. So, after convincing him to go to his place, we left the crime scene. I knew that he couldn't drive, and that was part of my escape plan. He started driving as badly and erratically as I had predicted. I knew the area well since I drove there to dance practically every week. I mentally planned my jump from the car as he swerved left and right, crossing the dividing line of the road. *I'll make my escape at the curve,* I told myself.

When he turned a sharp curve going around thirty miles an hour, I reached my hand from the back seat and slowly pushed the seat up. I opened the door quickly and jumped. As soon as I jumped forward, he caught my blouse. I was being dragged by my ripped blouse alongside the car! Thank God for a couple who was standing near the curb, kissing, after a date. The man was dropping his lady friend off for the night. I ran to them after the rapist finally stomped on the brakes, jerking the car to a halt. He still had to put the car into park before he could come after me. I got up with all my strength and ran like hell. It was closer to a stagger than a run, but it served its purpose as it got their attention.

"Help me! Help me! Please help me!" I cried out with the hoarseness of someone who had been screaming and shouting for hours.

The rapist came running over to me as I got to the man

and woman. He said to me, "Come on, baby." Then, he said to the couple, "She's just tripping off drugs. She did some acid, and she is hallucinating."

The couple had no problem putting the pieces of the puzzle together as they looked at my face and neck and saw the blood. Even though it was dark, they could see that there was more blood showing than there was skin. They saw that my clothes were ripped and drenched with blood and that my face was in horrible condition, looking much like I had lost a prizefight.

The guy said, "You can just go on, sir. We are going to take her inside and call the police."

This couple was on the larger side. The woman was around five foot nine, and the man was tall, over six feet three in height, much taller than the rapist, who was about five foot four at best. Their size was the greatest deterrent because he could not overpower the man and probably not the woman either.

They took me inside of the woman's apartment and called the police. The rapist ran back to my car, jerked it into drive, and sped away. Once the police came, I was first taken to the hospital, given my physical state. After I had received medical attention, I gave the officers a description of that animal. The police later came back to the hospital, after about three hours, and informed me that they had a man in custody.

By that time, my parents had made it to the hospital. Daddy just looked at me with an expression of concern, although he remained quiet and solemn. The police said they had gone by the club. They said that the man I had described had brazenly gone back to the club and left my car nearby, so they brought him in. I had to view him in a line-up as soon as I was able to leave the hospital. We left the hospital after three days, and, immediately, we went to the police station. I identified that rabid dog, and he was, then, indicted for rape.

My mother told me not to mention the rape to anybody in Neverwills if I was asked. Predictably, I was asked about it. There were rumors all over the school as well as the town. Mama worked on the scratches and the bruises that were all over me until I was presentable. In spite of the great treatment that I received from her, I didn't go to school for a week. I denied that the incident had even happened each and every time someone asked. My horrible-looking physical education teacher, who reminded me of the cartoon character Magilla Gorilla, kept looking at me with a smirk and smug look. I knew that she hated me and that she instinctively knew what had happened. She was silently celebrating with her smiles.

Before all this had happened, she said to me, "I don't like you because you're just a spoiled brat."

My mother met with that bitch, and she told my mother the same thing that she had said to me; she didn't bite her tongue.

My mother said to me, "Don't you worry about that woman, baby. The Lord will take care of her."

Years later, the man that Magilla Gorilla ended up marrying became hooked on heavy drugs. He, eventually, stole everything out of their home and sold practically everything that she owned to support his habit. She caught pure hell. I felt that she had brought every bit of it on herself. Karma, eventually, exacts its justice on everyone. I was not immune to the laws of the Universe. However, at that time, I didn't know that karma existed, but I would certainly become well acquainted with it.

That sick, rabid dog of a rapist was put in jail, and we had to go to trial in Jasper, Alabama. As a coping mechanism for the trauma that I was going through at the time, I tried to pretend as though the rape didn't affect me

Meleisa Betts

as much as it did. During the proceedings, I tried to answer the questions unemotionally, as if I was just taking a quiz. I guess that sentiment showed on my face during my testimony.

As I look back, I can see why the judge gave him only two years after the jury found him guilty. I didn't cry at the time of the verdict, and, for some reason, I kept the same somber demeanor. Afterwards, I cried whenever I thought of him, what he did, and how he had gotten off nearly scott-free, even though he was guilty as hell. He had to perform only seven months of that measly two year sentence. He was let go early because of good behavior.

I did not let what happened deter me, though. I continued to be a regular at the same club after I recovered. On one occasion, I would find, to my shock, in less than the two years after he was sentenced, that piece of dog shit was back! I was incensed when I saw that piece of filth standing on the wall of the club. He looked as hideous as he had before. I just lost it totally as I grabbed someone's champagne bottle and smashed it on that monster's head. He staggered a little, and then he turned around and looked at me as if nothing had happened. By that time, the owner and what seemed like every other man in the club had grabbed me in order to prevent me from trying to kill that bastard with the bottle.

It was good for his safety that the owner put his ass out of the club. In reality, the owner shouldn't have let me into the club in the first place because of my age, even though I never touched any alcohol. At the time, I guess my parents weren't thinking about a lawsuit. They could very well have sued him and would have probably owned the club.

I decided to sit my ass down after that incident and stay out of harm's way, at least, as far as my public exhibitions were concerned. I never went back to that club, and I remained out of clubs for years. I stopped dancing at that time, unless it was just me and my stereo or just dancing to the television shows where I had learned to dance. I shifted my focus at that point in my life to girls, girls, and more girls!

It was nearly five months later that I was told that Lewis, which was that bastard's name, was burned over ninety percent of his body by someone he had fucked over. Apparently, he was knocked out, doused with kerosene, and lit like a Molotov cocktail. Now, he was as physically scarred on the outside as I was on the inside. He would never be the same physically, and neither would I.

"So, in effect, he didn't escape his karma, and someone punished him where the courts failed," Karen commented.

"I usually don't wish anything bad on people, but that monster was not human. Hell, yeah! I felt that he deserved it, but, somehow, a part of me felt vindicated, yet another part of me didn't feel as good about his payback as you might think. That is the paradox of the many faces of Angiel," I sighed, and I smiled a smile which told little about the angst that I felt.

"Well, you do have a conscience!" Karen said, and we laughed together.

What was wrong with me? I had it all, but that still wasn't enough for me, at that time or at any time that I can remember. I would always want more. When I was around eighteen years old, I perpetrated a scam for money using my father's trust and carelessness against him. I would go to the grocery store to buy groceries with a blank check that he had pre-signed. I would always get some money for myself out of it. Ten or twenty dollars a pop was where the pilfering began. Unfortunately, that pittance was not enough for me. I got greedy, and I would go into my father's office while my mother was still in there paying the workers on Fridays. I would sneak about three or four checks out of his checkbook. My twisted and self-centered rationale was that Daddy had so much money that he wouldn't miss what I took.

Daddy couldn't read very well at all, but he could sign his name and count. He couldn't comprehend most of what he read and signed. In the evening, I would spend about an hour looking at his signature, practicing writing it until I perfected it. I would sign one after another blank check. Some days, I would cash it for one hundred dollars, or, on some Saturdays when I bought groceries, I would write the check out for fifty dollars more than the price of the bill and get the cash back.

I never thought that someone at the cash register might, in all likelihood, have been screwing my father. The thought never occurred to me that anyone would go back and tell him about my scam. After about three months of my larceny, one of his whores did, in fact, tell. Daddy came home and questioned me about it. I waffled, double-talked nonsense, and evaded the truth. He went from inquiry to point blank telling me what I had done. He was mad as hell, and no one could have blamed him. I had fucked up everything — my sweet situation and my free ride through life.

Daddy picked up a mop stick and broke it in half. I

wasn't a fool. I knew what that meant. So, I ran to the back of the house, to my room, and locked the door. Daddy came to the door with that stick and said, "Angiel, you better open this damn door!" His voice was a loud bellow that I had never heard in my life.

I opened the door, and he came rushing in and started beating the shit out of me with that half of a mop. He beat me like he was beating one of my brothers. I cried so hard that I pissed all over myself. It was so horrific and such an epic ass whipping that Mama cried, too, probably as much as I did, if not more. Before this check writing incident escalated to the exclamation point of an ass-beating, I had gotten up my nerve and brashly showed Mama what I had been doing with Daddy's checks.

In a sad voice, while shaking her head, she said, "Baby, if Daddy finds out, he will kill you. You got to stop this."

My hard-headed ass didn't listen to her. Mama tried to remind me about what happened to my brother Blaine when he shot my sister Alice in the hand with the BB gun that he'd gotten for Christmas one year. I should have paid attention. Daddy beat Blaine with an extension coil to within an inch of his life. Mama had to nurse him with salve and white clothes because his welts were so severe.

Yes, I had screwed up for real this time.

At that time, I had a limited edition 1981 white Trans Am that Daddy had bought for me, which was yet another new vehicle. Pontiac manufactured only five thousand of those vehicles that year. I had the only one in the entire state of Alabama. However, Daddy wasn't paying for any more car notes after my major screw-up. After the beating, I was riding around with my arm in a sling, and, to add insult to injury, I had no more perks. My freestyle life was fucked all to hell because of my greediness. The Littlefield family, with whom I still had an ongoing love-hate, but mostly hateful relationship with, loved it. He had told his bitches that he wasn't paying for any more of my car notes.

Daddy had a gas pump in the yard. Although this was primarily for his work trucks, I previously had unlimited access to the free gas. I had messed that up, too. I was not allowed to get any more gas out of the pump, even if my life had depended on it.

My life has always seemed to take some unexpected twists, although most of them were of my own doing. I just could not believe the events that had occurred in my younger years. Looking back at the events many years later, they all seemed so improbable. This is just one example of how my life is part enigma and part contradiction. Unbelievably, less than two years after the check writing incident, this time it was my mother who bought me another new car: a red Corvette. It was a thing of beauty. This was my fourth brand spanking new vehicle. She was able to buy it because she had started her own pulpwood processing business. This is still another example of why I thought that I was special. What other person in my hometown could boast that she had had four new cars in less than six years? While looking back on my life, I realize that this level of indulgence by my parents has had a residual effect on me subconsciously. I'm sure of it.

Sadly, the business didn't last because she had hired lazy, booze-thirsty alcoholics who didn't want to work. At the time, "Little Red Corvette" by Prince and the Revolution was number one on the charts. I was the big-shit queen of the world again. Of course, I guess I've always really felt that way about myself. The Corvette made me extra shitty.

Here was yet another ironic and paradoxical twist to my convoluted life. By this time, I had decided to get married to Wesley, who previously had been more of a partner and my pretend brother, as I alluded to earlier. Wesley wanted to marry me even though he knew of my craving for females.

I agreed because I actually did love him, but as a friend loves another friend. Shortly after we were married, Wesley went off to the army and was to be stationed in Korea. I told him that I wanted to stay in the United States.

I said, "Since you will only be there for one year, you go on ahead. I will be here when you get back."

He was furious, but he reluctantly agreed. We remained married for less than a year, but, in that time, I was getting a small stipend check for two hundred dollars every month because I was his wife. The two hundred dollars helped on the four hundred a month Corvette car payment. Since my mother's business had closed, I had to foot the bill myself.

Wesley wanted me to sell the car, but I told him emphatically, "Hell, no!" I figured that I had a trump card, in that Wesley had had two illegitimate sons with his next door neighbor's daughter, and I held that over his head like a sword.

"How can you tell me to sell anything, when you won't take care of your two damn sons from your next door neighbor?" I would ask that question to him defiantly whenever he brought up the subject of me selling my Corvette.

That was always my answer to that request. Even though my rationalization of using his sons had nothing to do with my defense of not selling my car, that was my stand, and I stood by it. Once again, our marriage was a microcosm of my chaotic and self-absorbed life. My life was one filled with contradictions and mixed messages.

On one hand, Wesley knew that I preferred women. On the other, even though we were intimate as man and wife, it was more of a perfunctory act that I went through for him than romance. Hell! I had made love with Claire Morton, my first love, who I kept in touch with, on our wedding night!

We had married for the most ridiculous of reasons — we loved each other as friends. We didn't ever want to lose that friendship. That reasoning was as flawed then, as it now seems to me today. The marriage caused a rift in our relationship that was irreparable.

Wesley transformed from buddy to husband instantaneously, and I was not having that at all. I was willing to accommodate his needs sexually, but I was not going to be ordered around like a passive housewife. The event that signaled the end of our union was when I had drove way out to someplace in the boondocks, maybe a six hour drive, to the military base where Wesley was leaving from. Chauncey, his brother, and I drove all that way to see him before he went to Korea. That drive must have been four hundred miles. We went to Fort Benning, Georgia, I think. Wesley told me beforehand that he had gotten a hotel for me and Chauncey, plus a pass to the military base. When we got there, we couldn't get on the base because his dumb ass hadn't arranged for the base pass. To compound that nonsense, I was hungry as hell. I hadn't had a thing to eat since the morning of our trip.

Chauncey had the bright idea to put on Wesley's military uniform, which we had brought with us to give to Wesley since he'd left it at our home in Neverwills. Chauncey used it to go into the mess hall for food. He, then, asked the servers to give him one more piece of chicken. He gave that one piece to me by sneaking it out of the mess hall in a napkin.

Wesley didn't even offer to get me any food after we finally caught up with him. That one chicken breast barely kept me from starving, but Wesley never acted as if he cared one bit. After that bullshit treatment, I'd had enough of being Wesley's wife and his friend. I hurried up and took my mad and hungry ass back to the comfort of my mother and Neverwills. It was a shame that we had to go our separate ways. We had gone through a lot of good and bad times together, but there was no doubt that we were ending on a down note. Wesley and I were divorced near the end of 1982.

Once Wesley went off to Korea and I was happily back in Neverwills, his sister Coco started calling me every day, asking me to take her for rides in my car. It didn't take long to discover that this request had ulterior motives behind it. She really wanted to have sex with me, and we did become intimate. However, it was sexual contact, such as kissing, fondling of breasts, and dry-humping but no oral sex. Yes, this was still my husband's sister! I was sort of cheating on Wesley with yet another woman, and this one was in his immediate family. It was just wrong, and, as I look back on it, many years later, I can truthfully admit as much. Even though I didn't approach Coco with any of the desires I had for her, I didn't decline the invitation.

What was wrong with me that I could even entertain the thought? It was as if I had this hate or some sort of unresolved issue in me, and sex was the tool that I used to try to resolve that hostility. Many times, people who have been sexually abused act out sexually. I had not been abused

in any way except for the sexual assault at the dance club.
I can only hope that I can find an answer to this perplexing
part of my psyche. I had no moral compass as to what I
should or shouldn't do. It was as if I was so self-involved
that I had no scruples whatsoever.

I can remember back to the time before all of this, when
we were no more than buddies and Wesley discussed with
me the fact that he was fucking this girl, Alison, when he
was fifteen years old. He got her pregnant, and, then, he
went back and got her pregnant again a year later at age
sixteen. I could not believe Wesley had gotten her pregnant,
not once but twice based on what he used to say about her.
However, as far as I was concerned, who Wesley was
screwing was completely irrelevant. At that point in time,
we were simply dance partners and good friends, so
whether he had been screwing Miss Alabama, Miss
Neverwills, or the creature that supposedly lived in the
forest, didn't matter to me one damned iota. I had women
on my brain solely, and that was just the way that it was.

Karen was silent with a pregnant pause, before she
spoke.

"Now, wait a minute! You had your father practically

giving you the world, and you ruined that by stealing insignificant money? He beat you with a mop? You seduced a fourteen-year-old girl? What about the rape ordeal? How in the world did you not tell me about this during the beginning of our conversation? This is pertinent information to your case. How did you go from being friends with Wesley to marrying him and then becoming sexual with his sister?"

"I don't know, Karen. Like I said, we wanted to keep the friendship, so we married. His sister came on to me," I sighed. I gave these reasons matter-of-factly, as if they were truly plausible.

"The way that you keep the friendship going is by sending him Hallmark cards, calling the man on his birthday, or taking him out to a club or for dinner from time to time, certainly not by getting married," Karen said.

"Hey, I can't explain it. I was young and stupid, I guess. Hell, I don't know, that was like twenty years ago. Haven't you ever made a mistake?" I said, laughing because Karen's expression was so incredulous. "Okay, there's more. I haven't gotten to the halfway point. How much time do I have left in this session?" I asked. I had been talking for nearly an hour, and the time had blown by.

"You have about eight minutes, so it's best to make the most of it. You should get busy talking," Karen said.

{Chapter 5}

After my short-lived marriage to Wesley, I decided to go ahead and trade the red Corvette in and get something a little cheaper. This time, I got a 1981 Nissan 280 ZX, still a flashy car, and something which I seemed to feel that I deserved. I drove it back and forth to my new job in Greenville, Alabama. I had gotten a job working part-time for my mother's doctor, Jesse J. Howard. My mother didn't trust any doctors in Neverwills, so she went to Dr. Howard, who was a black man of about fifty-eight, even though it was hard to tell for sure if he was older. I worked from four to eight P.M. Monday through Friday. I made about a hundred dollars per week and cleared eighty dollars after I paid for my gas. I learned a lot working for Dr. Howard. The most important and valuable thing I learned from him was how to administer injections.

This was a blessing because, three months later, I had

to stop working for him and help take care of my mother. Mama found out that she was a diabetic, and her blood sugar was constantly over four hundred. She had to start taking insulin immediately. I would give her an injection in the morning and one in the afternoon until she learned how to do it herself. Dr. Howard never tried to come on to me or flirt, as did other men, while I worked for him. He was very professional. His professionalism really struck me. If you are going to be about your business, do so, and keep your business and personal life separate. It was a rule that I tried to adhere to from that point forward, at least, as best as I could given my manipulative personality. As I had learned, nothing was ever as good or as bad as it seemed. Up to that point, things were never quite that good.

This was the time that I had made a semi-permanent move to West Palm Beach. It was after my failed marriage to Wesley. I had known that the situation with my parents was temporary, and I had to make a move in order to press forward in my life. I met two so-called religious "prophets" shortly after my arrival in West Palm. I had gone to them for some good luck and spiritual guidance. Low and behold, I became intimately involved with the first of the prophets in 1983. This religious swindler was an older white man who had the largest penis that I had ever seen in my life! I became pregnant by him because he told me that he couldn't have any kids. I foolishly allowed him to have unprotected sex with me. Again, for some reason, I seemed to live my life and make decisions as though there were no consequences.

Surprisingly, or maybe, more accurately, foolishly, I had never used any type of birth control. I had been amazingly lucky with my other interactions with men as to not have gotten pregnant. I, then, became involved with the second prophet three years later, this one was a slick, smooth-talking black man. He had a brand new white Rolls Royce, which seemed to be a perk of his being such a shyster. The car was, of course, a major attraction for me as I could envision myself behind the wheel.

He had the first cellular phone that I had ever seen. It was big, about nine or ten inches long, greenish-gray in color, and about three inches deep. He would flaunt his cell phone by talking with people while we were out at restaurants. It was probably costing him a dollar a minute, since they were new and expensive to own at that time.

He was "Mr. Everything" in my opinion. He was husband and father material in my mind, but I wasn't ready to have anybody's child. Even with this fact firmly in my mind, I became pregnant by this prophet, also. In both cases, I was young, materialistic, and gullible. I was seduced by their words and financial trappings. Those things mattered a lot to me as I have reiterated on other occasions. If you didn't have money, you could just forget about Angiel. If you had money and cars, you could get a piece of this pie and then some.

I cannot fully explain why I was sleeping with men, marrying them, and still craving the soft sensuality of women. Maybe, I was just being an opportunist, but, again, I did things that I could not understand. At that time, the term "gold digger" did not exist, but I do know that the term would have been an accurate assessment of me, particularly during my early years. I did take advantage of the fact that men wanted to spend their time and money on me.

At this time, I applied for a job with Universal Packaging, a national freight and delivery service. I loved the company, and I was especially in love with the red polo shirts that were a part of the uniform. They had a slanted gold U and P on the right of the chest and the sleeves. I received a letter from the Universal Packaging offices stating that I had passed the test and that I could start employment in sixty days. The problem was that Universal Packaging was not hiring pregnant women, and I was. The father was none other than the second prophet.

I had abortions in both cases because I was not going to be saddled with an unwanted child. I went back to Alabama for both abortions. There was yet another unbelievable assault on me during the second abortion. Both abortions were performed by the "professional" Dr. Howard, as I had considered him to be. During the second procedure, I woke up prematurely from the anesthetic to find that Dr. Howard was on top of me. Incredibly, he was having sex with me, after I had just had an abortion! I was so out of it that I only remember him saying, "It won't take long."

When I left his office, I couldn't say anything. I couldn't utter one single, solitary word. Eventually, I told my mother what Dr. Howard had done. She said for me to just try to forget about it. I tried, but, nine years later, I was still feeling the mental after-effects of the assault. Finally, I called the Alabama Medical Board to report him because I was having problems dealing with the trauma of it all.

The medical board informed me that Dr. Howard's license had been revoked for over five years. He couldn't practice medicine anymore. I asked them why, but, of course, they wouldn't go into any of the details. In reality, I already knew why based upon the unethical and criminal act that he had performed on me. I couldn't understand why he didn't try to date me while I was working for him. Why did he have to wait until I was lying defenseless on an operating table to make his move?

The only conclusion I could come to was that he was a rapist hiding behind the well respected and trusted white coat of a physician. I live with the regret each day that I didn't report him as soon as the assault occurred. I, also, wish that I had never had either of those abortions. I ask God for His forgiveness for those acts all of the time, but I'm just not sure if He has accepted my apology. If I had to base my belief on the way things have turned out up to the present, my answer would be no.

"Do you think he did anything to you the first time?" Karen inquired.

I paused for a moment before I answered.

"I don't know, but, if he could do it during my second visit, then who's to say that he didn't do it when I was there the first time?" I responded. I'm sure that Karen must have thought in the back of her mind that I was either making these things up or downright hallucinating, yet all of these instances were totally true.

"I heard some gossip a few years ago from a person in Greenville who claimed to know Dr. Howard. He alleged that they had found Dr. Howard in a hotel room stripped naked and tied up. There were syringes and drugs in the room. He had been drugged, assaulted, and robbed. They never found out who did it or why. I say that it serves that bastard right."

Karen looked straight ahead for a nanosecond. Then, she looked down and began writing in my file without commenting on my revelation.

I had decided to get married again. This time, it was to an affluent businessman who I had met in West Palm Beach. It was a short-lived union, to say the least. We were only married for three months. His name was Josh T. Martin. He was much older, about fourteen years my senior, and, of course, because I held true to my formula, he was not hurting financially. In me, Josh had both a lady and a perfect accompaniment to his lifestyle. Everything was perfect until he told me that my nieces couldn't come over to his house to visit me anymore.

"Why can't my relatives come and visit?" I questioned.

"They are too dark, and they look like black Mexican whores," he responded.

I cursed that bastard out with every profane word known to mankind, and, even then, I used words that I am sure no one had ever heard before. Maybe, I should have taken more time to get to know Josh properly. If I had, I would have learned that he was a racist bigot. He had probably dated black or Hispanic females before, yet he had a plantation mentality about minority women. Apparently, they were only good to have sex with in secret and not to be associated with in general. To be with or around Josh, you had to be lily-white, not black, Hispanic or otherwise. It was no major loss because he was the worst lover I had ever known. His two-minute-a-day sex was horrible.

Josh Martin held a secret that only he and I knew — that he was a latent homosexual. Under the guise of being open-minded, Josh would frequently ask me to dress as a dominatrix, complete with a leather outfit and a whip. He would ask me to beat him with the whip until there were welts. Then, he would request that I screw him with a strap-on penis. During the act, he would be on all fours, hollering and shouting, yet he would prod me on by shouting, "Do it! Do it! Harder!" The irony of this perverse sexual request was that Josh tried to appear as though he was a hard-ass to the general public.

During our brief marriage, Josh would put me out of the house all the time, especially when he wanted to be with his other women. Despite this fact, I remained faithful right up until the very end of our relationship. I even considered him to be a nice looking man until I found false teeth and a fake hairpiece in the bathroom. As I look back on it, Josh putting me out of his house wasn't that bad of a deal. The last thing that I heard concerning Josh Martin was that he was embroiled in a scandal because of some pictures that had surfaced of him with several men in compromising positions. Josh was involved in many public endeavors in West Palm, as well as being on the board of city commissioners. Those photos most certainly put a severe dent in the Josh Martin Empire.

I didn't love Josh Martin at all. I married him because I was tired of Aunt Rosie Bell, the relative I lived with until I established myself in West Palm. She did ridiculous things like turn off the hot water in her house in the wintertime to save money. There was no ventilation in the house at all. In the room where I slept, the windows were all sealed.

It was always hot as a furnace in her house. I paid the utility bills out of my personal emergency funds, so money was not the issue. My mother offered to put an air conditioning unit in my aunt's house, but she said no. My aunt's house was paid for, so she didn't ask me for any rent. It was just too stifling to be in such a closed-in space. I married Josh purely and simply to get the hell out of Aunt Rosie Bell's hot box of a house.

In between the evictions by my soon-to-be ex-husband, I met Andrew Bollinger. He really became infatuated with me. Andrew was seventy-two years of age when I met him, so he was fifty years older than me. He was about five foot seven and slender with no hair on the top of his head whatsoever but with white hair on either side, which he kept long and bushy, sort of like an octogenarian clown. He always had a cigar dangling from the side of his mouth, whether lit or not. It was Andrew Bollinger's green Rolls that I drove back and forth to Neverwills during my weekend sex romps with Sonya Littlefield. He couldn't have sex because of some medical problems, and his love of alcohol didn't help matters, yet it never stopped him from having many lady friends besides me.

It was pretty clear that the women who were coming by

Meleisa Betts

to visit him were doing so just to get money. He loved it. Just having women and vaginas and breasts around to look at was enough satisfaction for Andrew. Strangely enough, I really cared for him, even though he served no useful purpose other than to provide shelter for me when Josh inevitably threw me out. After a while, he even stopped giving me money, but I still wanted to be with him. He was so much fun, and he had the spirit of a twenty year old. It was perfect. No sex, just companionship. After my divorce from Josh Martin, I tried to get Andrew to marry me, but he wouldn't. Maybe he could see through the manipulation that there was nothing that I could offer him that the other women weren't already providing.

At this point, Karen wrote for about two minutes in my file. I watched her and wondered to myself what she must have thought of me. I could only guess how many clients she'd had who had problems and issues, but how many could have had as many complex and conflicting layers as me? She paused and adjusted her glasses closer to the bridge of her nose. She looked at me with a pregnant pause and then asked a question.

"Angiel, why do you think that you cared for and wanted to marry a man who was 'fun' in your words, but that was the extent of it? He was a man who was not a viable sexual partner, refused to give you money, and who could not truly be a husband to you," Karen asked.

This question had a tone of a friend asking a friend a question where the asking friend was lending a sympathetic ear and the other friend was being an absolute fool.

I closed my eyes and thought for a few moments before answering.

"I don't know. Other than, he was something that I couldn't have, I guess. Maybe, my thing is that I was so used to people giving me whatever I wanted, whenever I wanted it. Andrew's resistance to me made him more of a challenge. That's one of the reasons that I'm here talking with you, so I can make sense of who and what I am and why I am this way."

I started to tear up a little, and Karen offered me one of her tissues. It was in a lavender box, and it smelled of lavender. She probably had this scent for its calming properties, and it seemed to help.

"I feel better, for some reason, by telling you this, Karen. It seems that the more intimate that I am in these sessions, the more liberated I feel. I'm ready to get back to it now," I said, smiling through slightly reddened eyes.

Andrew had told my mother that he wanted her to come down to West Palm from Neverwills. He said that he was going to quick-claim one of his rental properties to me, so she made the trip. We were all sitting in the lawyer's conference room. The lawyer put the papers in front of Andrew Bollinger, and, for some reason that only he knew, he wouldn't sign the documents. My mother had come all the way to West Palm at his request only to see him change his mind right out of the blue. I was mad as hell, and it was at that point that I decided to let go of Andrew Bollinger for good.

Being the confused and twisted person that I am, I really and truly believed that I loved Andrew and that I would have been so good for him and to him. Why did I have this passion and affinity for him? I cannot tell you, but I really did. Maybe, it had something to do with the regret that I had for not spending any appreciable time with my Grandfather James, and, because of that, Andrew was a substitute for some sort of grandfather void that I had. Maybe, my love for him was confused in my addled mind with a family-type of love. Instead of the boyfriend-girlfriend type of relationship, it was simply the same as what you would have with a favorite uncle, but, for some reason, I could not process the fact from the fiction that was inside of my head.

Strangely, I often think of Andrew to this day, many years after his passing away. I had finally gotten a position at Universal Packaging. Andrew had had a great deal of influence in my receiving the opportunity to apply for and, eventually, getting that job. He died within the three months of my probationary period with the West Palm Universal Office. I didn't know that he had died until one of his friends happened to come by Aunt Rosie Bell's home looking for me.

I had gone by my aunt's house to get some sleep because I couldn't get any at the condo I had just purchased. My neighbor's ten-year-old, bad-ass boy, Jonas, was always climbing on top of my roof intentionally to awaken me. I finally called DFACS to lodge a complaint of child neglect and endangerment, and that put a stop to him.

"You called DFACS on somebody's child when there was no real child neglect?" Karen asked.

I responded, "I didn't want to do that, but his mother wouldn't do anything with his bad ass. I had to get some sleep. Hell! I was working the graveyard shift, and that little bastard knew it. He would do shit to deliberately wake me up. I will never forget that little green-eyed monster!"

"That was a very extreme reaction to a child being a child. Moving on. What happened when the man you referred to came by your aunt's home to speak with you?" Karen asked.

The man was standing outside on my aunt's porch. He was about sixty-two or so, tall and stooping with a face weathered by the sun. He was wearing one of those CAT tractor hats, which had seen better days. He said, "Angiel, I see that you are doing okay with the news."

I asked him, "What do you mean? What news are you talking about?"

He said, "You don't know, I see. I would have thought that, given how close you were with him that the family would have told you."

"Told me what?" I was getting impatient and annoyed with his stammering and beating around the damned bush.

"Andrew passed away about nine days ago," he said solemnly.

I could not say a word. I walked over to the rusty green and white porch chair that my aunt had had there for as long as I could remember. That metal chair felt as cold and as hard as anything that I had ever sat on at that point in my life. The man said goodbye and shuffled over to his red-rust and bondo filled Chevrolet pickup truck. I sat in that chair for three hours, just staring at the street and not seeing the cars go by.

I found it hard to accept that Andrew had died and that they'd already had his funeral. I called his sister as soon as I recovered from the shock. She said that she had tried to get in contact with me, but she didn't have any numbers for me nor did she know where my aunt lived. I was so hurt that I could not think of anything other than what I had found out. I said to myself that I knew that God meant for it to happen this way because I was under my probationary period, and I couldn't miss work. If I had known, I would have been so depressed. I probably would have called in sick for sure. In fact, I am certain that I would have done that, and I would have been unemployed.

Andrew had helped me get the job with Universal Packaging using his personal contacts, but, more specifically, through his drinking associate who was in management at Universal. In the afternoons, after he left work, he would go to the Sunset Lounge, his favorite watering hole. He always wanted me to meet him there.

He was usually full of alcohol, but he would keep his

wits. Andrew would always ask this one particular man, who always seemed to be at the Sunset Lounge, "Help my baby get on with the Universal office."

Finally, one day, the man said to me, "I want you to come down to my office tomorrow."

Hell, it was clear, given my history and my belief that I should be a kept woman, that I didn't really want to work, but Andrew Bollinger made it a point to get my ass up out of the bed whenever he got up for work. This day was no exception, and it was the most important day since I would finally be put on the road to becoming self-sufficient.

I went to the Universal Packaging office to see this man, whose name I can't remember, who apparently was the supervisor. He told me to sign up for the test, and then he directed me to the examination room. I took the test. It was somewhat difficult, but, within a month, I found out that I had passed with a high grade. This must have been Andrew's purpose in my life. Everyone we meet is put in our path for some reason, be it good or bad. Andrew had been placed in my path to make me a functioning member of society and a contributor rather than just being a user and a taker.

After Andrew passed away, his sister allowed the Rolls

Royce to sit in a garage and rust away. She could have given it to me, but, apparently, there was either some greed or resentment involved. I had the car all of the time when Andrew was alive, and my driving of the car amounted to more than two-thirds of its mileage. She never drove it at all, and, as far as I could remember, I never remember seeing her driving at all. She was always driven by her henpecked husband whenever she came to visit Andrew. It literally sat and rotted into a pile of green and rust-reddened steel.

I was a master manipulator of men who wanted my attention. I can remember, back in 1985, I was again living with my Aunt Rosie Bell. It was after Andrew and I were on bad terms due to my controlling and demanding ways. He had kicked me out of his house in order to show me who was really in control. With no immediate options and some issues that needed attention, I went to work finding a mark. A mark is someone a con artist targets to run his or her scams on. In this case, I was going to be as close to the con artist or grifter than an innocent victim.

I had heard about this young, black dentist who was single. I had two teeth in the front of my mouth that I badly wanted to have capped. They didn't look bad. However, I have to admit that those teeth made me look like a hillbilly because they were slightly bucked, and I had an overbite. I could tell that it was hindering me from getting a good job. Because of this, I made it my business to set up an appointment with this dentist to get my teeth taken care of. I, also, had a few missing teeth in the back of my mouth that needed to be replaced.

"I am doubly certain that there is a story behind your dental issues if the rest of your life's story, to this point, is any indication," Karen quipped.

"Well, the dentist that we had when I was growing up in Neverwills was nothing but a damned drunk. Every time someone had a toothache, he would simply pull the tooth. He was such a bumpkin of a dentist that he didn't know anything about root canals or any other method of preserving teeth," I said.

I arrived for my appointment. The assistant put me in a room. Eventually, the doctor came in. He was a nerdy sort, who looked like he had probably never slept with a real woman before.

"Hi! How are you?" he asked, and, for some reason, he looked a little nervous. The file in his hand that I was asked to fill out was shaking just a little in his left hand.

"I'm doing just fine, except for my teeth," I joked. I was

a little nervous, also, if truth be told.

"Well, what is the problem with your teeth?" He looked at me with one of those looks when a man is trying to be suave.

"When I was young, I sucked pacifiers and then my thumb for a while. Later, I just kept sucking on things, and here we are!" I said.

The dentist swallowed hard at the clear sexual innuendo that I threw at him.

"I'm going to set you up for an appointment to come back in a couple of weeks. I will see what I can do to change that," he said.

"I don't have any insurance," I sighed. I looked at him with a sidelong glance to make sure that he saw that I was flirting.

"We're not going to worry about that right now. We're going to go ahead today and clean your teeth. This will be on me. Just make sure that you leave your contact information with the young lady out front," he said.

I said okay to him while giving him my sexiest, most coquettish look. All the while that I was talking to him he was grinning like a Cheshire cat. His name was Jack Roberts. He was the complete visual definition of a nerd.

Dr. Roberts's hair was red and kinky, and it looked as though it had never been combed. I had never, in my life, seen a person with such bad hair. However, he was neither ugly nor handsome. He had a nice body to go with a beautiful smile.

Everything appeared to be falling into place when Dr. Roberts called me the same night at my aunt's house.

"Hello, Ms. Royal. Did I catch you at a bad time?" he asked.

Strangely, I was still a little nervous. "No, I'm not doing anything. Why do you ask?"

I knew full well why he was asking, of course.

"I was wondering if you would like to come over to my place," he said. Now, I was not expecting him to be that forward, but he was more aggressive than I figured.

"Well, it's late, and I don't feel like driving."

Once again, that was not quite the truth, but I was aware that the fish was on the hook.

"Where do you live? I can come over and pick you up," Dr. Roberts said.

I agreed to see him since he was picking up the tab for a lot of dental work. It was most certainly worth a little bit of my time. So, I had no problem accepting the invitation. I knew that the trade-off was sex for services rendered. I was more than willing to fulfill my end of the bargain.

Dr. Roberts drove me over to his apartment like he was driving in the Daytona 500. In a short time, we were getting down to business. Clothes were going everywhere. Lovemaking, if you can call it that, was quick and horrible! It was terrible, maybe even the worst sexual experience that I had experienced up to that point. The sex, however, was a necessary evil. I needed to have my teeth fixed, and my pussy was the only thing that I had to bargain with. Some people may call this prostitution, but I figured that I was simply using what I had to get what I needed.

Interestingly, he had never experienced oral sex, so it was a tremendous experience for him to have me go down on him. If I had known that Dr. Roberts was that much of a greenhorn, as it pertained to lovemaking, I could have taken his ass for a real financial ride, if I had chosen to. However, I needed the dental work badly, and that was it. Using him for anything more than what I needed would have required more energy than I was willing to expend at the time. Maybe, if the payoff had been more and if he had been a wealthy man, I would have invested more time in him. The fact that Dr. Roberts was no more than a beginning dentist was not enough of a financial incentive. Seducing him was not cost effective.

Dr. Roberts and I remained friends even after I moved to Valeria. The relationship, eventually, became one of his providing dental work for free and my supplying the medication to soothe the ache of his sweet tooth for females. Every time he came to Georgia, I lined up a beautiful, slender woman with long hair to accompany him for the weekend. After a few years, Dr. Roberts had gotten up the nerve and confidence to stay in contact with and date some of the women. After all, they were basically call girls, and I was acting as a madam by getting a percentage of what he paid. Eventually, he graduated to setting up his own sex appointments with the women and cutting me out as the middleman. Nowadays, I don't even hear a word from him.

"When was the last time that you actually heard from Dr. Roberts?" Karen asked.

"It's been a while now, like a year and a half or more when I last needed a root canal. The last thing I heard about him was that he was involved with one of those escorts. I understand that her name is Avalon, and she is smoking hot."

"I would imagine that, if he went so far as to be

involved with a hooker, she would have to be attractive," Karen replied.

As I think back to that era in my life, I would be remiss not to mention Gino Halliburton, even if he is nothing more than a footnote. Before Josh, Andrew, or the prophets, I was just trying on West Palm for size. I was just visiting to see if I wanted to make it a semi-permanent home, at least, as far as my nomadic lifestyle would permit at the time. I met Gino, and he instantly fell in love with me. I wasn't sure if I was going to stay in West Palm at the time or not. As I said, I was visiting.

I still had the red Corvette, so I was Post-Wesley, but just by a few months. Gino's parents had plenty of money. He wanted to get an apartment for me and move me to West Palm. I tried to see where this offer would lead. We had an intimate relationship, but I hated the sex. We only had sex once a week. It was all for his benefit, obviously. He complained about it, but I stuck to my guns. I just couldn't deal with his ugly ass. He looked like a goon. He was about two hundred eighty pounds and about six feet two inches in height. His hair was dirty brown and bushy. He had a unibrow which made him look like a caveman.

He had a monstrous dick though, about eight or nine

inches long and two and a half inches wide. That size was too much, considering that I was not that attracted to him, and I would not get lubricated. Even though it was painful at times, I endured it because of the circumstances. Maybe, it could be said that I took advantage of the situation, but Gino approached me with the proposal and not the other way around. I was not in a position, financially, at that time in my life, to have been too selective.

One Friday night, when Gino came home, something was in the air, like the atmosphere was charged with some sort of energy, and it was not positive. I just knew that something was going to happen or that I was going to instigate whatever it was that was going to happen. It turned out to be the latter and a self-fulfilling prophecy. At around nine o'clock, I asked Gino for the four hundred dollars that I needed to send home to my mother to pay my car note. He told me that I had to wait a while because he didn't have it right then. I, then, made the mistake of letting my emotions control my mouth, and I yelled these three words before I knew that I had said them: "YOU STUPID MOTHERFUCKER!"

That bastard stood up from the chair that he was resting in, and, in one continuous motion, slapped me so damn hard that I saw stars. I knew that he regretted that he had hit me, but, at that moment, it was a gut reaction to my smart mouthed insult. But, by that time, there was no turning back, and the wheels were set in motion for my departure.

Gino was so mad that he couldn't speak to me, so he just left the apartment seconds after I slumped into the lounge chair in the living room. As soon as his ass hit the pavement, I went to the bedroom, packed the few clothes that I had with me, and put them behind the seat of the Corvette, and I headed back to Neverwills. By twelve A.M., I was on the turnpike headed north.

Gino called and called some more, probably fifty times, and, each time, he begged me to come back. He asked my mother if she would speak to me on his behalf. My mother had met Gino and his entire family, and, though she had an opinion, she decided to remain neutral. She told him, and later me, that it was up to me to make the decision on whether or not to go back to him or to stay in Neverwills.

I said, "Mama, I am not going back. He hit me, and that was that."

I later heard that he married the same girl he'd had his child with. That was really where my four hundred dollars went on that Friday night. Hell! He might have thought so, but I wasn't stupid by a long shot. Once again, this was an example of my thinking in ME terms about what someone could do to affect ME, and that played a part in my decision and my life at that point.

"Ms. Royal, you are confessing to me that you were pregnant by two fake prophets. You were raped in your sleep by the doctor who performed the abortions. You married your best friend who was no more than a friend romantically. You married a white man who hated dark women, even if they were Caucasian and who was probably a closeted gay man. You were in love with a seventy-two year old man who was old enough to be your grandfather. You had sex with a man who disgusted you sexually just to keep an apartment, and these examples are just a short list of your confessions. Ms. Royal, you were one confused and convoluted person at that time, and I can say, without a doubt, that your life events are the most controversial of any that I have ever heard. To be quite blunt and honest, there is little wonder why you are in therapy," Karen said.

I started laughing before I could speak. "Shut the hell up, Karen! If you had gone through as much as I have, then you would be crazy, too!" I said between the laughter.

"Okay. You can leave the rest for your next session. Your time is up for this week's session," Karen said.

"This is more than you ever thought you would ever hear about me, huh?" I asked as I bent over to pick up my Gucci handbag.

"The things that you have recounted to me are, without a doubt, some of the most bizarre stories that I've ever heard," she remarked.

"There's more, doc. A lot more. With me, it seems that there always was," I said as I picked up my pocketbook from the wooden-paneled floor and exited the office. I stopped to say good-bye to the receptionist with a wink, a wave, and a smile.

As I left the building, I had an epiphany. I realized that, in order to better understand who I am now, I have had to continually re-examine my past and the people who influenced me.

{Chapter 6}

On my next appointment on the following Tuesday, Karen seemed to be more energetic and ready for the session. It began promptly at one P.M., and she was ready. She had my file opened and her pen in hand.

"I am sure you have a hundred interesting stories that you have remembered since last week," Karen remarked.

"One hundred is way too small. It's more like a thousand."

"Well, if you have that many offbeat stories, then we had better get started. You only have fifty minutes, you know?"

"I know that, Dr. Oppenheim. Like I have said before: be careful what you wish for," I said as I took a tube of cherry lip gloss out of my bag and moistened my lips for the revelations to come.

I can recall with clarity my acquaintance with a woman named Dottie Mae four months after my marriage to Wesley was over. At that time, she was a big-time drug dealer from Tuscaloosa, Alabama. She came to Neverwills a few times a month for "business" and to see me. I had met Dottie Mae at the local convenience station while I was there filling up the Nissan 280ZX, which, again, was the replacement vehicle that I had traded for my beloved red Corvette.

As Dottie Mae pulled up in her big luxury sedan, she looked me over from top to bottom. Dottie Mae was the embodiment of a dike. She had big blond hair that was combed back like a country singer. She had a gravelly voice and a face prematurely wrinkled from chain smoking Marlboro menthol cigarettes. After I introduced myself to her, we struck up a conversation. She told me that I was her exact type, and, if I hung with her, I would have everything that I would ever need or want. Of course, she was speaking my language, the language of money.

I took her over to my parents' house to meet my mother because I wanted her to know who I would be visiting while I was in Tuscaloosa. Mama didn't know that Dottie Mae was a drug dealer, and I saw no real reason to reveal that

Meleisa Betts

information. Even if she had known, she was always nonjudgmental and would have reserved her opinions, unless I asked her what she thought. Dottie Mae was around fifty years of age, so she was considerably older than me. She had this big, black Lincoln Continental and a driver. He drove her around the state to pick up her drugs and make her deals, just like a rich woman would, or, for that matter, a mob boss. She gave me money every time I saw her in Neverwills or whenever I visited her in Tuscaloosa, and that was practically every day for about a month. I even went with her on a couple of drug runs out to New Orleans.

"Let me interrupt you for clarification. Was this BEFORE you moved to Palm Beach?" Karen asked.

"Yes," I said. "I know my stories seem to go back and forth in time, but I have to tell you this way to show how I seemed to be influenced by money and power. It didn't matter if it was a man or a woman with the money and power. Also, my mind jumps around like that, from thought to thought, but I'm trying to keep to the theme of how I manipulate people for money. Maybe, by just telling you what comes to mind this way, something will jump out at you that will give you insight into me."

"Excuse me, Ms. Royal, for the interruption. And just for the record, I'm not concerned with the chronology of your life's events but rather how they make up your psyche. You may proceed," Karen said.

Dottie Mae would snort cocaine while being chauffeured around by her driver as I sat in the middle seat of the car. I was a young, stupid ass, oblivious to how dangerous this woman could be. I never told my mother about Dottie Mae's personal life, and she never asked me one question. I would just tell her that I was driving down to Mobile or wherever Dottie Mae was headed and that I would be back later on in the evening.

That was as forthright and open as I could be with her at the time. If I had told my mother of what I was doing and the bad situations that I could have been involved in, it would have crushed her. It was bad enough that Dottie Mae had a huge home with a lot of people coming and going all of the damn time, but she, also, wanted me there with her practically every second that I was around her.

On one occasion, she was snorting this drug that they called "skag" on the street. It was really just heroin. Anyway, Dottie Mae seemed to enjoy being high all of the time, so I decided to try it, just to see what the big deal was.

I figured that, since she did it, and, since people paid her for this drug, it must have been something else. What in the hell did I do that for? I found that this skag was something else altogether.

After I snorted a little of the skag, I, immediately, became paralyzed from the top of my head down to the tips of my toes. The only things that I could move were my eyes. I laid on Dottie Mae's couch like a mummy for two hours. I could hear and see everybody walking by me as they came into her house, asking questions to Dottie Mae and her henchmen.

"What in the hell is wrong with her?" people asked that and variations of that same question as they saw me laying there, immobilized, like I was a wax dummy.

They, meaning Dottie Mae and her accomplices, would say to the "customers", "She'll be okay. Come on in. So, what do you need?"

She proceeded to do her drug transactions around me as if I was a coffee table. I was so scared because I was laying there, incapacitated, for what seemed like days. I tried to use my brain to tell myself to get up or move my fingers or anything, but it was useless. More than two hours passed before the paralysis was finally over. After that incident, I got what little things that I had with me and stormed out of the house without so much as one word of goodbye. I left Dottie Mae's house, drugs, cars, and money in the dust, and I never called her again, never answered her calls, and never went back to her house.

Later that year, as I watched the nightly news at my mother's home, lo and behold, there was Dottie Mae and her cronies and thugs being busted for drugs. They were herded into police cars and vans and driven away. I heard from another woman, who knew her, that Dottie Mae had received fifteen years of federal prison time for distributing cocaine.

As I think back on that time, I realize that, if I had continued on my path of association with Dottie Mae, I probably would have been serving time, also. As I look back on my mindset during that period of ten or so years in my life, I can see that I was either attracting negative people toward me or, at the very least, constantly putting myself in precarious situations. Once again, the question is why?

This brings to mind another older woman, who I had met many years before Dottie Mae, when I was about fifteen or sixteen years old. This lady's name was Nicole. She was, at least, thirty- three years of age at that time. She was very attractive with a beautiful smile, an attractive figure, glowing brown skin, and golden hair. She drove a sporty car with T-tops. It was a luxury vehicle, but I cannot remember its make. She always kept a big bankroll of money and would always flash it in front of me. She would always have, at least, two thousand dollars on her every time I saw her.

Now that I think about it, the allure of maturity and money was intoxicating to my young, materialistic mind. Those two factors have been the common denominators in many of my relationships with men and women. I fell in "love" with Nicole which, in hindsight, probably meant that I was in love with her cash. I knew that she had plenty of money, but I had no idea how she came into her finances because she never seemed to do anything but spend, spend, and spend some more. I had imagined that, maybe, she was a model, an actress, or, even— to not discount the seedier side of life— a stripper or a prostitute. I never asked her for any money, but she would always give it to me, and I, of course, would not turn it away. Nothing really came of my infatuation with Nicole at that point in time, but we kept in touch. It became clear, as time went on, that the feeling was mutual.

One year after I graduated from high school, Nicole

and I rekindled our friendship. I ended up moving out to New Orleans to live with her. I came home every other week with Nicole whenever she came to visit her family. I ended up living with her for six months.

Eventually, things started going really badly for Nicole. She became heavily involved with drugs, which set a torch to her bank account. By that time, I had discovered that the money that Nicole was flaunting was a windfall settlement from an injury her husband had suffered while working on an oil rig. They had been living high and mighty on borrowed time, but the money was not enough to support their lifestyle forever. Around the fourth month of my living with her in New Orleans, she told me that our arrangement would only be temporary. She said that, if I needed to live somewhere permanently, I needed to move in with Rick, who was one of her male friends that she got high with. She said I could get money from Rick to pay my car note every month. So, I did just that. It was either get a job or use that alternative. Those were my only two choices at that moment, and, of course, I was not getting a job. I found the Rick Option to be the best choice. I had to fuck his old ugly ass almost every other night. It was awful, just horrible. I hated each and every minute of it. Rick was like a cowboy who came in from the farm after roping calves. He smoked cigars and liked bourbon, so he always smelled like a nightclub mixed with a barn. He was short and thick with sausage fingers, and his dick matched him perfectly. His hair was combed over, and anyone with eyes could see that he was bald.

Nicole's husband, Morgan, was a spineless jellyfish. She treated him as though he was a child, and he took it without so much as a peep. She screamed at him constantly, and he acted just like a little puppy. This guy was a giant, about six feet five, and, at least, two hundred and fifty pounds. When I lived with them, Nicole and I slept in the same bed every night, and he never said one word about it.

My understanding of the situation was that Morgan was injured pretty badly on that oil rig where he worked, and, allegedly, he could no longer have sex. This was what Rick had told to me, so I don't know if this information was fact or hearsay. I had my suspicions that Rick was fucking Nicole, as well, because he did everything she told him to, showing the same lack of backbone that Morgan revealed. Even though he paid my car note for about two months, the experience was so revolting that I couldn't deal with him or Nicole anymore. I left them both, and I, once again, went back to Neverwills.

I believe Nicole, eventually, became jealous of Rick giving me the money that she could have been getting from him. Her drug problem had gotten progressively worse as her money situation deteriorated to a nearly zero bank account. Nicole's addiction had taken her from marijuana to powder cocaine, and, eventually, to crack in a relatively short time.

During the time that I lived with Nicole, I met this guy named Daniel at a gas station. He, instantly, fell head over heels in love with me. We would talk on the phone for hours while I was in New Orleans. We even continued conversing after I moved back to Alabama. I started visiting him at his home in Port Sulfur, Louisiana. It was an hour and a half away from New Orleans. I didn't mind the long trips or the conversations because I genuinely liked Daniel.

Daniel never pressured me into having sex, and I never brought the subject into our conversation, so we never did it. Incredibly, he gave me five thousand dollars for no reason other than the fact that he liked me. I held on to that money from 1983 up until 1987 when I started working for the Universal Packaging Service. During my ninety day probationary period, I used the five thousand dollars as a down payment on that same condominium that I couldn't rest in because of my neighbor's little bad ass, green-eyed boy who constantly slammed against the walls and roof. That was a real waste of a lot of money.

Daniel began mailing me two hundred dollars every month beginning the very first month that I met him. Again, I never asked for the money, but I was never one to turn down free cash as I have been honest enough to admit. Amazingly, he kept sending me money for nearly twenty years. The reason that he finally stopped the payments was that he became hooked on crack cocaine really bad, and, as a result, drained his bank account. He had, also, started fucking prostitutes. Both vices would take a large chunk out of anyone's bank account.

We still remained friends for many years, despite his problems and his lack of money. I comforted him via the phone when his dad and brother passed away and whenever he needed moral support. I tried to persuade Daniel to move to West Palm once I moved there, but he didn't want to. He had visited me there a couple of times, but, as usual, there was never any sex involved. There you have it: a man who actually supported a woman who he was attracted to, yet, who he never was intimate with. Here was just another in a series of examples of stories in my life that defied logic.

The last real contact that I had with Daniel was when I spoke to him right before Hurricane Katrina devastated the state of Louisiana in 2005. I wrote him letters, and they all were returned as undeliverable. I have tried to find him over the internet, but I haven't been able to find any information concerning him or his family. I am too afraid to contact the Red Cross because they might tell me that he and his family are dead. This would hurt me as I loved Daniel in my own special way. I cared for his family, and I often think about him, his mother Margaret, and his sister Jennifer. I hope he and his family are alive and doing well. If they are, I wonder if Daniel ever thinks about me. One day, I am going to get up enough nerve to call the Red Cross just for the sake of knowing. I wasn't in love with Daniel, but I cared for him and loved him as a friend. I told him as much, yet he still wanted to marry me badly, even though he had no intimate knowledge of who I was. He knew what he wanted, and it was me. It was just too bad that the feeling was not mutual.

As the years passed, I so desperately wanted to get closer to my mother. In 1991, I finally received a transfer from the West Palm Universal Packaging office to the South Georgia branch.

It wasn't very long afterwards that I fell in love with a very sophisticated and worldly woman named Paula. She was twenty-two years older than me. She was beautiful with thick, full lips, as well as a beautiful body. She had deep auburn, shoulder length hair, and the deepest brown eyes that I had ever experienced. She, also, happened to be my manager at my job, which lent itself to the dicey nature of our relationship, as well as its intrigue. After I was intimate with Paula, I vowed to never be with another man, but that vow didn't last forever, of course. To this day, I believe, now more than ever, that she was the one woman who truly convinced me of my affinity for women or, at least, that I liked being with them very much.

Paula had class, style, and grace. To describe her as my ideal woman would not be a stretch. She had it all! In her, I found the woman I had been searching for.

I had never discussed my sexual inclination toward women with my mother, but my gut feeling told me that she was aware of what was going on, but she never told me of her suspicions. What let me know that she knew the truth was a discussion that I had with her concerning Paula receiving a promotion to a higher paying position.

Paula was supposed to move a distance of eight hours away, and I didn't know what to do. I couldn't ask her to turn down this advancement, and she wouldn't have, even if I'd had the nerve to ask. I needed to be consoled by someone, and my mother was the best person in the world at making me believe that everything would be alright.

I called her at eight in the evening, about three weeks before Paula was to leave.

"Mama, Paula is leaving me to take a new position, and I don't think I can take it! I can't live without her, Mama!" I wailed into the phone.

My mother was perceptive. I had said that "I couldn't live without Paula." That was a statement that someone makes about a lover, not just a friend. This was, in effect, my disclosure that I actually was romantically involved with Paula, and this statement probably allowed my mother to connect the stories of my alleged relationship with Sonya Littlefield and my long-standing connection with Dottie Mae. She was probably thinking, _My baby likes women, but it doesn't matter. She is still my child._

After listening to me speak and bawl and feel sorry for myself for about thirty minutes, my mother spoke.

"Baby, listen. If that's what's supposed to happen, it will. You have to trust that everything will work out the way that it should."

I could just imagine her nodding her head as she did whenever she talked me down off of one of my emotional cliffhangers.

"Mama, it seems like nothing works out for me!" I sobbed into the phone, feeling sorry for myself.

"You just have to trust that the right thing will happen to you as long as you are doing what is right by God," she answered.

I said goodnight after we talked for a few more minutes. Then, I settled in to consider what she had said. Was I doing what was right? Was I thinking of Paula? Or was I only thinking of my own selfish ambitions?

In that instance, the circumstances ended up working in my favor because the promotion did not happen. It seemed as though there was some sort of mystical intervention. Paula was a virtual lock for the position, and, then, the opportunity disappeared. I've always wondered why, but she never mentioned any of the details. Maybe, she had decided that she didn't want to move away from me and turned down the promotion. Whatever the case, I never asked her to decline the promotion, so my conscience was clear, and the love of my life wasn't going anywhere, at least, for the time being.

Paula and I were together for a total of eight years. After I met Paula, I felt that no love that I'd had for any woman in my life, either past or present, could compare to the love that I had for her. However, things changed after the sixth year. Prior to that time, we were very happy, but it was at the six year point that sex between us stopped completely, and we began to fight. Ironically, even though we were in a lesbian relationship, the so-called lovemaking for those six years didn't involve oral sex.

"I'm curious as to why you and Paula never engaged in oral sex since that is a major component of a lesbian relationship," Karen said.

"She didn't like oral sex at all," I said in a slow, deliberate, and ashamed tone for reasons I could not understand. The answer simply came out that way for whatever reason.

"So, what, then, did you do that served as sex for the two of you?" Karen asked.

"I used a strap-on dildo," I said bluntly without a pause or a waver in my voice. "It's strange because I was a female and a lesbian, yet, on looking back on it, Paula could have been heterosexual but liked me for who I was. It's confusing, but I am confusing, huh?"

"Of course, given what you have divulged up until this point, the fact that you are, as you call yourself 'confusing' goes without saying," Karen said rather whimsically.

The fighting between us had accelerated from being just verbal altercations to actual physical abuse on my part. I even put my gun to her head once and threatened to kill her if she left me. That threat kept Paula with me for another two excruciating years, and I can honestly attest to being the source of her agony. She, finally, left me in 1998 for some other woman's husband, and, to add insult to injury, I caught them having sex in our bedroom.

I was so emotionally devastated. My sensibilities were assaulted. After the shock of seeing the two of them writhing in my bed, it took years before I was able to get myself together again. The paradox of being me is that I was the person who had created the problem, like an abusive husband or boyfriend, but I was regretful, probably in the same way that abusers are.

"If she were standing here right in front of you and you

could say one thing to Paula now, what would you say to her?" Karen asked.

I said, "If I could say one thing to her right now, it would be that she didn't deserve the treatment I gave her. I would say to her, 'Baby, I am so sorry. Would you please forgive me and give me one more chance?' Of course, I am sure that apology would fall on deaf ears."

"Realistically, no sane human could blame Paula for leaving you. You beat that lady, and you claimed to care for her. I can't believe that so many women stay in abusive situations and don't have the courage to leave like Paula," Karen said pointedly.

"I don't know why I was doing that in the first place. Maybe, if Paula had just fought back, I might have stopped. That just goes to show that you don't have to be a man to abuse a woman," I sighed.

"Why do you suppose that you could beat up Paula, who was taller and bigger than you, but not fight off a rapist who was closer to your size?" Karen asked.

"I think there's a big difference between being mad and being scared. It was like I had extra strength when I was pissed off at Paula. I don't know. Just let me get back to this story because I know I only have thirty minutes left for this week," I said.

After my missteps with Paula, I started to question whether or not things were ever going to go my way in terms of finding love. I knew that I was my own worst enemy on one hand, but, on the other hand, I refused to actually blame myself. Paula was involved with a married man. The fact that I had caught them together was concrete visual evidence. It was a hard thing to stomach, but it was the truth. She cheated on me even though I had forced her hand, but there was no turning back. I loved Paula more than I had loved any other woman. Apparently, my love was not good enough for her. I had to rationalize the situation in my own twisted self-talk, but the reality was that I had driven her into another's arms.

In my self-directed mind, I thought that I had given her all of the love that she needed, but the fact that she had to find love in the life of someone other than me was the crushing blow of reality. I can't deny that I am pretty much the one to blame for my failed relationship with Paula because I abused her verbally and physically. How do I justify hurting the one woman I professed to love more than any other person that I had ever been involved with? For what seems like the hundredth time, I must admit that

I was the driving force in creating my own misery.

A few months after Paula and I broke up, Becky, who years ago had alerted me to the Littlefield sisters' ambush after school and who had been my friend since the first grade, confessed to me that she'd had an affair with a woman. Becky knew about my relationships with women. She had, however, never hinted that she had any such inclinations. Surprisingly, Becky suggested that we get together. I agreed because I was single and because it was just sex. Even though that should have been out of bounds — screwing around with a friend — as I have revealed, I had no such boundaries.

This time, I should have thought the situation through because the sex was horrible, and she was so physically unappealing. She had a wide ass; her tits hung like a cow's udders, and she had a gut like a middle-aged man who drinks a six pack of beer every night. Nevertheless, despite my lack of physical attraction to Becky, we were intimate three times. The only reason that I could rationalize doing it with her was because any female contact was a balm for my pain over losing Paula. I used Becky like a person uses a drink of cheap alcohol— to soothe and to forget. Those acts were entirely selfish, and they had nothing to do with

Meleisa Betts

how Becky felt during it.

After Becky, it was female after female with the occasional male thrown in. The men had something that could benefit me. They wanted to give me what I needed in exchange for the opportunity to sleep with me. With men, it was primarily business, but, with women, it was personal and physical. I still had my old policy in force — if you didn't have money, you don't have Angiel, and that was that.

I met a woman, after my debacle with Becky, named Danielle. She was employed in a profession which paid her well over six figures. She was attractive, to boot. I felt as though I had hit the jackpot with Danielle. She really dug me. After two weeks of dating, we ended up at my place. We couldn't make it to my bed. We were kissing and heatedly tearing off each other's clothes. Right in the midst of this, Danielle abruptly stopped.

"I have something to tell you," Danielle said with a somber tone of voice. She was not making direct eye contact.

I was thinking to myself that Danielle would say that she had a boyfriend or even a girlfriend.

"I have herpes," Danielle revealed. She said this while looking at my chest, as though the revelation was meant for my blouse.

I, instantly, went from burning hot to ice cold. It happened in milliseconds.

"How did it happen, Danielle?" I tried to ask with concern, but, as far as I was concerned, it was a clinical question that a psychiatrist would ask rather than a potential lover.

"I was raped by an African man who had the disease," Danielle answered. She wasn't making any eye contact at all.

I became saddened after talking with Danielle for hours because it was a tragic story. However, I knew that there was no future between us. I knew that the inevitable question was coming.

"Is this going to change anything between us?" Danielle asked with a pleading look in her eyes.

I said no, but she could sense that it was not the truth. Of course, this was a game-changer!

"Are you sure?" she asked again with a tone that suggested she was pleading her case rather than seeking reassurance.

"Yes, Danielle," I said and kissed her. "Let's go to sleep."

Danielle and I spent that Saturday and Sunday together

until she had to leave, which was that Sunday night. I didn't call her much after that revelation, and I didn't answer her calls. One weekend, Danielle came to my door and banged on it for nearly an hour. She, eventually, took the hint after many brush-offs that I was no longer interested in being involved with her. Danielle must have been very much in love with me, or, at least, she hoped that she had found someone who understood. I was sympathetic, but I was not putting myself in that situation for anyone.

I don't know if my experiences with the rapes were the catalysts that began the mental and sexual indifference that I developed towards men, but I can only say that I have no ongoing desire for men from a sexual standpoint. In other words, there is no physical "craving" to have a man like there is for me to possess a woman. One thing that I feel, for sure, is that my life would have been vastly different if I had never been raped.

Those traumatic experiences had not changed my desire for women, but they were contributing factors to all the confusion and thousands of bad and questionable decisions that I have made. Without that trauma, I probably would have had a clearer perspective at a much younger age. I think that the rapes started to mess with me years later. Only after I sought treatment did I come to grips with the incidents. Between my job, my own actions, and running into dishonest people, I began to wonder if I was cursed, but I never thought that, maybe, the curse was self-inflicted.

I have never truly loved a man, as far as I know. I have cared for men such as Wesley, Andrew, and Daniel. But did I love them? The answer to that question is an emphatic NO! However, I admit that I am a paradox wrapped in an enigma with a question mark as the crowning bow.

I was the only child out of the six in my family who ever went to jail. I went to jail because the tenant of some property that I owned told a lie on me. At that time, I was using what I had learned from the men that I had been involved with. They taught me that owning property was a great way to make money. Being the money loving person that I am, I saw this as a way to get rich without working very hard at it. As was my history, though, nothing in my life is ever that clear-cut.

The tenant lived in a beautiful house that I owned in a nice area in Alabama. She claimed to the police that I had threatened to use a knife on her if she didn't give me the rent. I had done nothing of the sort. I had come to the house to verbally evict her if she didn't have my money. She and her sister were getting ready to whip my ass over my not letting her skate by with the rent being late. I picked up a big stick, which was on the ground, to defend myself. I told them to get back as I waved the stick as I attempted to walk back to my car. As soon as I got in my car, police seemed to come from everywhere and nowhere at the same time. There were, at least, four or five police cars that surrounded my car.

I have to point out that her sister was the mayor of this little town, so I really didn't have a chance at a fair trial. The charge that was brought against me was assault with a deadly weapon, but there was no "deadly weapon" anywhere to be found. Was I wrong to try to protect myself from an ass-whipping? I say no, but I ended up in jail. That bitch had conveniently forgotten to mention that she and her sister were getting ready to beat me up over money that the sister owed me. I remained in a holding cell for twenty-four hours. It was a nightmare from hell without a doubt. After calling every person that I could think of, I finally convinced one of my cousins to bail me out.

I was so depressed and scared that I was going to lose my job because I had been charged with a felony, which is an absolute no-no when working in a federal government position. Because of my worrying and my overblown belief that my career was over, I attempted suicide for the second time in my life. The only difference was that, this time, I used sleeping pills. The last thing I remembered was calling my sister. I told her that I didn't want to live anymore. There were some things that happened to me in jail that I care to never talk about or even think of. When I look back on that terrible time, I think that I was crying out for help more so than actually trying to end my life.

If I really was trying to kill myself, then I wouldn't have called anyone. I would have just done it, and that would have been the end of me. When I woke up from my self-induced semi-coma, I was in the hospital. My stomach had been pumped, and I was cuffed to the bed. My sister Rebecca's face was the first thing I saw when I opened my eyes. If it wasn't for my psychologist at the time, who came to the hospital at an ungodly hour to sign my release form, I would have been hauled off to a mental institution. Thank God she was on call that night.

"I sincerely hope that you are well past the feelings that caused you to try and take your life," Karen said.

"I'm not, Karen. That's why I'm in therapy with you. My former psychologist said that I was in a good mental state when she released me from her care, but I am still struggling with these things that keep haunting me, like the parts of my life that either seem like a dream or things that I surely did, and there is evidence that I did them, but there is no memory that I have of having done them," I said with my face in my hands and my elbows on my knees. That was the only support that kept me from toppling over onto the hardwood floor of the room.

"Still, I need your assurance that you will not act out of despair again. Promise me that, if you get those feelings, you will also call me at home, regardless of the time," Karen insisted.

"Karen, I promise you that I will do that if I need to," I said.

This time, I looked up from my cupped hands with eyes red and stained with tears.

To add to my other issues with tenants and my love life, my mother's health deteriorated rapidly between 1994 and 2003. She'd had a stroke in 1994 that left her paralyzed on her right side, and her speech was severely impaired. As a testament to her strength and character, my mother fought back from the awful effects of the stroke and lived for almost ten more wonderful years.

In 2003, I was serving as a primary caregiver to my mother, who was still in Neverwills, so I had to come home to Valeria to get some papers. My intent was to get what I needed and to get right back on the road to Alabama, but, as soon as I started upstairs to my condominium, I smelled shit. I was horrified to find that it was painted all over my door, as though someone had used a paintbrush. I called the police, and they came out and investigated. The police found the culprit. It was my psychotic neighbor. The neighbor confessed to the police that he had shit-painted my doorway because he believed that my dog had shitted in his yard. This was not true because I never took my dog anywhere near his "yard". Plus, we lived in condominiums! Nobody personally owned a yard! He forgot to mention that his flamingly gay neighbor had a dog. In addition, we lived in two separate buildings that were divided by a partition.

The police officers came to me and said, "Ms. Royal, he admitted to doing it and is willing to clean your door or buy you a new one."

I told both of the officers, "Hell, no! My mother is in Alabama on the verge of passing away, and I had to come home to find SHIT on my door? I don't think so! His ass is going to jail tonight!"

They didn't want to do the report, so I asked to speak with their superior officer. This request made them write the report. They handcuffed this psychopath and took him in. I had to go to the police department to file charges. This took, at least, four hours. This was four hours that I could have been with mother, instead of dealing with this bullshit. He was later found guilty and was sentenced to clean both the Humane Society and the public transit vehicles.

"That was really bizarre," Karen said.

"Hell, yeah! It was! He was crazy and stupid for even admitting to doing something that psychotic," I said as I looked at Karen with a wide-eyed look that probably made me appear a bit psychotic, as well.

After dealing with that incredible situation, I drove back to Neverwills that morning at five o'clock with no sleep to speak of. It was the month of August, so it was extremely hot outside. The fog was so thick that I could hardly see the lines on the road. Finally, I made it home, and I rushed to my mother's bedside.

"Mama, it's me. Are you doing okay?" I found strength enough to say, even though I was about to fall asleep. My eyelids were so heavy.

"Baby, I'm still here," she answered as her eyes opened. She seemed to have been waiting on me.

"Don't leave me, Mama! Please don't leave me!" I pleaded.

I sat at Mama's bedside and told her about what had just happened. I would always let her know about what was going on with me. She could just barely hold her eyes open, as well. It took all of her energy to speak to me, but I knew what she was thinking even though she never said a word. My mother's eyes told me what her question was. She was asking me, "Baby, what have you gotten into now?"

I had promised her that morning, before I left for Valeria, that, no matter what, I was going to try my best to stay out of trouble.

I said, "Mama, you know it's always something with me. I don't always bring things on myself, but problems just seem to follow me. Why that is I don't know, but I promise you, Mama, that I'm gonna try to avoid any type of confusion. I promise you that, and I mean it," I said, crying. "Mama, you don't have to worry about me. I'll be alright. I know that you've been worrying about me all my life, but, Mama, I'm a big girl now, and I can take care of myself. You can be at peace now. Don't worry about me anymore."

Meleisa Betts

Tears were flowing down my face like a mini-waterfall. Deep down, I knew that I wasn't a big girl at all. I was still somewhat immature and childish. I was still that same adolescent who acted impulsively. What was I going to do without my mother? My baby sister Allison put her arm on my shoulder to comfort me. I lowered my head to catch a breath as I sat like a statue next to my mother's bed. Instantly, my chest felt like it had begun to swell. I was gasping for air! It felt like my heart stopped beating. My arms, my legs felt numb. Tears began to run down my cheeks like a flowing river. I couldn't stop crying. I watched my mother take her last breath. "JESUS, JESUS, JESUS, help me!" was all that I could say. My mother closed her eyes. Then, she was gone.

My baby sister said, "She's still with us, Angiel, and she always will be. Please don't be so sad. Please. Whenever you need to see Mama, just look in the mirror."

While my mother was lying in the funeral home, I'd heard that bitch, Jenny Littlefield, and my daddy's new whore Velma had gone by to view her body. Incredibly, Velma was yet another member of the Littlefield family! How stupid and money grubbing could those sluts be? They had all consented to fucking the same man that three others had been openly screwing, and they didn't seem to care a bit. I was so mad that my daddy had the audacity to bring his present and former whores to see the woman that they had tormented for so many years of her life. I told Deputy McDaniel, a deputy sheriff of Neverwills that knew my family very well and who was aware of our contentious relationship, that, if they showed up at the funeral, it was gonna be a fight right there in the church and that somebody would get hurt. Deputy McDaniel knew that I meant each and every word, so he went to my father and the Littlefield whores to tell them to keep their distance.

"That really took a lot of nerve on their part," Karen stated.

"Karen, it would have been hell to pay 'cause I was going to raise hell and kick their asses," I said with my eyes glowering like a cat looking at a dog.

My daddy cried like a baby on the day of my mother's funeral. Given the way that he had treated her, I never imagined he would have reacted that way. All I could think of doing was just standing up and bashing him in the back of his fucking head because of how he had cheated on my mother over and over with those Littlefield tramps. I was suffering and angry at the same time. None of my so-called friends, not even Paula, who claimed to love both me and my mother, showed up to support me. In looking back on the situation, I guess I couldn't very well blame Paula, given the fact that we were on such bad terms, but, in my grief, I could not be rational.

Because of that grief and lack of emotional support during those difficult times, I, eventually, had to receive professional help from a psychiatrist. If it wasn't for this help, my faith in God, and my dog Christy Bell, I don't know what I would have done.

Even to this day, there are times when her absence hits me, and I spontaneously shed tears. Those tears, most often, come at night as I try to sleep. My pillow is my silent confidante as it receives all of my tears. Some mornings, I feel like it was just a bad dream and that my mother is still at home. I attempt to dial her number, but then reality sets in. I often find myself wishing that my mother was still here. I miss her more than words or emotions can describe. I love her so much. I, sometimes, ask, "Why, Mama? Why did God have to take you? Why?"

I find myself remembering the times I combed her long, pretty hair. I recall the sound of her laughter, the way she held me, and told me I was beautiful and special. These are comforting memories.

"To listen to your description of her, your mother seemed to be a wonderful woman who I would have loved to have known," Karen said.

I'm so glad I listened to God and my inner spirit back in 2001 and named my dog Christy Bell. This was the name on the social security card that Mama received in the mail back in 1984. It said Christy Bell, instead of her given name. From then on, I called her Christy Bell. She even started to answer to it. Eventually, everybody else in the family started calling her Christy Bell.

Back in 2001, I called Mama and said, "Mama, guess what? I got a puppy, and I named her Christy Bell."

She laughed and laughed. Everybody fell in love with my little doggie. Now, it seems like Christy Bell is always getting into something, like I did as a child. Cute and full of herself, she is the canine version of her owner. Christy Bell is a comfort for me. She helps ease the pain.

After I finally recovered from my relationship with Paula, I met my so-called next real girlfriend Heidi, whose nickname was Deborah. I met her at a nightclub. We began dating, at least, a year before my mom's passing. I could tell, from the moment we met, that she was a stripper.

Deborah had 38 double D breasts that complemented an already gorgeous body and beautiful face. Everywhere she went, heads turned, as one would expect. Because of this, she never took any other vocation seriously. She only stripped one week out of a month. She made enough in seven days to cover a month's worth of expenses.

During this time, I was dealing with my mother's death, and Deborah didn't make the situation easier. She wanted to come to Alabama to my mom's funeral, but I insisted that she not. I needed to be alone with my family, and I was sure that she would be a distraction. All she wanted to do was argue and pick fights it seemed.

All the fighting that we were doing was negated by the fact that we had a good sex life. The sex life neutralized the times when I tried to break up with Deborah, but then she would call to apologize, always promising to change her ways. Then, we would end up having sex. The cycle repeated itself several times over our tumultuous three-year relationship. Eventually, her personality cancelled out the sex life that we had. I had a confrontation with her the week after my mother's funeral because I was tired of the stripping. As I look back on the situation, I believe that I just got tired of her sorry ass in general.

"What happened? There must have been something that was a breaking point as there usually is some event that triggers the person to say, 'That's enough,'" Karen asked.

Well, one night, we were watching television, and she decided that she wanted to order Chinese food. She placed the order over the phone as though she was treating for the dinner.

I asked, "Are you paying for it? You just placed an order, and it seems like you got your favorite meal."

"Baby, you know I don't have a job," she said, smiling, while posing in a stance like a swimsuit model. I guess she figured that her looks were all the payment that she needed.

This statement struck a nerve in me, and I reacted.

"Why don't you go out and get a real job?" I asked in a tone which did not lend itself to civil conversation, but I had meant for the question to come out harshly.

"What I need a real job for?" Deborah had her hands on her hips, and she was leaning forward. The coquettish look on her face had, now, changed to angry bitch mode.

"Aren't you tired of being a whore? All you do is sell your body and soul for a few dollars in tips!" I said angrily.

"Your mama was a whore!" she said, leaning forward.

Her eyes were as wide as fifty cent pieces, and she looked like a wild animal to me at that moment.

Before I realized what I was doing, I had grabbed my .380 automatic pistol from inside of my entertainment unit and withdrawn it from its holster. As we struggled and wrestled, I dropped the gun to prevent it from going off. With that action, I, also, dropped my defenses. We began to kiss and fondle each other, which ended in our making fiery love. What an absolutely ridiculous outcome to such a heated confrontation that could have led to someone being shot or killed! That was just the nature of our relationship. There was a part of me that was attracted to the conflict, I guess. Eventually, being with Deborah was too emotionally draining. I got tired of the day-to-day drama. I, finally, broke up with her despite her pleading.

"So, you stayed with her for TWO MORE YEARS, after she called your mother a whore, you two fought, and you had to draw your pistol on her?" Karen asked incredulously.

"What can I say? The reason that I stayed with her was because the sex was good, I guess. I'm just being honest with you. I'm coming clean, so I can admit that I was probably thinking about myself more so than anything else," I said. "All we did was fuck and eat and argue and fuck. We fucked everywhere. We had sex in movie theaters, the back seat and front seat of my car, in restaurants, and in public restrooms. One time, we fucked on her roommate's dinner table. She was the 'turkey', and I basted her ass. That's just the honest truth. I'm telling you things about me that I'm sure you never could imagine. I gained twenty pounds within two months after Deborah and I broke up. Maybe, I was eating from the boredom that I experienced after we broke up."

"Yes, people often fill the void left after a breakup with food or some other diversion. I appreciate the fact that you are being open and honest with me. Your honestly can only help you come to a good place in your life," Karen said. This time, there was eye contact with me, and she did not make any entries into my file.

"Right now, you know more about me than anyone else on Earth," I said.

"It's true. Sex does help one keep the weight down, especially the energetic kind," Karen giggled.

{Chapter 7}

There was a period of time, near the end of 2002, where a black female supervisor at Universal Packaging began to cause me a lot of problems. She harassed the hell out of me. She harassed everyone that she didn't like, and, unfortunately, she was my immediate superior. My supervisor had had, by far, the most Equal Employment Opportunity Commission (EEOC) complaints filed against her, more than any other supervisor in the region. No one in upper management wanted to help me. I mentioned to Peggy, one of my co-workers, that I needed an attorney, but it was hard to find one with balls enough to go up against the federal government.

"One of my friends used to work for the EEOC within Universal Packaging. He has knowledge of the EEOC process," Peggy said.

"Is he a lawyer?" I asked.

"No, but he is very familiar with the EEOC process. He was an examiner for claims, I think."

I asked Peggy for this person's phone number, but she balked.

She said, "First, I have to check with him. Then, I'll get back with you."

I had no other choice in the matter, so I waited for her to contact him. I got her friend's number a few days later and called him.

The Universal Packaging service has their own in-house EEOC branch. This is fundamentally different from the other national delivery services. Almost everything, for Universal Packaging, is in-house. This is why it's so hard to fight them. They have judges downtown, who generally rule in their favor in grievances. Well, this one particular female supervisor where I worked cared more about harassing the workers than getting the public's mail out on time.

"Didn't you guys have a union?" Karen asked.

"Yes, we did, but most of the local union stewards are weak-assed bastards. The weak outnumber the strong. Maybe, one day, we'll get a strong leader," I replied.

"What about the Universal Packaging director and CEO? Don't they care about managers focusing on mind games rather than doing their jobs?" Karen asked.

I steered her away from this line of questioning. "Let's get back to what I was saying. I have gotten off the subject," I said.

The name of the man that my co-worker referred me to was Thomas Walters. I called him that very evening. *What a pleasant voice on the other end of the phone?* I thought. I heard such a caring tone in his conversation. I never asked him what his present vocation was, but he stated that he was a former case worker for the EEOC. I explained to him in detail about how my supervisor was harassing me. He mentioned to me that his wife, also, had a complaint with the EEOC. He claimed her supervisor had assaulted her and that she had required medical attention afterwards.

I, later, spoke with his wife, Brandi, over the phone briefly. I only asked her a couple of questions about her case against her employer. Her story was that, at the time, she was a union representative in the district where she worked. She had made simple protests concerning working conditions, yet, along with the alleged assault by her supervisor, the employer had mounted an all-out assault on her. They had used tactics such as defamation and outright personal retaliation.

Brandi stated that someone was sending people to her home in order to vandalize her car and she had received threats on her life. I can still hear her voice crystal clear in my head, from the cadence of her words, right down to the tone and nuances of her gravelly voice. She seemed honest about her story and genuinely fearful of the fact that the company was paying someone to get rid of her. She had stated that Thomas felt that she was connecting the dots and had come to the wrong conclusion.

Thomas met with me at my home to discuss my case further. He was as impressed with my home as I was depressed about my situation. Thomas talked about my home as if he had never seen anything in his life that was nice. I really didn't care about his compliments because they were irrelevant to my situation.

As he droned on and on, I thought, *I'm hurting, man, so shut the hell up!* I wanted to say to Thomas, "Can't you see the frustration on my face? Let's get on with the EEOC conversation. I know you heard it over the phone. That's why you are here now to discuss my situation. Shut the hell up about my condominium p-l-e-a-s-e!" My expression was telegraphing a message that he was obviously oblivious to.

Finally, the nonverbal messages that I was sending him must have worked because he shut up with the blathering questions about where I had gotten this painting or that vase. Thankfully, we began to talk about the government and how I was being railroaded into submission. I mentioned my prior EEOC complaints and went into detail about them. He wrote on a notepad as I spoke. I started to warm up to Thomas, and I became more and more impressed as we conversed. He asked all of the right questions, and I never had to repeat myself. It seemed as though he understood the situation as I went along. The last thing I needed was to be aggravated by some person who didn't really know the EEOC process or who wanted to use me to gain his experience.

Thomas listened to me when I told him that I was so sick and depressed over the harassment. I spoke of having no peace of mind for days and no sleep. I intimated that the situation was so taxing that I threw up constantly. I couldn't eat. I cried all the time. Thomas made me feel as though he was the only person in the world who understood my pain. He kept reminding me that Brandi was going through some of what I was going through, as well. He said that she threw up frequently, also. She was sick and depressed all of the time.

The next day, Thomas, who was acting as my counsel, called my managers. He, also, called the lead manager. He called everybody that I had named who was involved in my case. _Thomas really cares about me_, I thought.

The calls to upper management didn't do any damn good. Thomas told me that he was going to write the EEOC for the first process and that he wanted to meet with me to sign the complaint. First, he wanted me to proofread it. I met him a couple of days later at the QuikTrip convenience store around the corner from the building where I worked to proofread the document.

When Thomas got into my car, the first thing he started to talk about was my Lexus. I thought, _Oh, shit! How long is this going to go on?_

"Well, how does a person work for the government, drive a Lexus, and live in a penthouse on Devonshire Drive?" Thomas asked in a tone, which I took to be skeptical and accusatory, but I didn't act on that feeling. The fact is that probably everyone who knew anything about me may have thought something similar to this at one time or another.

In addition to my luxury vehicle, my condominium was located in Devonshire, which was a prominent area in South Georgia. I took a deep breath and thought, *Damn! That's a good question.* In the back of my mind, I knew how individuals did their social math. They thought that prosperity coupled with an average paying job or profession usually equaled some kind of illicit activity. I revealed my secret weapon to him, so he would give me the fucking papers to sign. The secret that I gave him as the reason for my nice things was the dot-com boom, which, of course, was an excuse that I fabricated. I needed to speed things along because I was almost running late for work. He already knew more than enough about me for only having known me for a few days.

Finally, I got to read the complaint. I was so amazed by his writing skills that I became very optimistic. In the back of my mind, I said to myself, "Wow! This is brilliant!"

Thomas had taken down every word that I'd said that first day. He'd even added to my words, thereby, creating the best EEOC complaint I had ever seen.

Originally, I had contacted Dot Weston, a top-notch employment attorney out of Philadelphia, Pennsylvania.

She had won many EEOC cases against the government. She was one of the best attorneys who specialized in prosecuting EEOC cases against the federal government. She had worked on a case for me back in 1996 against the government, and I had won.

We were so sure that this current case was, also, a winner that she didn't even charge any upfront fees, not even when she flew to Georgia. This was how sure she was of the outcome in our favor. Unfortunately, there was a conflict with a major employment litigation case, and Dot had to remove herself from my case. I could have probably sued her, but, since she had charged me nothing, I decided to move forward. After all, she was the best attorney in her field, and she believed that my case was an open and shut, surefire win. Now, I just needed to find someone to represent me.

Even though she had to back out of my case, Dot's professionalism left an indelible impression on me. Thomas was the male equivalent to Dot. I say this based on his mastery of vocabulary and caring and selfless manner. These were the same characteristics that Dot had shown, and that gave me supreme confidence in his ability to bring the case home. I even sent a copy of his complaint document to Dot for her opinion, and she was impressed.

In light of the stellar impression that Thomas had made on me with his literary skills, I signed the complaint and moved forward with him as my counsel. He said that he would send it certified mail the next day. I gave him the money to mail the document. He never really had mentioned any other money at that point in time. He did say that I would probably win my retaliation complaint and receive monetary damages. In subsequent conversations, Thomas began to tell me about the attorney that Brandi had — Billy Donavan. He said that Billy would even take cases on a contingency basis.

"What would happen if he doesn't take the case?" I asked, now feeling anxious about this new person being discussed.

He said, "He has Brandi's case, and I'm sure that I can talk him into taking yours."

As long as I won my case, it didn't matter who defended me. However, I was under the impression that Thomas was going to take my EEOC complaint from beginning to end based upon our conversations. I should have known better based on the fact that he was not a litigator. Well, at least, I was satisfied with the beginning of my dealings with him, and that meant something. I felt relatively comfortable around Thomas, but I always tried to keep the conversation geared toward what we were meeting for. He always tried to talk about other things like my dog or my condo or my car, but I stayed focused on the job, which was the complaint that I was filing. Eventually, all mentioning of the ballyhooed "Billy" ceased completely. Again, I was in a situation where I was not thinking. Instead, I made my decisions based on appearances.

The truth of my work situation was that I had literally absorbed my supervisor into my mind. That bitch was always the number one topic in my thought processes. My supervisor was in my dreams. More accurately, they were nightmares. There was some real shit going on in my head! I really didn't want to talk about anything else but my job and how my supervisor kept fucking with me every day. I felt as though I must have had a big sign on my head that read PLEASE SCREW WITH ME.

Despite all of the big talk and numerous conversations, we never went to mediation in my case. Thomas actually seemed to be paranoid about going to mediation with me against the Universal Packaging lawyers, and he abruptly changed his mind about representing me.

Meleisa Betts

"It might mess up Brandi's case if I'm involved with you and your EEOC case. That would be a conflict of interest," he said to me in a conversation that we had about two weeks before my hearing.

"How could it mess up her case? We're two totally separate circumstances, and we are not related," I said with anger in my voice that was unmistakable.

"The government inspectors will come and harass me at my house. They did it with Brandi, and they will do it to me. I know it. They will try to make me stop representing you," Thomas pleaded.

That whole theory was from outer space, but he was convinced of that so-called truth.

"You should have known right then that he was sort of suspect. It sounds like he believed that he would be targeted by black ops government assassins," Karen stated.

"You're right. I should have suspected something. Why in the hell would the government try to harass him for taking an EEOC case?" I said, shaking my head.

"Never mind his reasoning. The fact is that his statement should have been a red flag to you. It seems that one of your hallmark methods of making decisions is to disregard what your instinct tells you, and you, instead, go with what seems easy and what will get the desired results. You did not think that something was wrong, but you had indications. We won't dwell on it, but there are patterns that seem to repeat with you."

"What exactly are these 'patterns' that you see?" I asked with equal parts anger and skepticism.

"I will discuss them with you eventually, but, at this point in our discussion, it is not the proper time. I assure you that I will give you my diagnosis at the appropriate point," Karen said, while looking at and making notes in my file and making no direct eye contact with me.

"What? After you have made enough to pay for your Mercedes?" I quipped.

"No, it actually will be after I pay for my timeshare in Boca Raton," Karen quickly shot back.

"Well, since I'm paying for your vacation home, then I better get my money's worth," I retaliated.

Thomas began to tell me about the cases he'd read while he worked at the EEOC. This is the same branch of the federal government that he now had refused to fight. In his explanation of why he was backing out on me, he told me about one case where a manager actually raped several women. According to Thomas, the manager had called certain females into his Universal Packaging office and forced them to perform oral sex on him. Many of those women suffered nervous breakdowns because of the horrible things that were done to them and what he had forced them to do for the sake of their jobs. During the investigations, Thomas alleged that the same manager was simply transferred to another location. This disgusting slime ball of a supervisor had supposedly done the same thing to several females over a number of years.

Thomas said, "None of these females ever knew of each other because the government would settle the cases in secret. Each time the manager was moved, no one ever knew the real reason. The manager kept doing the same thing over and over, and the government just kept moving him. The government inspectors would just break into people's homes with no just cause. One morning, Brandi and I woke up to find all four tires on both cars flattened. We knew the Universal Packaging inspectors had done it."

"Did you call the police?" I asked, looking at him intently.

He responded, "No, we just got new tires." He looked up into space while answering.

Emphatically, I said, "You should have called and

made a complaint. Not calling the police over that kind of vandalism doesn't make sense!"

Thomas didn't say anything to that statement. I felt so sorry for him and Brandi at that point. It was on my mind for the rest of the night! *The Universal Packaging Service should not do that to that poor man and his family*, I thought. My heart wept for him and Brandi. At the time, there was no way on Earth for me to know that Thomas was a liar.

"You must have had a pretty good record to get a transfer from West Palm to Valeria, I'm assuming?" Karen said.

"Hell, no! My record was much better than just good! The problem with Universal Packaging transfers was that generally they don't grant them unless you have a damn good record," I stated. "I had to get closer to my mother because it was too taxing for me to drive from Florida to Alabama. I had to find a way, and I did. I used the best means that I had at my disposal," I said.

"Let me guess. Your solution probably involved using sex in some form," Karen joked.

"Of course, it did. 'You have to use what you have to get what you want' is my motto, if you recall. Did I tell you that?" I joked.

"Was it a man or a woman that you used your feminine whiles to captivate?" Karen asked.

"Okay. First of all, don't judge me because I did what I had to do. Karen, sometimes, you do bad things for good reasons. This time, I did a questionable thing for the best reason in the world. I lucked up and got an interview with a manager who loved young, single women."

"He loved young, single women, meaning?" Karen asked with a leading tone.

"Meaning. He wanted some of this vajayjay. So, I gave him some to get what I needed. What's wrong with that? We, women, have been using that weapon for years to get what we need, and men keep paying the price, right?" I laughed.

"So, in effect, you had sex with a manager to affect the transfer," she stated.

"I didn't give a damn about him or how good or bad it was, Karen! Hell! I needed to be closer to my mama. To tell the truth about it, the sex was taking so long with that dude that I had to fake an orgasm," I laughed.

"I am surprised at your propensity over and over to use your sexuality as a weapon, which seems to be an overriding theme in your life," Karen said defiantly.

"Okay, but can we get back on track, now? We're getting closer to what this crazy-ass bastard did to his wife and what happened to him," I stated. "First, I need to tell you a little more about the EEOC case, so you will fully understand the entire picture. We have been talking for almost an hour, and you still haven't heard the real stuff."

"This must be serious since you seem to be ultra-focused on revealing whatever this secret happens to be," Karen said.

"I'll let you be the judge of that," I replied.

I had my EEOC complaint in process at the same time my mother's health was failing. I requested a revised work schedule. I wanted to work and help my sister take care of my mother, but it was denied. I decided the hell with them. I took off for the rest of the time that I needed. It didn't matter how long of a leave it was going to be because nothing was going to keep me from being with her. The federal government had kept me from going to my Granddaddy James's funeral back in 1988. At that time, I didn't know any better. I had gotten an official discussion on my attendance and the next step was a letter of reprimand. I was too scared to take off from work and go to my own

Meleisa Betts

granddaddy's funeral.

"I find it hard to believe that they wouldn't let you off, knowing your mother was really sick," Karen said slowly.

"That's what I've been telling you. They do shit to employees just to make them miserable!" I screamed. "Hell! I wasn't lying to you earlier nor was I bullshitting you."

"Again, that's really hard to believe," Karen said.

"Well, you best believe it 'cause it's the damn truth! I've lived with that decision every day because I loved my grandfather. I should have just taken off, regardless of the consequences," I said.

"That's just pure evil if what you are alleging is true," Karen said quietly.

During the time my mama was on her death bed, I made a couple of promises to her. One was concerning the job. I knew how my mother felt about me filing complaints on the job. For that reason, I promised that I would drop the EEOC complaint and any other grievances. I kept my promise to my mother for nearly three years. I worked very hard at trying to get along with my supervisor. Let the truth be told. I had no energy to fight.

Thomas and I didn't talk for years after that initial encounter. Nevertheless, I kept his telephone number, just in case I needed him in the future, even though he had been useless when I had needed him the most. If I could have foreseen the future, I would have flushed his number down the toilet.

I returned to work after being out on leave because I had been assaulted. Two females had beaten me severely in the hallway of my building. They had met me at the door of my condominium after an incompetent gate guard had allowed them access to my building without my permission and without me even being on the premises! The principal assailant was arrested and charged; yet, the damage had already taken its toll on me.

I tried to sue the property management, but there were too many people on their security staff who stated that I had given the females access to the property at all times. No one but an idiot would pay for the security of a gated community and then allow anyone to come onto the property. Still, defying all of this logic, I lost the case against Devonshire Properties. For all that I paid to be secure, I was left with a black eye, bruised ribs, a badly injured back, and lips that looked like I had gotten collagen injections that had gone horribly wrong.

I was on a shift known as "tour one". I went in at eleven

P.M. and got off at 7:30 A.M. Because this shift wasn't working for me, I put in a revised schedule. The traffic was heavy, traveling to downtown Valeria. My new hours were twelve A.M. to 8:30 A.M. Now, this schedule was much better for me. I came to work every night on time for, at least, two weeks. Then, the same supervisor started to fuck with me. She was the day shift supervisor, and her reporting time was seven A.M. She really should not have had any contact with me, but she made it her business to find me every morning and page me throughout the building.

"What happened to the manager who gave you the transfer?" Karen asked.

"They sent his ass somewhere. Who knows?"

This bitch began to turn the other managers against me. Because they were weak-minded individuals, they all gradually changed their ways toward me. I felt like a leper.

One morning, around seven o'clock, I re-injured my back while lifting heavy trays of mail. I sat at a table and tried to get myself together. I cried a flood of tears because of the pain. The bitch approached me, requesting that I report to an area which was against my restrictions. She saw that I was crying so damn hard and that I was in pain, but that didn't deter her.

She yelled, "Report to the area!"as she pointed.

"I'm really in a lot of pain," I said, while sniffling through my tears. "Can I just sit here at the table?"

She said, "I'm instructing you to report to the area," while continuing to point at nothing.

"I need to go to the hospital," I pleaded.

"Go to the manager's office," she said, pointing in the direction of the door.

I went to the office and waited for a supervisor to take me to the hospital. They, finally, found someone to do the paperwork, so I could be treated for my injuries. The supervisor was very hostile to me in front of everybody while all of this was transpiring. I was in too much pain to respond to her ignorance. They waited until ten in the morning, before deciding to take me to the hospital, and then I was just dropped off.

"They waited that long to take you to the hospital? Why? What would they gain by denying you medical attention?" Karen asked.

"It was just another form of harassment," I responded.

While at home, I thought about the entire ordeal and decided that I was treated wrongfully. I wasn't going back to work under that monster. It was too stressful. I, also, thought about the promises that I'd made to my mother. I got on my knees and asked her to forgive me. I couldn't let them get away with this!

I called Thomas after having not spoken with him in nearly three years. I discussed the situation thoroughly with him. He said that he would come over to my house and go over the EEOC claim with me. During the conversation, Thomas casually mentioned that Brandi had passed away earlier in the year. I felt a sense of grief for him. We, then, set up a date to meet once more. He came by and took very detailed notes just like before.

When he got ready to leave, he said, "I'll call you once I've completed the papers. I'm only charging you four hundred dollars to process the paperwork and go to mediation."

It all seemed fair, so I wrote him a check without thinking about what had happened three years earlier. I was so adamant about getting back at Universal Packaging that I couldn't see the forest for the trees. Thomas called a few days later and gave me directions to his office. I went there to expedite matters because I was ready to do battle with the Universal Packaging office.

Once I arrived at his shop, I was quite impressed with

the decorations and the general setup. I seemed to be overly impressed with looks rather than the fact that Thomas was not an attorney, but I had basically paid him a retainer as though he was one. However, it looked as though Thomas had achieved a level of success based on his surroundings. His affiliation with Georgia Upholstery contributed to the ambience. Thomas was one of the principal owners of Georgia Upholstery, which carried a variety of furniture for the home and office. He had two part-time workers, Britney and Tracey. Britney was at the shop on the day I stopped by. I signed the EEOC papers on that day, as well.

"So, Thomas went from working a temporary job at the Universal Packaging service to repairing and reupholstering furniture? Oh, my word! What a dream!" Karen said.

"It turns out that it was a 'how can I sit on my ass' dream," I quipped.

My co-worker, Celestine Martin, was familiar with the EEOC process within the Universal Packaging Service. So, I put Thomas in contact with her via my cell phone. In my mind, I wanted to create a "dream team". To me, the combination of Thomas and Celestine was the perfect match, but, when Thomas finished up the call with

Celestine, ten minutes later, he said, "Celestine is not a paralegal. She's a Universal inspector and that doesn't help your case or do it any good."

"It's clear to me that Thomas just wanted all of the money for himself. He knew that Celestine wasn't in the legal profession or with the EEOC. That was just plain nonsense to dismiss her and say she was invaluable when he wasn't even a lawyer!" Karen said in a tone that almost suggested that she couldn't believe my rationale for my decision making.

All night, I pondered the possibility that I was misinformed. Celestine couldn't be a Universal Packaging inspector! Despite my misgivings, I took Thomas's statement for what it was worth. I forgot about the dream team idea and just resigned myself to letting Thomas handle the case on his own. I was 100% convinced that Celestine was not a government inspector, but I never insisted that she be a part of my case. *Thomas is just having a hard time dealing with Brandi's death*, I thought. Even though, three years later, that fact should be irrelevant to my case. I did, however, remember him saying that he believed that the inspectors had slashed Brandi's tires three years earlier. I wanted to believe that it was just paranoia on his part.

Before I left the shop, we decided to get something to eat. We ate at a place he was familiar with called Polazzo's. They served authentic Italian cuisine, and it was located in the most posh area of Valeria. For this meal, I picked up the tab, which was relatively costly. The second time that we dined together, he paid for some cheap meal at a local delicatessen. I refer to it as a "cheap meal" because the meal I had provided for him was nearly fifty dollars, while the second meal that he provided couldn't have been more than ten dollars total.

During the second meal, I mentioned to Thomas my idea for a modeling agency. At first, I was a little reluctant to expound on my concept, but Thomas kept asking me about my ideas. Finally, I relented, and I went over the idea detail by detail. I wanted a modeling agency devoted to undiscovered beauties in the South Georgia area. I knew the concept would sell if it got enough exposure and positive press. Not only did I need to obtain a small business grant in order to swing the deal, but I, also, needed someone to write the grant proposals. At first, he didn't seem overly interested in the modeling concept. However, the next day, I got a call from Thomas, and he seemed excited and enthusiastic. He said, "I thought about your idea, and I think it's great. Can you come by the office?"

"How could Thomas have known anything about managing a modeling agency? He ran an upholstery shop," Karen asked while looking at me over her glasses.

"Remember, I told you how good his writing skills were? Well, I needed a writer to put together grant proposals, and I figured bringing him along would give him incentive," I rationalized.

"It would have been logical to have gotten someone that worked in that area of expertise, not someone who covered torn furniture," Karen replied forcefully. "Your typical mode of operation seems to be some form of manipulation, be it the promise of sex or money."

"My belief was— and it still is to some extent— that money and sex are the things that drive men, so like I said, I used what I had to get what I needed. That has been going on since the beginning of time," I said with a laugh. Karen simply looked at my file and made what seemed like the thousandth entry.

On a Thursday evening, I met Tracey for the first time, and it was at Thomas's upholstery business. We were all sitting on the sofa and table area, which was right outside of his office. Thomas's main concern was a name for the modeling agency. He wanted it to be called the Model Shop. Now, I should have known that something wasn't right with that picture, but I ignored the signs. I had already told him that I wanted it to be called Total Dime Modeling Agency. I told him that I had chosen this name because of Chyna, my friend who had died. I wanted to keep her dream alive.

I'll never forget the day I received the news of her death. I had gone out of town for the weekend. When I got back to work on that Monday, a co-worker ran up to me. She asked if I had heard about Chyna. I was thinking that she was going to tell me that Chyna had finally made it big. Instead, my co-worker informed me that Chyna had been killed in a car accident over the weekend. I nearly fainted when I heard the crushing news. I cried for weeks, which seemed to turn into months. Even though we had ended on bad terms, I still cared for her, and I had promised myself that I would honor her by using my nickname for her. I called her "Chyna Dimes".

Thomas asked Britney and Tracey what they thought about the various names he had thrown out. Most of them escaped me because I had no intention of signing off on anything that they agreed on. I sat and listened for two damn hours. As the sun set, I knew that I wasn't going to make it home by dark. That was a problem. I told Thomas about my religious beliefs and that I was supposed to be home before nightfall. After I declared my religious belief, Thomas, then, declared that he was Jewish. The only black Jew that I'd ever heard of was Sammy Davis Jr., but I gave Thomas the benefit of the doubt. His beliefs had nothing to do with the fact that I was leaving, and it irritated me to no end that he had to use any topic to try and one up me in conversation. Finally, fed up with the useless brainstorming, I declared to them all that the modeling agency would be called Total Dimes and nothing else. I gathered my things and said a sharp good night. I didn't see why we were even having the conversation about my business plan. It was my idea, and it had absolutely nothing to do with my EEOC case, which had taken a back seat to the modeling agency talk.

Thomas had taken up my valuable time, and I was agitated. Possibly to reinforce his religious claim, before I got to the door of his building, he demonstrated how he could write my name in Hebrew by scribbling it on his notepad and rushing to the door to show me before I left. He wrote something on a piece of paper in a script I'd never seen before. To this day, I don't know whether or not it was real or a made up lie. My bets are on the lie. *Who gives a shit about all of this?*, I thought as I exited his office.

"He told you that he was Jewish? I'm Jewish, and everything that he has stated and allegedly done according to what you have said does not fall in line with my beliefs!" Karen laughed.

"Yeah, he was lying through his ugly-ass mug. I try to give everyone a chance, though."

"I'm sorry to interrupt you, but that was a clear lie," Karen said.

"Hey! My guardian angels were giving me signs, but I ignored them," I sighed. "I have done that for my entire life."

"He seems to lie far too much for me to claim him as one of my own!" Karen chuckled.

"I try not to question any man's religion. I'll leave that alone."

All the signs were there. Little angels were on my shoulders whispering into my ear. One was telling me to go ahead and trust Thomas, and the other one was telling me to be careful. I wasn't paying attention to the other one at all.

Meleisa Betts

I agreed to yet another meeting with Thomas and his female associates on the following Monday. My instincts told me to move away from him. Yet, I listened to the bad angel whispering in my ear. I use this as a metaphor, but it seems that, at times, my mind is controlled by good and bad angels.

After we again finished discussing possible names for the modeling agency, despite the fact that I had declared that Total Dimes was the one and only choice, Britney and Tracey left the office. This was when Thomas asked me to tell him about Chyna.

I told him the full story about how I had met Chyna and, eventually, asked her to move in with me. She was going to accept, but she met her untimely death. I told Thomas all of this. I allowed him a level of intimacy that he was not worthy of. However, he began to tell me some personal things about himself. The most interesting thing that he revealed was that he was thinking about marrying an African woman that he had met on the internet.

I asked, "Have you two met in person?"

My first thought was *Hell, no!*

I wondered if she had seen a picture of his big, ugly ass, and, if so, then why on Earth would she still want to marry him? The only answer, which made sense, was that she had to be ugly herself or she was looking to marry an American citizen in order to get a green card.

"We haven't met yet. She lost her husband to cancer a little less than a year ago. The thing is that, through our long and deep conversations, I find that we have a lot in common," he said.

"Thomas, I'm not so sure that you've finished grieving over Brandi. Chyna died back in March, and I still think about her every day," I said.

"Well, wherever she is right now, I know that Brandi would be happy for me to move on," he said, appearing to stifle back tears, but it seemed to me as though he was trying too hard to look sad.

"Excuse me for getting personal, but are you receiving anything like social security?" I asked as he nodded, wiping a tear from his eye."Is it enough to supplement your income?" I, then, asked.

"I only get fourteen hundred dollars a month," he said, while staring at the wall.

"You do know that your benefits will stop if you marry again?" I asked.

"I guess it depends on whether or not she's worth it,"

Thomas said in a rather businesslike tone.

The signs were there, and they were starting to mount up. It seemed as if there now was an angel and a devil on my shoulder just like in the cartoons. One told me to turn tail and run. The other said to stay and listen.

"Thomas, what about the kids? How do they feel? Have you mentioned it to your kids?" I asked.

"I really haven't talked with them in depth about it," he said.

"Do you get any help from the mother of your oldest kid?"

"No, I don't receive any support for him. His mother is dead, too," he responded sadly, almost despondently.

I was too sorry to hear about the tragedies in his life, so I left the subject alone. *Damn! Those bastards at the Universal Packaging killed Brandi!* That was all I could think about while he lamented. I, also, mentioned my lawsuit against the condominium complex where I lived. I told him the full story about how the gateman had let the two young women in without my permission, how they had waited for me in my hallway, and how they had ambushed and beat the hell out of me. There was so much going on at that time in my life. Since hindsight is 20/20, I know now that I should have never shared such personal and intimate information with Thomas. But I did, and it would come back to haunt me.

I told Thomas the story about a particular female who had assaulted me. I told him about how I had mentioned to her that I wasn't looking for a relationship when I first met her. I was still grieving over Chyna. I told him about the crazy signs I started to recognize. She had lied about her age. At first, she'd told me she was twenty-one. She had a picture ID with her that told the same. I, later, saw a basket in her apartment filled with nothing but fake IDs. The reality was that she was nineteen. As I was telling Thomas the story, I began to feel a little skeptical about whether or not he was even listening. It seemed like his mind was on another subject.

"What were the crazy signs that you saw?" Karen asked.

"One Thursday afternoon, the girl called me and asked if she could go to Bible study with me. I didn't mind, so I picked her up from the train station. Once we got to the church, I happened to look down at her black bag and noticed that it was moving. I asked her why her bag was moving. She responded, 'Oh, that's just my dog.' I hurried up and took her ass home."

"That seems too bizarre to be real!" Karen said, laughing.

"I'm for real. No lie!"

We both laughed.

"Now, let's pause for a moment and try to get to the truth. Why didn't you like this girl? Tell the truth," Karen demanded.

"We were simply a bad match. She was fake from head to toe with fake breasts and a fake ass. Apparently, she had gone to a back alley bootleg plastic surgeon," I said. "No real professional would have done such shabby work."

"I knew there had to be another reason," Karen said.

"I guess you THINK you know me, huh? After all, I have told you just about every secret known to man."

We both laughed again.

Thomas, then, went on to talk about how, when he was in college, he'd had a friend who experienced being with another male. I didn't say a damn word or ask any questions while he went into this diatribe, which lasted nearly an hour. As it became monotonous and unbearable, I jumped in and said a few things about myself. With this change of direction of the subject matter, Thomas became enamored with my stories, and, because he was so involved with me now, I had to cut all of my answers short. He was asking me how this or that felt, looked, smelled and tasted. It was as though he was becoming aroused by the subject.

With all of the questions he asked, I can honestly say that this was the first time that I had ever felt so uncomfortable over the subject of my sexuality. For the most part, I simply let him do most of the talking at first. After I had opened up to him and he had become focused on me, I tried to steer the conversation toward another subject, but he would bring everything back to the subject of my sexuality. He even said that his mother was open-minded to different things. I had to cut the conversation short again because it now seemed like this bastard was trying to come on to me. I don't have anything against fat men as a rule since I've had my share of big men and big women. The difference was the women were sexy and big, and they had pretty faces.

This was why I felt so damn uncomfortable. Every time I took a look at him, he looked more and more like Caesar from the movie _Planet of the Apes_. To me, Thomas's face looked like a gorilla's face, and that was my most accurate assessment. One thing I didn't want to do was make him

Meleisa Betts

feel upset. I knew I needed him to answer my questions involving the EEOC.

Thomas phoned me the next day to continue the conversation about the modeling agency. He was hyping it up to be something potentially great. This kind of pep talk was just what I wanted to hear at that time. He wanted to take the lead. He proposed that he become the assistant manager. Once again, my ambitions caused me to overlook the fact that there was still no discussion of my EEOC claim.

"I'll be responsible for keeping the records and getting investors. I'll write all the grant proposals," he said confidently over the phone.

I wanted to hear positive feedback from my potential grant writer. He would be the one writing the majority of the proposals. I needed him to make this dream of mine, as well as Chyna's, come true.

"You should have left when your instinct told you that something was wrong," Karen said. "How could Thomas magically transform himself from repairing furniture to being a manager for your agency in no time flat?" Karen said. "Not to mention the fact that the EEOC claim was not being discussed."

I was fighting depression like I was in a war, so

anything that sounded uplifting was what I focused on. I overlooked the negatives. I didn't think about how Thomas bounced from one of my projects to another, even though he had no expertise in either, because the prospect of making money was clouding my judgment.

At the end of this very lengthy conversation, Thomas asked, "Would you like to spend New Year's Eve over at my mother's house? I'm making gumbo for all of us," he said.

Thomas knew through our conversations that gumbo was my favorite dish. I was excited because I had no plans for the holidays, but I would only attend on one condition — that I bring my dog.

Thomas said, "Oh, I love Christy Bell! She's my favorite dog."

I could not see it clearly at the time, but Thomas seemed to be calculatingly saying and doing all of the right things.

He said, "I just need to OK it with my mother first."

I replied, "If your mother doesn't like dogs, I completely understand."

He responded, "Let me call you back in a couple of minutes."

He called back and said it wasn't a problem. This was

yet another sign that I was given, which I ignored. If his mother cared for dogs as Thomas had claimed, he wouldn't have had to get her to OK anything. The truth of the matter was that his mother probably didn't like dogs. He probably told her that he had a plan for me and that it required her cooperation. Part of the scheme was for him to make me feel as comfortable as possible. His mother, of course, went along with him and so did his oldest son. I didn't realize it at the time, but, again, my guardian angels were giving me signs through my skepticism that I continually ignored.

"Neither one of those boys had a mother? That is a really sad situation brewing there," Karen said.

Previously, I had told Thomas that I didn't eat pork. So, he made sure to buy turkey sausage. Whatever I wanted in the gumbo was what he put in it, and he was in full please mode. New Year's Eve finally came. Christy Bell and I met Thomas in front of his mother's house. He invited me in, and I met the oldest son, Barry. He was a light-skinned boy with gray eyes who looked as though he was of mixed heritage. He was around thirteen. Thomas spoke glowingly of that child, as though he was his most prized possession. Thomas gushed over Barry, and he played and joked with him. It seemed as though he was most proud of the way Barry looked, and it seemed as though he was ashamed of the younger son, Little T. I asked him which side of the family Barry had gotten his gray eyes from.

He said, "He got them from my mother's side of the family."

He took me aside, away from the boys, and he quietly explained that his grandmother or one of her ancestors had had gray eyes. He told me that his grandmother had been raped by her own brother, which was not necessary for me to know in order for him to answer my original question, of course. Thomas, then, went on to say that his mother was raped and impregnated in college by a white professor. This man would have been Thomas's father. Thomas didn't, however, look like he was bi-racial at all. He spilled his family secrets to me without me even asking. Then, all of a sudden, he stopped talking. He started crying. I had believed everything he told me even though my instinct was shouting at me to keep on guard.

"Do you think his mom really had been raped?" Karen asked softly.

"You know, I just don't know, but I had no proof otherwise," I answered obligingly.

Then, I met Little T, which, of course, was short for

Thomas. He was a brown-skinned little boy who looked nothing like his brother. He looked like a typical African-American child, not biracial like Barry. I sensed that he had a lot of anger simmering on a low boil within him. He constantly whined throughout the time that I was there, which was several hours. He was extremely rude and pushy. It's not normal for a child around his age to be mean and indifferent to a little dog, but he shunned Christy Bell every time she attempted to play with him.

Then, I met Thomas's mother. She was nothing like Thomas had described. She was not unpleasant, but I could sense a little deception going on in her speech and in her mannerisms. His mother tried to appear cordial, yet it was strained. It was as though she was forcing herself to act nice. Once again, I continued to ignore the signs. Next, a short man came downstairs. Thomas introduced him as his mother's fiancé. Later, yet another man came down-stairs. Thomas introduced him as his uncle. Earlier that week, Thomas had mentioned that his uncle lived with him.

He said, "He gets on my nerves because he doesn't wash his hands after he goes to the bathroom."

I asked, "How do you know whether or not he washes

his hands?" This was a strange thing to be perceptive of.

He answered, "I listen for running water, and I never hear anything but the toilet flush."

This was yet another sign I ignored. He was unusually deceptive and invasive of people's privacy to a degree that went past normal. I couldn't see this at the time. In retrospect, it was all too clear. The last time Thomas came by my house, he was impressed with my library. One of the books he was especially impressed with was titled _The Prince_ by Niccolo Machiavelli. We were sitting in his mother's living room watching television when his son Barry started talking about that particular book. Thomas had obviously coached him prior to my arrival, telling him to mention the book and act as though he had read it. Thomas hoped that Barry's diverse literary catalog of reading would impress me. From a rearview mirror's perspective, everything was clearly set up. I could see it happening right in front of me.

"I feel sorry for the woman that marries his oldest son. He is going to be a lot like his father," Karen surmised, concerned.

"Yes, he is," I responded.

There I was in the presence of what seemed to be one big, jovial, and close-knit family. They were very well-spoken individuals. They were probably all coached. Their verbs all fell neatly into place. To the casual observer, it seemed that they all got along so well. Whenever I was in the presence of my family members, they always seemed to be screaming and yelling. In contrast, Thomas's family was such a perfect family that they reminded me of a television sitcom.

It was only a minute later that I heard an argument break out in the kitchen. It was Thomas and his mother. I sat and thought, *Wow! I can't believe he's arguing with his mother*. They were talking to each other as if they wanted to fight. Barry spoke out and reminded them that they had company. The argument subsided after he had spoken up. This was yet another harbinger of what was to come. Thomas invited me to come to the table and take a seat. We began to eat dinner. I said my grace before beginning to eat as I always did. I didn't see any of them doing the same. Thomas, who was supposedly Jewish, gave no thanks for his food. This was not necessarily a bad sign, but it was food for thought. Pardon the pun.

Truth be told, the so-called gumbo wasn't good at all. It tasted like a bunch of odds and ends mixed up together. It tasted like chicken soup with seafood in it.

After dinner, we watched the countdown to the New Year on television.

"How did you like the gumbo?" Thomas asked out of the blue.

At first, I was hesitant, but I felt I could be honest with him and that he wouldn't get offended.

I answered, "Thomas, it was good, but it wasn't gumbo like I am used to eating. You have to remember, I go to New Orleans all of the time, so I am used to authentic gumbo."

"It didn't taste like gumbo?" he asked with a semi-offended tone.

"No, it was good, but it tasted more like seafood soup," I offered.

He looked to be more than a little disappointed, but I was as honest as I could be without hurting his feelings.

"Maybe, you should have said, 'Yes, it was very good, Thomas,' and just left it at that," Karen said flatly.

"Karen, I didn't want to lie. If he wanted to call it gumbo, then he should have learned how to actually cook it."

It's time to stop talking about that fucking gumbo, I thought as the clock ticked down—five, four, three, two, and one. HAPPY NEW YEAR!

The honking of the toy horns and the clanking of champagne flutes was sweet music to my hurting spirit. I drank punch with the two boys. Everybody else drank champagne. His mother and her fiancé were upstairs celebrating with the uncle. I thought it was a little rude, but I didn't say anything since I was a guest. Thomas tried his best to get me to drink alcohol, but I insisted and said no to his invitation.

"Hmmm… he was trying to get you drunk. I wonder why?" Karen asked, with a slight chuckle.

It seemed to be, at that time, a big relief from the pain of the previous year. I had made it through another holiday season. My New Year was coming in pretty damn good. I was surrounded by what I perceived to be wonderful people. Thank God I didn't have to spend it by myself. It was a good celebration. This was a vastly different situation. It was wonderful, unique, and pleasant. I forgot about the argument between Thomas and his mother. I didn't ask him anything about it. After we brought in the New Year, I waited about ten minutes. Then, I went home. I didn't take any leftovers with me for obvious reasons.

The next day, Thomas called. He asked me to come over to his shop. I wasn't doing anything at the time, so I put on some clothes and drove out to his shop. When I arrived, I went inside and sat down. I watched as Britney and Tracey did repairs on a couple of chairs.

Thomas said, "I'm going to start training them on how to write grant proposals and solicit investors. Would you like to watch?" he asked.

I wanted to critique them as well. I thought it would be fun to act like a CEO, so I agreed.

Britney and Tracey went out to get some food for lunch. That was when Thomas decided to present me with the contract. He charged a fee to write the proposal for the agency and to get investors. I took a look at it. It bothered me that he was charging me for the proposal, while he was trying to be a part owner of my business.

"Come by the house later, so we can talk in more detail," I said in a monotone voice. I couldn't understand certain parts of the contract because it was mostly legal jargon.

"Okay. I don't have a problem with that," he said.

"I'm getting ready to leave. My head is killing me."

I gave him a check for four hundred dollars, which was for the first part of the EEOC claim representation and for his drafting the proposal for the modeling agency. As I gathered my belongings to leave, Thomas presented a contract which stated that it would take twelve thousand dollars to start up the production of the modeling agency.

"No way! I don't have money like that!" I said, completely flabbergasted.

"Well, we can crunch the numbers a little. So, what can you come up with?" he asked without a hint of emotion.

"We'll talk later about this contract and the money. My head is pounding, and I can't concentrate on this right now," I said as I left his business again, wondering if I was making the right choice.

Thomas called me the next day.

"I want to stop by and talk to you about the modeling agency. It's not out of my way."

"I'm a little bit tired. Can't we do this later in the week?" I asked.

Thomas said, "If you're gonna do the agency thing, then you should move ahead with it. If not, then I have other things to do."

Damn! He sure is pressuring me, I thought. *If I don't do it, he might steal my idea, and then I'm out of my money and my idea.*

I was so confused. I knew the modeling agency could

turn into something big. All I needed was a photographer, along with someone to write the proposals for the grant money. This would have been the point where Thomas came into the picture if everything would have gone true to my plan.

"It is perfectly clear that he took advantage of you. He knew you suffered from depression from your previous EEOC claim and the other things which had gone on during the last few years." Karen seemed disturbed.

"If I could have separated the truth from the fiction and from what my ambitions were, I could have made better decisions," I admitted.

Thomas came by within the hour. We sat down and discussed the contract. I asked him about the 45% profit share that he wanted as compensation, which seemed a bit much.

"Well, I am going to be doing most of the work. Forty-five percent is not even half," he stated with a heavy tone.

"If he got 45%, was he paying any expenses out of it?" Karen asked.

"I was responsible for all the expenses," I admitted.

By this time, a puzzled look crossed my face that only I could see. I knew where Karen was headed.

"You should have listened to your instinct and never let that scoundrel into your house, let alone your life," Karen said in a measured but serious tone.

"If only I had followed my instinct!"

She was 100% correct, and I had nothing to rebut.

"Thomas, the first thing we need to do is go to an attorney and get the agency incorporated," I said.

"We'll do that in a couple of days. The first thing is the financing."

"Will seven thousand get this started?" I asked, opening my pocketbook to get my checkbook out.

"Yes, that will do as a starter amount."

Thomas nearly jumped off of the sofa when he heard that amount.

I just knew we could make this happen. I was so excited that I felt like a child at Christmas. We went over to my dining room table, and I signed the contract. Then, I gave him the check for seven thousand dollars, and he could hardly contain his excitement. We both had original copies of the agreement.

"Well, I'm not going to stay. I have a lot of work cut out for me. Between my upholstery shop and your agency, I need to get started," Thomas beamed as he packed all of the information into a folder and then into his brown briefcase.

"Okay! So, I'll call you tomorrow," I said happily. My face was plastered with a grin as wide as could fit on it.

As soon as Thomas left my condominium, I started calling all of my friends and acquaintances to tell them about this new adventure. I called friends who had successful businesses, and I asked them to invest in the modeling agency until I received the grant money. I explained to them that they would be reimbursed once I got the grant money, and I promised that they would get a share of my profits as an incentive. By the next day, I had two verbal commitments; they totaled thirty-six hundred dollars. I had, also, gotten verbal commitments from twelve models that would be featured in the business. Everybody was excited and optimistic that the modeling agency would be a success. The only thing that the models needed was a release paper to take to their photographer, and my friends needed a contract with the agency's name on it to make the document official. These people were not just going to be handing me checks without legitimate agreements. I picked up the phone and called Thomas.

I asked, "When are we supposed to be going to the

attorney to become incorporated?"

"Well, they're busy, but I'll get Britney to make an appointment this week," he stated as though there was not an issue.

"I'm probably gonna have to track down Ms. Chocolate, so she can do the Iceberg photo shoot that we wanted to do as our first assignment. Her regular dance club caught on fire last week, and I didn't have her phone number or address," I said.

Ms. Chocolate, as you could guess, was a dark-complexioned black woman who was a popular exotic dancer in Valeria, but she also had the look which allowed her to do print work. For some reason, she preferred the naked work over the more acceptable modeling.

Thomas asked, "How did a strip club catch on fire? That story sounds kind of shady."

"This kind of stuff goes on all the time in the exotic dancer industry. People get killed, contracts are taken out on owners, women end up missing and everything you can imagine. Do you remember the time when this guy was accused of burning down Club She She's?"

He said, "Not really. I usually don't pay much attention to those stories since they are on the local news every night it seems."

I proceeded to tell him the story about a male dancer named Marlon who was accused of hiring someone to break the mayor of Valeria's legs. I told him that I had heard about it and had seen it on the news.

He said, "Well, I heard Mr. Cortez say on his radio show one day that the mayor was actually gay." Mr. Cortez was a local shock jock who loved to keep stories brewing in Valeria.

The mayor of Valeria, at that time, was under fire for a series of indiscretions and was eventually indicted for several offenses. As a result, the mayor was convicted and sentenced to prison. It was mentioned during the mayor's trial that a man named Luey had been living in his basement for years without paying any rent. This was not only stealing from the government by a noted official but, also, an example of the corruption that was hidden from view. The mayor, also, had his hands on the exotic dancer industry by taking kickbacks and using police force manpower to guard the clubs with the city's finances.

Allegedly, the exotic dancer Marlon was in a relationship with the mayor, and, when the mayor decided that he was through and had gotten all that he could from the association, he, then, cut ties with Marlon. As retaliation, Marlon placed a contract hit on the mayor to have his legs broken. When the hit man was caught after assaulting the mayor, he confessed that Marlon had paid him. After a lengthy trial, it resulted in a hung jury. Despite not actually suffering the broken legs, many would say that the mayor, eventually, got what he deserved with a broken political career.

We, also, discussed the two women who had kicked my ass in my condominium building and other things. By this time, the conversation had gone way off on a tangent, onto subjects that had nothing to do with the tasks that we had united to accomplish. I didn't know it at the time, but the subject matter would be used against me in an extremely improbable fashion.

After this conversation of part pertinent talk and mostly gossip, I told Thomas in a highly excited voice about my progress in getting investors for the agency.

"Guess what, Thomas? I got two investors today. They're willing to commit to thirty-six hundred dollars already!" I said.

"Wow! That was quick! How did you manage that?" Thomas asked.

"Remember I told you that my dentist friend and my friend who owns a custom tire rim shop were going to invest?"

"Your doctor friend should be investing in my elite upholstery shop," Thomas stated with an air of certainty, as though his business was the real project and not the modeling agency.

"Why do you say that? What does a furniture store have to do with a modeling agency?" I asked, with a part questioning and part pissed off look on my face.

"Well, he's a doctor! I need investors for my furniture shop. You know I just started it," he said. Thomas was rolling his eyes as though I should have been thinking his thoughts and sharing his feelings about his business. I didn't give a shit about his furniture building one way or the other, but it was clear that he had a separate agenda.

"I have a concern about the models. Some of them may be strippers, and I don't feel comfortable having them coming in and out of my shop," Thomas said, sounding rather soft and timid.

"So, what do you propose we do about that?" I asked.

"You could rent the office next door for the photo shoots. It would only cost eight hundred dollars a month," he said as though eight hundred dollars was the same as eight dollars.

"No, the agreement was to do the photo shoots in the back of your shop. We'll just stick to that," I objected.

"Okay, then. Now, back to your doctor friend. I think he should consider investing in my shop since it's already established. When we get the grant money coming in for the agency, I'll give you back 20% of the profit share," Thomas said.

I quickly cut him off by raising my hand in a crossing guard-type gesture.

"Hold it! Let's get something clear here. I did mention your furniture shop, but he only wants to invest in my modeling agency."

I hadn't mentioned a damned thing to my investors about his shop, but I had to shut him up and return his focused to my project. Why would he even think that someone would want to invest in a damn furniture shop when sex sells? This was the point when a major red flag finally went up in my head. At this point, I knew that, even though the contract stated that Thomas's obligations were to get investors for the agency within four weeks, his true agenda was to secure investors for his furniture shop. I realized that, when Thomas made that statement about my friends investing in his business, he was only thinking about investors for his shop during the entire discussion and planning phases. He was talking about the modeling business to humor me and to get money to put into his personal plans.

Thomas couldn't have cared less about my welfare and the best interests of my investors. It was becoming clear. I attempted to call him the next day after our meeting, but he was too busy to speak with me. About three hours later, I made three calls to his cell phone, and, again, he wouldn't answer. Thomas apparently had turned his cell phone off in order for me to be unable to speak with him. Now, I was concerned.

The very next day the same thing happened again. I called both the office and cell phone numbers that Thomas had given me, and, again, no answer. After this nonsense, I was pissed off to no end, so I called his shop as a customer would. Britney answered the phone. After I insisted on speaking to Thomas, she gave him the phone. He had all kinds of excuses as to why he neither answered nor returned my calls. Less than a minute into our conversation, he said, "I'll call you back in about an hour."

Meleisa Betts

Hours passed with no call from Thomas. I called him nonstop until I finally reached him at around two in the morning. He tried to sound as though he was groggy and so completely out of it that he could barely speak.

"Thomas, this is Angiel. I've been calling you all day. What in the hell is going on here? You promised me that you would call me in an hour, and it has been sixteen fucking hours of me calling you!" I snapped.

"Angiel, you have to understand that I have a medical condition. I have vertigo, and I stay tired a lot. I don't know why my clients think they can just call me at any time of the night and at this time of morning," he insulted in his half-sleepy drone.

"Thomas, you were calling me at two in the morning, just days ago. And it was okay then. Now, it's a problem?" I said sharply.

"Don't call me at two in the morning!" he shouted.

"You don't have to worry about me calling you this early anymore, but, if I can't reach you during the day, then what are my options?" I asked. "Thomas, if you treat your clients this way, then I see why there's a problem in your business and why you need investors. I'm sure you answer and return your rich clients' calls," I said defiantly, feeling very insulted by the implication that, it was me, and not him, who was being unprofessional and unreasonable. It was clear that Thomas wanted to argue, but I was focused on my business.

"I'm coming over to your office to see the progress report on the grant proposals," I said, stating more of an order than a request.

The next day, I was at Thomas's shop at eleven A.M. in order to see what he had accomplished. I looked over the grant proposals, which were legible but not overly impressive. Allegedly, he had spent three days working on them. He, also, claimed he had paid Britney and some of her friends to write up the proposals, which was a contradiction that I didn't confront him with since I just wanted to get things moving as smoothly as possible. The next day, I wanted to speak to him, but, again, I couldn't get to him on the phone. This time, I waited four hours, and I called him once more. On this occasion, he answered rather than avoiding me altogether.

"Thomas, I need all my receipts!" I demanded.

"First of all, I gave the graphics design firm a check for twenty-two hundred dollars to begin the project. Then, I had to pay Britney and her friends cash for their work," he said in a tone, suggesting that I had no reason to question the veracity of his statements.

I looked at the telephone receiver with a wide-eyed stare, which mimicked one of his best saucer-eyed looks.

"You mean to tell me you paid someone in cash!" I almost yelled.

"Yes, I did," he responded as though there was no problem.

"Thomas, please tell me why in the world you would pay a bill in cash? You need to get Britney to go back to each one of her friends that she paid or you paid and get me those receipts. You, as a business man, should know that receipts and checks are the only evidence that you can use to prove that something was either paid or owed. By the way, how much cash are we speaking of?" I asked forcefully.

"It was three hundred dollars," he said, still using that superior and defiant tone.

"I need receipts, Thomas. Once again, you know that anytime you have a business you always get receipts, if for no other reason than for records and tax purposes. You should know this, Thomas!" I demanded.

"Well, it's Brandi's birthday, and I'm grieving. Can we

just do this some other day?" he asked, with a sound of hurt that could have been real, but was more than likely faked.

"What are you telling your high-profile clients when they walk into your shop or call you? So, you're telling them you're grieving? Thomas, I grieve every day over my mother. Another thing: how can you be grieving so hard when you said last week that you're going marry some African woman?" I asked.

I was looking at the telephone receiver as if I could look through the fiber optic lines and cables and see his pumpkin pie face. My eyes were like lasers traveling over the phone lines, burning a hole into his fat head.

"I'm sure Brandi would want me to be happy," he sobbed, sounding much like he was a soap opera character.

"Well, I'm getting dressed as we speak. I'll be there in a couple of hours."

At that point, I hung up. Barely five minutes later, I had received an email. It read:

Britney has the receipts you requested. I spoke with my photographer today. We're both excited about the modeling agency. He's excited to work with the girls. We came up with a name for your agency. I'll be printing the business cards tomorrow.

What in the hell is this guy talking about? What is this "we came up with a name" bullshit? I called him immediately after reading his email, and, this time, he answered.

"Hello, Thomas. I read your email. I'm interested in knowing the name that you and your photographer came up with."

Unless the name was a vast improvement on Total Dimes, it was a moot point.

"We came up with a great name! The Alley," Thomas said with an enthusiasm that seemed insincere.

"The Alley is the name of a European modeling agency! Didn't you know that? What happened to the name I came up with?" I asked defiantly.

"Well, I checked with the secretary of state, and the receptionist said that the name, the Alley, was available," he responded.

"Thomas, this is why we need an attorney. The name the Alley is already taken. The Alley is probably under an umbrella of other businesses," I shot back.

Thomas was silent, but only for a moment. He knew that he had made a mistake. I, also, asked him about the business cards.

"Thomas, how can you print up business cards without first speaking to me and then an attorney? You should know how important it is to get incorporated. This was the first thing we were going to do. What's the damn problem? If you had printed the cards using the name the Alley, you would've had to throw all those cards away," I fumed.

He was silent, and I was fed up at this point.

"You know, Thomas, you've gone back on your word more than once. You've tried to rename MY modeling agency. First, it was the Modeling Shop, and now it's the Alley. You claimed you didn't have receipts for what you paid Britney. Then, you email me five minutes later, saying that you have them. Where did they come from so fast?" I asked. "Also, when I call, you don't answer. When you do answer, you're either busy or grieving. Then, you want to argue with me just because I asked you for my receipts, which I am entitled to. So, at this point, I think you should just give me all my money back. I think we need to end this association!" I demanded.

"You and Brandi are just alike. Let me call you back. I have to step out for a couple of hours."

"No! Damn it! You can leave Brandi out of this! You

need to give me my money back, Thomas!"

That asshole hung up the phone on me! I called him right back, and he picked up.

I immediately said, "This is not like you and Brandi! Don't you ever compare me to her again! We're talking about seven thousand dollars! This is serious. Some people call it blood money when it's all they have, and they will hurt you if you fuck with them!"

Thomas became very quiet for about ten seconds. At that point, he began to defend himself.

"What about all the materials that I've researched for your agency? What about the money I've paid to people?" he asked.

"You said that you were gonna hire a market research team. Supposedly, it was the same market research team that did work for *The Apprentice*. So, what happened to them? Thomas, I want my money back because you're playing games!" I shouted into the telephone.

I had gotten tired of Thomas's shit, and I could see that there was a confrontation brewing.

"You're just like Brandi!" he said once more, and this made my blood boil. I couldn't contain myself anymore at this point.

"Didn't I tell you not to ever compare me to your and Brandi's ordeal? This is BLOOD MONEY, Thomas! I'm gonna call everybody in your area and tell them about what happened to me with this money deal. Thomas, I'm, also, gonna call the Valeria Chamber of Commerce!" I shouted. He became very hostile, said a few choice words, and then hung up. I went straight to my computer and did an internet search for the graphics company that he claimed he had paid the twenty- two hundred dollars to. I found them, and they were listed.

I took their number from the webpage and called the graphic design firm. A young man named Rodney answered, and I told him who I was. He was the person who was going to put together a web page for the agency, complete with flyers, calendars, and business cards.

"Were you given any money to do work for my modeling agency?" I asked.

Rodney responded, "Your business partner Thomas Walters gave us a twenty-two hundred dollar check. It had your name on the memo line, but we credited it toward his past due account of twenty-two hundred dollars. We can never start up a new project if there's an outstanding balance on another account."

Meleisa Betts

I told him about my situation and how Thomas was apparently trying to swindle me.

Rodney said, "Hold on. I'm gonna call Thomas on three way."

During the conversation, Thomas said, "Rodney, don't worry because I'm on the phone with the district attorney's office as we speak. Just go ahead and credit my account. I'll pay Angiel back out of my personal account."

Thomas, then, abruptly hung up.

Rodney clicked over from the connection, and it became a two way conversation. "Well, I hope everything works out for you." He said as we said our good-byes.

The tone of his voice had a ring of doubt. He knew that I was in for an ordeal with Thomas as they probably had been in trying to get their payment. At least, one of us was happy.

Within three days of my conversation with Rodney, I received six emails from Thomas. He said that I had threatened him and that he was afraid for his family's life. In the emails, he wrote that he knew that I was in a gang that was involved in burning down buildings and breaking people's legs and hiding in bushes waiting to beat people up. The letters were so well constructed that whoever read them surely would have believed every word Thomas wrote. He had cleverly used our previous conversations and my intimate revelations against me. He had twisted my statements to create the worst human that I had ever heard of in my life.

At this point, I'm wondering who or what in the hell I was dealing with. This man was a tremendous con artist.

I asked God, "How could this happen to me again? What is Thomas planning to do?"

I had fasted over my decision before I finally decided to sign the contract with him. I had convinced myself that there were no signs of anything wrong, but, in fact, there were clear signs that I had ignored. The red flags were flying high during the New Year's Eve celebration with Thomas and his family. In looking back, God was giving me the intuition of what to do or not to, but I wasn't paying close enough attention. I wanted what I wanted, which was a successful modeling agency and to win my EEOC suit. I wanted to believe in what I was doing and to believe in someone. My mistake was putting all of my trust and my friends' money in Thomas Walters. Maybe, my biggest mistake was that I had been serving two masters.

Meleisa Betts

"What do you mean by that exactly?" Karen asked.

"I'll get to that, but there are a few more things I need to say about this," I said.

I began to enter into the worst state of physical depression over my misstep with Thomas. It was a feeling that overloaded my entire soul. It spilled over into my physical world. I could barely walk, and, when I did walk or stand, I moved like an invalid, shuffling and moving in a slumped position. My voice became weak, and my face became frail and drawn, as though I had aged ten years overnight. I wondered if God had forsaken me. I wondered if He was punishing me for being so self-centered. I kept calling out to Him, asking Him to please give me strength. He had always been there for me in the past, despite my transgressions. I couldn't let this debacle stop me. I couldn't let Thomas get away with his thievery.

"I'm glad you didn't let this bad experience turn you away from God," Karen said softly.

"Yeah, some people turn away and never look back!" I stated.

Finally, a couple of days later, my strength began to come back. I decided to file a theft by deception warrant against Thomas. It was theft, and it was deception. At the time, I couldn't think of anyone better to call on than an old familiar lawyer named Mike. He had caught my attention while I was in court on another occasion. He was wearing a silk suit. He had a unique style about himself. Mike was so suave. I had asked Mike for a business card because I just had to get him to go to court with me.

Ironically, the case had involved ten thousand dollars, and it was, also, theft by deception. Although it took over a year for me to get my money back, thanks to Mike, I did. So, because my previous experience had been a success, I called Mike and made an appointment to discuss the Thomas debacle.

When I arrived at his office, he still looked like the Mike that I had met years ago. The only difference was that he just had a few hairs missing on the top of his head. I explained to him in detail about my situation with Thomas, and, as I concluded, he rolled his eyes in amazement.

"What do you think is the reason for these kinds of things always happening to you with these types of individuals?" Mike asked.

"Always happening with these types of individuals? What do you mean by that?" I looked at him with a wide-eyed stare.

"The last time I represented you it was another guy, as I recall, 'ripping you off'. Now, this Thomas fellow is scamming you," Mike said rather condescendingly.

"Mike, the previous theft by deception case was a business deal that has no relation to this one. So, let's get this straight! My situation with this man is a business deal with totally different aspects. So, don't misunderstand the facts. Hell, I've had bad experiences with females, too," I said defiantly.

I got him back on the right path real quick with my response.

Mike requested that I give him six hundred dollars as a retainer. He said, "In the meantime, I'm going to try to get your money back without having to go to court. Hopefully, we can just get a settlement."

"It would be great if you could manage to do that," I said.

"Do you have the graphic designer's phone number?" he asked.

"Yeah, I have the number right here," I said as I looked in my address book and gave him the number.

He called the designers while I was in his office. He put the conversation on his speakerphone for me to hear.

Again, Rodney was the person who answered. Mike asked a few preliminary questions, and Rodney was quick to comply.

"Thomas gave us twenty-two hundred dollars, but it was credited toward his past due account for the same amount." Rodney freely disclosed this information without coercion.

Mike, then, asked Rodney to send him an email with all of the information that he had just revealed to him. Again, he was happy to be of help, and the information arrived within minutes. At that point, I wrote Mike a check for six hundred dollars, satisfied that he would again do the job. He was showing an aggression that was reassuring.

As I was endorsing the check, I asked, "Now, Mike, you are gonna show up for court, right?" I had to be doubly sure about things.

"Yes. Of course, I will. Do I need to give you a contract to make this binding?" He asked in a "you can bank on me" tone.

"No, dude. I trust you! I can always sue you for breach of contract if you don't show, right?" I said.

We both laughed as I left his office. I should have realized that my truth mirrors fiction most of the time, but surely not now?

The days were long, and the nights were sleepless. I couldn't help but think about the entire ordeal. How did I let this happen to me again? At night, I rehashed my business deal with Thomas over and over. I mentally repeated every word of all of our conversations. I thought about the meetings that we'd had at the shop with Britney and Tracey. I thought about the New Year's Eve celebration at his mother's house. I concluded that it was all orchestrated. Yes, Thomas had planned out this entire con game to the smallest detail. Thomas had never even seriously thought about the modeling agency. Hell! He had never thought about investors except for how they would benefit his business! He pretended that he had researched the viability of the modeling business by going online. He had used images of different models without them physically being present and without their permission for the shoots to make everything look legitimate. Thomas basically typed out information about the models to coincide with their pictures. This simple process probably took all of ten minutes.

Thomas knew that I suffered from depression. He thought he could use that information to get the best of me.

He thought that I would just go away, but he was so wrong! The case was finally scheduled for court. In the meantime, I couldn't get this crazy shit off of my mind. It was in my dreams and waking thoughts, and I carried it with me throughout the day. I was constantly obsessing over the case and, in turn, talking about it with anyone who would listen.

One night, I was awakened around two in the morning by an image that looked like a thin black woman. I was shaking like hell. I was so scared! In my dazed condition, I wasn't totally coherent, but I thought that I could hear the apparition say, "Find out about Thomas's first wife." Then, the spirit faded away, or, at least, I thought it did.

I didn't forget about what Thomas had told me the week before I signed the contract with him. He had told me that Barry's mother had passed away some years ago. I remembered asking him about getting married to the African woman. His ensuing response was, "It depends on whether or not it's worth it." I just sat there in bed, thinking about what I had seen and heard that day. I had so many pressing questions concerning Thomas. I wanted to call Peggy right then. I decided, however, to wait until the next day. I called Peggy around noon.

Meleisa Betts

After exchanging a few pleasantries, I decided to cut right to the chase. I asked, "Peggy, what happened to Thomas's first wife?"

Her revelation blew me away. It was incredible! At first, I thought Peggy was just kidding with me because she could be a big-time jokester at times. She assured me that her story was one hundred percent true.

Peggy began her story. "Thomas told me that Barry was a product of a rape. It occurred while Barry's mother was in college. It was a white college professor that supposedly raped her. After Barry's mom made the allegation, she had to leave the college. Supposedly, the administration there made things so hard for her that she was forced out. While she was pregnant, she met and fell in love with Thomas. They, eventually, married after about eight months of dating. Less than eighteen months after they exchanged vows, Thomas buried his wife. He's now raising Barry as his own son."

Now, this story was in complete opposition to what Thomas had told me. He had told me that both of his son's mothers were deceased, but he had never even implied that Barry was not his biological son. He said that Barry got his gray eyes from his grandmother's side of the family, which would lead anyone to infer that Barry was a blood relative of the Walters family. He didn't mention anything, at all, about Barry's mom being pregnant when they met each other, nor had he mentioned that Barry was the product of rape. Peggy went on to drop the second bombshell.

"Angiel, you want to know what happened to Brandi?" she asked cryptically.

"I already know. She died from health issues caused by dealing with the Universal Packaging harassment," I said.

"Nope. The fact is that Thomas killed her. Whether on purpose or by accident, he killed her," she said without so much as a pause.

"Peggy, I'm not in the mood for any games. How did he kill Brandi?" I asked, with a strong tone of skepticism in my voice.

Peggy said that she went over to Thomas's home right after Brandi's death to show her sympathy. When she went to hug Thomas, he turned away from her and said, "I've been smoking."

"Smoking what? Marijuana?" I asked.

"I don't know, so I can't comment," Peggy waffled.

"Don't you know what marijuana smells like?" I asked.

"No, I never tried it," she answered. I was sure that that was a lie.

"Hell! You've been around people that smoke it. I'm sure."

"No, I haven't," Peggy said angrily.

"Bullshit, Peggy! You expect me to believe that? By the way, your friend Thomas cheated me out of seven thousand dollars! Are you sure that it wasn't crack that you smelled?" I snapped.

"You can believe what you want. I don't know how drugs smell. As far as the swindling talk goes, I have nothing to do with that part, but he says that you are the problem, and you say that it's him." She was now scowling.

"So, you guys have been talking?" I asked.

"We spoke for just a few minutes. That's all, but he said that you were psycho and all kinds of things that I wouldn't get into with him," she said this as though she had been defending my honor to him.

"Peggy, just finish telling me what you and Thomas talked about. It's pretty clear that something was going on with him since he wouldn't let you hug him. It was guilt or shame for the smell, but there was something to that scene," I said with disgust.

Peggy said she found that comment to be strange because she had never known Thomas to be a smoker, but she ignored it. Thomas, then, intimated to her that he had changed Brandi's medicine.

Thomas said, "Brandi kept screaming out in pain, so I gave her eight hundred milligrams of ibuprofen every two hours, just to shut her up. That's when Brandi began foaming at the mouth. Mucus was coming out of her nose, but I didn't think anything of it."

Peggy began to really spill information. She said on several occasions that Thomas would say terrible things about Brandi to her. She said that she had even heard Thomas's mother telling him to get rid of Brandi.

His mother had said, "She's too sickly, and she's just holding you back, Thomas."

Peggy said that she had even witnessed an argument between Thomas and Brandi during a telephone conversation.

"Thomas slammed the phone down after he had argued with Brandi for about thirty minutes. Afterwards, he kept saying, 'I wish she was dead! I wish she would go ahead and die!' He kept saying it over and over," Peggy said.

This shocking account left me speechless, but only for

Meleisa Betts

a moment.

"Peggy, you didn't tell me this story when I was questioning you about whether or not I should go into business with him!"

"What do you mean?" Peggy asked.

"What in the hell do you mean by 'what do you mean'? You more or less said that he would make a good business partner!" I virtually screamed this into the telephone.

"Angiel, I wasn't thinking about all of this at that time." Peggy sounded as though she was taking no responsibility.

"Peggy, how in the hell could you forget about what you just told me? If I had been in your place, I would have called the fucking police."

"I'm sorry! I'm sorry!" It sounded as though she was crying.

"If I had known all of this shit, there's no way I would have gone into business with Thomas! Why didn't you tell me this?"

I was as livid as anyone would be after such a confession.

"I didn't think Thomas was serious about wanting her dead," Peggy said.

I sat for a second and wondered how much of a dumb

ass she was, trying to act so naïve and innocent. I, then, realized that I was just as much of a donkey as Peggy was because I was fully caught up in the trickery — if not more so because I was out of a nearly ten thousand dollars.

"What was the explanation for the eight hundred milligrams of ibuprofen that she was given? That much medicine once every two hours means that, in eight hours, he had given her 3200 milligrams. That's over 12,000 milligrams in a day. That's more than overdosing. A person with a third grade education can read the label and know that the normal level of dosage is four hundred milligrams every six hours," I said forcefully.

"I just didn't know what to think," she said as though that simple answer would suffice.

"You could have, at least, told me," I reiterated.

At that moment, I had a feeling that came over me, and I believed that it was the spirit of Brandi. I could, in fact, feel her presence or, at least, the presence of someone or something. I had been seeing apparitions over the past few weeks of a black woman in a white gown. Now, I just knew that whatever I was seeing was Brandi. Yes, it was Brandi, and she was coming to me, prodding me to find out the truth about what really happened to her.

"So, you are visited by ghosts?" Karen interrupted.

"Yes, although they don't try to hurt me, it's still a scary thing. They just scare the piss out of me. That's all," I chuckled.

"That Peggy character sounds like a really weak woman," Karen stated.

"Yes, she's full of shit if she claims that she didn't suspect something."

"Didn't Thomas tell you that his own mother was, also, raped in college by a professor?" Karen asked, casting a sidelong glance.

"He sure did. He's a lying sick bitch," I said, shaking my head.

That following weekend, I began an internet search on that wretched unknown and yet to be convicted criminal. Thomas had literally gotten away with murder. I went from web site to web site, trying to come up with information on Thomas. I, finally, found a web site called Net Detectives. I found information on Thomas and his entire family with the exception of his father. I, also, found Brandi's brother's telephone number and address. It took a lot of nerve for me to call him, but I needed answers.

Thomas had mentioned to me that he and Brandi's

family were not speaking anymore for some reason. At that point, I began to pray over making the phone call to Brandi's brother.

I asked God to guide and direct me. I didn't want to call him and have him hang up on me, thinking that I was some telemarketer or, even worse, a lunatic. I, basically, didn't want to get my feelings hurt, but, if what I suspected was true, then Thomas needed to be punished. I found out through Net Detectives that, before Thomas married Brandi, he had been married to a woman named Bernice Walters. I found Bernice's address and phone number. I mustered up enough courage to call the two numbers that the website listed. Both numbers were to a homeless shelter in Chicago. Thomas and his entire family had migrated to Valeria from Chicago. When I called the first shelter which was within a hospital, I found a trail of information. I found out from the first shelter that Bernice was only forty-four years old.

After pretending to be a detective and asking those probing-type questions that law enforcement officers ask, the clerk at the shelter offered some tangible information; "Oh, yeah! You're talking about light-skinned Zoë. That was our nickname for her."

He had offered the name without resistance. "When I

say 'light skinned', it was hard to tell if Zoë was just a really white woman or an Albino because her skin was so pale. Does that fit the description of the woman who you are looking for?"

I said, "Yes," hoping to get more information, but I didn't need to prod him. He started flowing information like a geyser.

He said, "I haven't seen her in two years, but, yeah, she used to be a nurse here. Are you a family member?"

"Yes. Can you have her to call this number if you see her?"

He took down my number. I, also, tried to sneak in a question about Thomas.

"Did you know her husband Thomas?"

He quickly said, "I don't know anything about a husband. I'll give her this information, though. I've told you too much already, and we're not supposed to give out any information, especially over the phone."

I thanked him for his help, and we hung up. At least, now, I had a good starting point.

I, also, tried to call back at different times to the shelter. I tried to get the same man, but now I seemed to get a different person each time I called. I couldn't get any of the other receptionists to give me any information. Bernice, obviously, either didn't want to be found or was being so well hidden as to be virtually invisible to the regular world. Then, it dawned on me why the man at the shelter put so much emphasis on light skin. Bernice must have had an extremely bright complexion. She must have been or looked almost white.

All of the evidence was now adding up. Thomas's oldest son wasn't from a rape in college. Given the unlikelihood of Thomas's two stories, that both his mother and wife were raped in college, means that nobody was ever raped in college. It was all a lie to make his improbable life interesting and to gain some sort of sick sympathy. This was, indeed, Barry's mother, and she was not dead. A question formed in the back of my mind. *Why doesn't she have her son?* The ultra light-skinned or white woman named Bernice is still alive! Those "facts" made me wonder if Barry even knew that his mother was still alive.

"I would think, in all probability, that Thomas would have told him that his mother was dead!" Karen said matter-of-factly.

"Karen, you're probably right," I nodded.

Why would Thomas keep Bernice a secret? Why would

a forty-four year old nurse be forced to live in homeless shelters? I wondered.

All the pieces were starting to fit together into a puzzle that ironically still made little sense. I, also, found out, through Net Detectives, that Brandi's home was in Thomas's uncle's name. Thomas had somehow managed to convince Brandi to sell her old home in South Georgia. He had probably used the proceeds from the sale to put toward the home that he had purchased using his uncle's name. I found out that even his mother's home was in his uncle's and mother's fiancé's names.

"You would make a very good detective!" Karen stated.

Peggy, also, mentioned to me that Thomas had met Brandi over the internet. He told Brandi that he wasn't moving to Georgia until she married him. According to Net Detectives, Brandi went to Chicago to be with him. After Brandi became pregnant, Thomas married her. He, then, moved to Georgia and brought his entire family. During that time, Thomas got a position with the Universal Packaging Service as a temporary employee. He, somehow, managed to finagle a detail into the EEOC department. This kind of rapid movement is unheard of. This branch of the government possesses very personal files, involving private medical histories on individuals throughout the United States.

How in the hell did Thomas manage this? Even to this day, the government has kept his methods secret, but one can only wonder how he ascended so quickly up the ranks of such an important organization. Maybe, it was to cover their own asses as to how easily their protocols and security could be breached.

To check on how Thomas had beat their system, I contacted a close friend of mine in the personnel department. I asked him to check and see how long Thomas had worked for the government. I gave him all of the names that I came up with through Net Detectives. He put me on hold for about eight or so minutes. Then, he came back to the phone.

He said, "I can't find him in the system. It's like he has never worked for Universal Packaging."

"Are you positive about that?" I knew the answer, of course.

"I did a twenty year search. No one by either name could be found to match his demographics," he said.

I asked my friend to check Brandi's records. He found Brandi easily, and he reported that she was an employee in good standing.

"Who does Brandi have listed as her spouse or beneficiary?" I asked.

"Brandi doesn't have anyone listed as a dependant or as a beneficiary," he stated.

From there, I called the supervisor of timekeepers. I asked for the manager. Marilyn, who was the supervisor, came to the phone. I told her what had happened with the seven thousand dollars and what I now suspected Thomas of trying to do to me. She understood. She, then, looked into the system files to reconfirm what I had already been told.

"No one by that name has ever worked for Universal Packaging!" Marilyn stated in a tone which sounded strangely shocked.

I responded, "Marilyn, there must be a mistake! This con man was even an EEOC representative supposedly."

She said, "No, the system would pull it up if he ever worked in this district."

I asked Marilyn if she would call down to the EEOC department and ask about Thomas because I knew, for a fact, that he had worked under Ms. Jiles. She agreed to call the department and to check. She said to me, "I'll get back to you with the results of the conversation."

I was antsy. I waited twenty minutes. Then, I called Marilyn back. She said, "I called down to EEOC, but no one knew of or had heard of a Thomas Walters."

I was certain that they would have told her the truth since she was a manager. When I called the EEOC, they quickly told me that they couldn't give out any information on persons who had previously worked there, which I had figured. Now, I knew, for sure, that Thomas had worked for Universal Packaging because Peggy had worked with him in the computer room before Thomas got detailed to EEOC.

So, what happened in the EEOC department with Thomas if he had, in fact, worked with them? I found it hard to believe that a cover up wasn't going on. How could he be an examiner for the EEOC and now have his records wiped clean? It was like some high-level CIA operatives working on a mission and then covering their tracks. The thing is, if that was the case, why?

I thought about what Thomas had said. He told me that management had harassed Ms. Jiles so badly that she'd had a nervous breakdown. I did remember seeing Ms. Jiles several times in the cafeteria. She looked as if she had a nervous problem and was on the verge of being committed to an asylum. Ms. Jiles's unsightly appearance was so noticeable because she had once been a very beautiful female. She could now be seen sitting in the cafeteria alone and despondent. She had gained so much weight that it was obvious that something drastic had happened to her. I wondered if whatever happened to her, had happened while Thomas was working with her or if he was directly responsible. Thomas may have stolen records to manipulate his situation and all of the blame for the theft could have come back to Ms. Jiles since she was in charge. The end result was Ms. Jiles was demoted and harassed until she could not take any more. Then, she physically and mentally broke down. Whether or not Thomas was the central culprit in all of this may never be known.

Thomas told me that Brandi had brought up a lawsuit against Universal Packaging because the supervisor had hit her. I had my suspicions that Thomas was feeding me bullshit about the truth about her case since his existence within the government was a lie. Apparently, he had used an alias since no records could substantiate him having ever been employed at Universal Packaging. The evidence I had uncovered pointed to Thomas possibly stealing files of cases that had been won in order to assist with his filings of Brandi's case.

At that point, I decided to call the county hospital to see why they didn't investigate Brandi's death. I, also, called both the district attorney's office and the county examiner's office. I wanted to know the protocol for patients brought in for what seemed to be a case of drug overdose. They all said, "If the doctors think anything is suspicious, they contact the medical examiner's office." At that point, I contacted the medical examiner's office. At first, he couldn't pull up a Brandi Walters. It was on a Friday afternoon, so all he wanted to do was order the death certificate and get back with me on the following Monday.

That weekend, I managed to reach Peggy. I said to her, "I get the impression from the medical examiner that Brandi didn't die in the county she lived."

"Is that really what happened? That is a shock since Thomas never said anything like that. If what you are saying is true, then none of this makes any sense at all," she responded.

I was truly in shock over finding this out and so was she. At least, she sounded surprised. Monday morning finally came, and I received a call from the medical examiner's assistant. She said, "Brandi Walters did, in fact, die at the local medical hospital."

I was unknowingly spelling her name wrong. I found out that Brandi's first name was spelled with an 'I' on the end, instead of the normal spelling with a 'Y'.

Obviously, the doctors didn't suspect foul play. That's why they didn't do an investigation, I thought.

The assistant went on to say to me that, "There's no way for the county to initiate an investigation since there's no body to examine." She continued, "The family would have to hire an attorney to get the medical records, and then go to the district attorney's office with sufficient evidence."

I thought, *With the facts at hand, there's enough evidence for negligence.* None of these people at the medical examiner's office wanted to seriously consider what I was saying. I could only imagined what families had gone through with district attorneys, prosecutors, medical examiners, and police detectives when they suspected that a loved one had been murdered by a husband or wife. Maybe, this inaction was why the cases were, so often, simply abandoned after a few months and became cold cases. Now, I knew that I had to put together enough faith and courage and strength to call Brandi's brother, and I did. I called her brother, and, lo and behold, he answered the phone. I immediately identified myself. I quickly went on to say that I knew Thomas Walters and that I was involved in a legal issue with him.

I said, "I'm so sorry to hear about Brandi's death."

I said all of this to him in what felt like one breath. He was quiet, and I was nervous as hell.

I went on to say, "I've been having many sleepless nights. I prayed that you would, at least, be open-minded enough to listen to me." I made it clear that this had nothing to do with any vengeance toward Thomas.

He reassured me by saying, "Okay. I'm listening."

I went detail by detail from the business arrangement with Thomas to my conversations with Brandi. I told him everything Brandi had said to me.

After listening to me, he said, "That's a lot for me take in."

I managed to get past my initial nervousness and that allowed me to get a few questions into the conversation.

I asked, "Did you know that Thomas was married before he married Brandi?"

He answered, "No, I didn't. That piece of information

is news to me."

I mentioned to him that I had tried to find Thomas in the personnel system of Universal Packaging and that he could not be found. The brother found that to be strange because to his knowledge Thomas had, in fact, worked for the EEOC as a temporary employee.

"Did the immediate family request to have Brandi cremated?" I asked.

He said quickly, "No! Thomas went and had that done without our consent. We were very upset because we wanted to have a burial for Brandi." He, then, asked for my number. After I gave it to him, he said, "I've got to call my brother, and, if we decide to pursue the issue, we'll call you back."

I replied, "I think that you all should look into this because something's not right here. Sir, please don't think that I'm trying to get back at Thomas. This has really been bothering my heart. I truly believe that he deliberately killed your sister, so he could get the money that he needed to get his furniture business off of the ground. Did you know that Brandi received a settlement from Universal Packaging back in December or January for sixty-eight thousand dollars?"

He became quiet, so I assumed that he didn't know

anything about the money. This silence was the very definition of a pregnant pause. I could only speculate as to what he was thinking as he was wordless for about fifteen seconds.

He responded, "We'll call you back later in the week."

We hung up, and that was that. I didn't know what to think about how everything went, but, at least, I was doing what I could.

After several days went by and I didn't receive a call from Brandi's brother, I thought, _He's not gonna call back. Damn! Thomas is gonna get away with murder!_ I have to admit that I was only 95% sure that Thomas had killed his wife. Finally, I got a call from both brothers and one of their wives. I had to stand firm and be strong. I told them the story just as I had initially explained it. These individuals were very articulate, so I had to make doubly certain that I was being very clear.

I could only imagine how sweet of a person Brandi was. I imagined her to be strong-minded. And I had imagined her to be someone who had unknowingly gotten caught up with the devil's apprentice. The apparition that came to me, though hazy, was tall and gaunt. She looked sad. I truly believed Brandi could have lived longer if she had not been in such a sad situation. I've known people who have suffered from different debilitating diseases, yet they have managed to live productive lives. Those people couldn't have survived with any stress in their lives though, and Thomas and his family had created a great deal of stress for Brandi. Thomas, of course, had deliberately done as much as he could to cause her distress since his plans did not include her. According to her brother, Thomas had known of Brandi's illness through their correspondences via email before they had married. He admitted to Brandi's brother that he was only marrying Brandi for her employment benefits. The brother, then, told Brandi exactly what Thomas had admitted. The saga was beginning to come together, yet the logic of it all still made little sense to me.

"Did he really admit that to you, knowing you were gonna tell her?" I asked.

"Yes! He sure did! At that point, we pretty much started to suspect that his intentions were not good for my sister. We practically begged Brandi several times to leave that stressful situation," the brother stated.

"Did you know Thomas filed for a divorce? I think that you should check into her beneficiary money from

Universal Packaging. Brandi didn't have either Thomas or her son down as a beneficiary. I know that Thomas is trying very hard to get this money, but he can't," I explained.

Brandi's sister-in-law was in agreement with me. She wanted Brandi's death to be investigated.

She said, "Thomas was rarely at the hospital during the time Brandi was admitted. He was away taking care of his shop, as though Brandi was no more than an afterthought."

According to the brother, the doctor who attended to Brandi asked Thomas why he hadn't brought her in sooner.

Thomas told the doctor, "I didn't know that Brandi was giving herself all that medication."

The brother stated that the doctor seemed curious since the circumstances were suspicious. He kept asking questions, but Thomas kept giving him answers which explained each question. I can only imagine what he was saying with his forked serpent of a tongue as he pretended to be so distraught.

The brother said that the doctor stated, "Brandi has the worst case of renal failure that I have ever observed during my medical career or even heard or read of!"

Despite this blatant medical situation, she was not

placed on dialysis. Apparently, Thomas had refused to allow it for some reason. This was crazy, and it made as much sense as a three-dollar bill. This was how she could have been saved, yet no one could see through the confusion and figure out that Thomas had killed her in plain sight!

"Angiel, I'm surprised the brother didn't hang up on you the first time you called. Why should any rational person think that someone who had nothing at all to do with Brandi would be so obsessed with her so-called murder?" Karen offered.

I was now shaking with anger, not of fear, and my eyes were filled with vengeful tears.

"That bastard has taken money that I needed, and I trusted him to use it to help me, and he screwed me over, not to mention my friends who entrusted their hard earned money with me! Now, it looks like that low-down piece of shit has killed an innocent woman, who gave him a child, for money. He is a monster who is just hurting people, and I just refused to let him get away like that. You just can't use and hurt people like they mean nothing. I just had to do whatever I could to get him, whether it was by the courts or whatever!" I half-shouted and cried. Karen made notes in my file, but she didn't add anything at all to my rant.

I had prayed about it before I made that call. All of the relatives were in agreement that, when Brandi died, Thomas had shown absolutely no remorse. He acted quickly to have Brandi's body cremated before any one of them could say anything about it. It was now clear that this was done to eliminate any physical evidence of his crime — purposefully overdosing her with ibuprofen. He wanted there to be nothing used or tested that could possibly convict him of wrongdoing.

The sister-in-law was on my side concerning Thomas. Our strong belief was that he had intentionally poisoned Brandi. She wanted to move forward toward justice, but the brothers had become a little reluctant. They were not quite as adamant about pursuing justice as they had been in the beginning. I felt as though the brothers feared Thomas and his possible retaliation, or, maybe, it was pure apathy and laziness on their parts. I could only rationalize that something must have happened in the past seven years which the family was not revealing. There was no way a family, who truly loved their sister, would just let a revelation like this simply be swept neatly underneath a rug of deceit without investigating the allegation, especially if they felt there was foul play involved. I wanted to believe that Thomas had put fear into Brandi's family, rather than the fact that they just didn't give a damn.

Before we ended the conversation, I told them that it was now up to them to proceed. I had done what I felt was right. It was as though that image of Brandi had prodded me to do so, which was to reveal the truth to them. I had basically done all the homework for them. I had found out things that they probably would never have known otherwise. I can only hope that the spirit of Brandi can find some peace.

Karen asked, "Didn't you say earlier that Thomas and Brandi had gotten a settlement from Universal Packaging?"

"Yeah. Brandi had gotten a settlement from her EEOC case three weeks prior to her death. So, Thomas couldn't say that he didn't have the money for her final expenses," I responded.

According to the sister-in-law, after dealing with Thomas for seven years, they really didn't expect him to cry or show any emotion concerning Brandi. The sister-in-law, also, said that their experiences with Thomas over those seven years had been quite an ordeal. She said that he was a hard person to deal with. I could only imagine the hell that he had put her family through and the certain chaos that he had caused Brandi.

I told them that I wasn't going to mention what we had spoken about at the application hearing, and they were happy to hear that. Brandi's brothers were most concerned about Thomas not letting them spend any time with their nephew, especially if he knew that we were having such intimate conversations. They said that he would do something like not answer their calls or cut off communications completely. I told them that Thomas wasn't taking care of his son, that he was living at his grandmother's house.

I recalled Thomas saying to his son on that New Year's Eve night, when he had started to whine about something, as he had done the entire night: "Stop it! Dry up those tears and be a man."

He said to "stop it and be a man" to a child who was no more than seven years old. I thought that was a bit strong for a kid to interpret, especially after dealing with his mother's death at such a tender age. His emotional indifference was what was wrong, the thing that I couldn't put a finger on. Now, some things were becoming clear. Thomas neither loved nor cared for anyone but himself, and he would take advantage of or destroy anyone, even family, if it meant that he would get what he was after. He just had to be stopped!

My conversations with the family had generally gone well. After doing the additional groundwork, I found that there were grounds in which they could take Thomas to court. According to the detectives and the medical examiner's office, if the family had decided to pursue filing any charges against Thomas, they could do so, but they would have to retain an attorney to propose the suit, as it would have to be a civil case. I, also, gave them the name of an attorney that I had met, who seemed to be an ideal choice for the task they were facing. Her name was Cathy Sparks. I had spoken to this attorney over the phone a day before my conversation with Brandi's family. I felt as though she came across confident and strong.

I was caught between a proverbial rock and a hard place with no attorney and little time. Mike, the attorney whom I thought I had secured days before with a check and no contract, did not return my calls to confirm our court appointment. Consequently, I had to take whomever I could get as it was now days before my court appearance. Eventually, I met with an attorney named Jay Cross. The meeting lasted thirty minutes, which was odd considering that most consultations lasted an hour or more. Jay had his son with him at the office, and his son was a little hyperactive, and he kept coming in the room every minute it seemed. Although this was an unconventional situation, I found Jay to be satisfactory, so I gave him a check for five hundred dollars as a retainer.

The day before the hearing, I was at home thinking back to the time I had first met Thomas. I tried to put myself in his place to see how he had viewed me during that time. Obviously, his perception of me was that I was weak, and he was right. Thomas had only seen me when I was severely depressed. He had yet to see the strong person that I could be when I had the time to marshal my forces. Thomas met me during a time when I was being harassed by my supervisor and was simultaneously dealing with my mother's sickness and all of the other problems that seemed to have arrived on my doorstep all at once.

"Did Peggy go to court with you to testify on your behalf?" Karen asked.

"I asked her to come, but she claimed she had something to do."

The day of the application hearing, I imagined that court would be a little difficult. I knew Thomas would be very convincing in front of the judge. I could just feel without even hearing one word of his testimony that he had convinced his attorney of his total innocence.

Karen stated, "I think Thomas may have promised his attorney as an incentive for winning that he would give him a profit share once he got your modeling agency. He seemed to be big on promises based on your story."

"I'm sure he did. He probably promised Peggy a share, too, even though she was not an investor. Maybe that's the reason she refused to testify for me," I said sadly.

Even though I had retained Jay during my haste to secure representation, I had left a voice message for an attorney by the name of Katherine Stone. She sounded so competent and forceful over the voice message. She returned my call right away, and we briefly discussed the details about my case.

"Katherine, would you feel comfortable with another attorney appearing with you in court?" I asked.

"I can handle it myself. I don't need anybody appearing with me."

Jay's meek demeanor was overwhelmed by what I was hearing from Katherine. I was sure that Thomas would have strong and aggressive counsel. I couldn't afford to be represented by a milquetoast. I needed strength and confidence. So, I made a choice. I decided to go with Katherine.

"You had already retained him. How could you switch like that? Didn't you sign an agreement or something?" Karen asked.

I was willing to lose the five hundred dollars versus losing the entire case. I called Jay to inform him of my decision. He was cordial, and he wished me well. I met with Katherine four hours prior to the hearing to retain her, and, in doing so, I flushed the retainer that I had paid Jay right down the toilet. I did this, as usual, on a whim and based on impressions, but she was nothing like what I had imagined.

She was this plain looking, regular, and nondescript older white woman. There was nothing outstanding about Katherine. *Damn! She's not a Katherine. She's more like a Kate,* I thought. *I like women, but I wouldn't touch that trailer trash looking road whore with a ten foot pole.* We shook each other's hand and sat down to discuss the situation. Her handshake belied her force on the phone as it was weak, clammy, and placid. A negative aura surrounded her. She seemed like a bigoted, backwoods cloud to me. That was what she

Meleisa Betts

emanated. I was not comfortable with her at all, but it was a last minute decision that I had to live with. I had dismissed Jay, so I needed an attorney to appear with me, so I could get the theft by deception warrant issued.

"Angiel, you should have stayed with Jay. What were you thinking?" Karen said.

"Karen, it's obvious that I wasn't thinking! That's part of the reason that I'm here with you. It seems like I'm thinking with two brains at times," I joked, but it was a half-truth.

Initially, everything seemed to be going well, but, one hour after speaking with her and after some deliberation, the true Katherine erupted.

Katherine abruptly stated, "This seems to be a civil issue and not a criminal issue."

"What? Why do you say that?" I asked, and she didn't answer.

During the fact-finding session, she had spoken with my former attorney Mike over the phone. She asked him for the email that was sent to him by Rodney concerning the twenty-two hundred dollars. Katherine completely glossed over the fact that the seven thousand dollars was not theft by deception. Hell, it was quite obvious that Thomas had used the money to cover his outstanding debt with the graphics design company. That was downright stealing! If you write a check for seven thousand dollars, and your bank account has absolutely zero dollars in it, then you go to jail. *How is this a civil case now?* I wondered.

It was now down to an hour and a half before court, and I was caught in a web of problems. I asked myself, "What in the world am I going to do?"

Katherine kept saying to me, "This case is civil and not criminal." She was beginning to sound like a scratched CD.

"Why are you just now saying this? You didn't say this at the beginning of our conversation when I agreed to retain you?" I asked with a quizzical look.

She responded, "I kind of felt that way from the beginning."

This was a misrepresentation of the facts. She never told me that she felt that way until an hour into our conversation on that day. Initially, she had made it appear that it was definitely a criminal case. She even said that she was going to subpoena Mike to testify. Now, it was a different story altogether. It was less than an hour and a half before court. I had told Jay not to appear. Now, I was stuck with this country bumpkin hick of an attorney. Hell! Mike literally took my six hundred dollars. I forfeited the five hundred dollars to Jay. And now, there I was, sitting in this office with this old hag who was telling me things that were completely different from what she said over the phone. She had said whatever it took for me to hire her as my attorney.

"Can you, at least, put up a good argument for it being a theft?" I pleaded.

"I don't think the judge will issue a warrant based upon the information that you have," Katherine stated, in her harsh, hoarse, gin and cigarette soaked southern drawl.

Time was not my ally as I had to be in court in one hour. In addition to this dilemma, I had three co-workers waiting on me. I needed to meet them to make sure that they went to the right courtroom. I just knew that my brother Blaine would be there to support me. I had called my father earlier when the problem first began, and I had kept him updated on what had been transpiring. My father told me that he would get in touch with Blaine and that he would be there for me for some added support.

My father had told me that he had spoken to Blaine and had told him, "I want you to be in that court room with your sister, boy."

To this request, Blaine had responded, "Yes, sir. I will. I promise."

Well, he wasn't there as he had promised my father, but I wasn't surprised. I was prepared, as usual, for one of my family members to let me down when I needed them. I was too mentally tired to both call Blaine and look for my co-workers at the same time. I was having stomach cramps from hell, and my head was hurting.

There was just too much happening too quickly. I knew right then, without a shadow of a doubt, that I had made a big mistake by replacing Jay with Katherine since my body was showing the signs of the newfound stress that I was under. The problem was that I was too involved with her to turn back at such a late stage in the proceedings.

At that point, I started preparing myself. It looked as though I was going to be the one convincing the judge of the merits of my case. If I started telling my story from the beginning, omitting the trivial things, mentioning the most important details, then I hoped that would be just enough to persuade the judge.

There was no time to think about the aches and pains. However, while waiting, taking a moment of relaxation before the court proceedings began, I had a revelation as to how I had arrived there.

{Chapter 8}

Karen stopped me by raising her hand, as though she were hailing a taxicab, and said, "Are you saying that, in the midst of all of the turmoil that you were experiencing, you finally had a moment of self-actualization?"

"I may have had that moment if you kindly explain to me what in the hell that means," I said.

"Self-actualization is when a person finally sees his or herself honestly from the perspective of truth and reality. This is the point where the individual really learns himself and is honest about what rights or wrongs he may be doing or what flaws are present. There are no more lies, only personal accountability," she said in a clinical way, but her explanation was somehow soothing and reassuring at the same time.

"I would have to say yes to that. That was the point where I stopped blaming others for the hell that I had created for myself. Everything from my relationships to the Thomas situation had been created by me or my desires."

"That is a positive revelation. This lets me know that you are trying to be honest with yourself. Before you can improve your mental state, you have to be honest on all fronts," she said.

The previous year, I had begun going to church more. I started attending Bible study classes every Thursday night and church every Saturday. Despite my having attended services so often, I, sometimes, went right back on Sundays. This schedule was the one that I kept for, at least, three times a month. I even went to the extreme of buying a DVD recorder in order to copy Thursday night's Bible study. I would copy the DVDs and pass them out to strangers who I conversed with. I had a zest to learn the Bible. It was rewarding. My life, at the time, was equally wonderful.

It was the month of October, and Pastor Dale was hosting a special event on the first Thursday night of the month. Hot 105.6, a local urban radio station, and a lot of rappers were there. The atmosphere was electric. The event was primarily for teenagers, even though adults attended.

Since I went to Bible study on Thursdays, this didn't interfere with my schedule, but I knew that I had to get there early since this was a big event. I wanted to get a seat in front to be close to the action.

When I arrived at church, there was a line of people that stretched around the building. To compound matters, it was about twelve degrees outside. I tried to go into the church using the side door. Since I was a regular patron, I didn't think it would be a problem. I walked up to the side door and found that a deacon was standing at the door.

"I'm sorry, but you're going to have to wait in line like everybody else," the deacon said.

"Sir, I can't stand for long periods of time because of my back," I pleaded.

"I'm sorry, but you have to get in line, miss," the deacon said, standing firm on his convictions.

"Sir, I'm by myself. There's no entourage to worry about." I felt as though I was making a legitimate case for myself.

"Miss, will you step back? I need to shut the door," he said rudely. Apparently, my pleading was useless.

"It's freezing cold out here. I see people going in and out!" I said defiantly. "It seems to be ridiculous for me to be standing out here freezing, sir!"

The deacon replied, "The ones that are going in and out are doing some type of work."

After standing and waiting for an hour, I began to see members of the church bringing in friends. I saw faces who were not members. They were coming in and out of the proceedings without being questioned.

"Can I come inside now? It seems to be more than just workers being allowed in."

He said, "No," and there were no further words. I was upset, yet I spoke to him with reason and calmness.

"Sir, I was coming to this church when Pastor Dale was over on the east side speaking from a big podium with a microphone in front of him. There were just a handful of members. I followed him here. I'm known as a regular member, so you're telling me that I have to stand outside as if I was someone off the streets? I helped to build this new church by paying my tithes diligently," I said in a strong and forceful tone.

"I'm sorry, but you still have to get in line, miss." This time, he was looking past me as if I was invisible.

After arguing with the deacon off and on for over two and a half hours, he finally let me in. The church was packed. They were sending people back. By the grace of God, I was able to find a seat in front. Nevertheless, I was so hurt in my spirit by the way I had been treated. It bothered me to the point that I couldn't fully enjoy the service. I didn't go back to Bible study nor could I, in good conscience, attend services on Sunday mornings. I was so disappointed in the church. I stopped listening to Pastor Dale's sermons on tapes. The DVD recorder turned out to have been a waste of money. After the fiasco with the church, I seemed to drop out of the world of religion completely. After I dropped out, all of my problems seemed to drop in. I don't mean that I stopped believing in God. I love Him with all my heart and soul. I simply was slowly, but surely, descending into a pattern of alternately losing, gaining, and losing faith in human beings.

After this falling out with the church, I decided to take a trip to New Orleans. While I was there, I consulted with voodoo doctors. There had to be something causing this negative cloud which was hanging over me and causing me so much grief and turmoil. I was sure that someone had done something to me. Maybe, someone had put a spell on me. It was hard to justify my belief in God while using an occult practice, but I was desperate. In the war between good and evil that had been waged in my life, evil had been winning the battle. I knew, at times, that I was my own worst enemy, but, on more than a few occasions, even when I had nothing but the best intentions, bad things still happened.

"How did you reconcile your belief in God with a religion which is based upon spells and spirits?" Karen asked.

"Karen, as I understand it, there are good voodoo doctors and there are bad ones, or so I rationalized. I went to the good ones, the 'white magic' makers," I said.

I bought a book to read while on the flight to Louisiana called *Voodoo & Hoodoo*. It was written by Jim Haskins. In it, he said to be very careful when dealing with different voodoo priests because some male priests would try to take advantage of a female if they know that she is already vulnerable. This happened to me on my visit to New Orleans. A priest tried to bilk me of money, while, also, trying to get sex from me.

I had spoken with one voodoo priest, in particular, numerous times over the phone prior to my decision to take the trip. I told him that I wanted to take a flight to New Orleans to visit Marie Laveau's grave, since he had mentioned it. According to the priest, Marie Laveau was considered to be the greatest voodoo practitioner in history. There's a belief that her powers even extend beyond the grave. Her followers believe that, if you leave three X's on her grave and three pennies, your request will be granted. Also, if you take a piece of her gravestone, your luck will improve. I had to get there. I was hoping God would forgive me for disobeying Him this one time. The voodoo priest suggested the trip to the gravesite. He had taken many of his clients to that site, as part of the fee that they paid him. I was gonna proceed with him, and my plans hadn't changed until the day before my flight when we had a conversation which revealed his true intentions. I called him less than twenty-four hours before my flight.

"I have my flight plans in place. I'm anxious to go to Marie Laveau's grave. Hopefully, this will get this negative curse off of me. When I get to New Orleans, what do I need to do? Do I call you once I get there?" I asked.

"Don't you have ya hotel reservations, yet?" the voodoo priest asked. He had a thick Cajun-Louisiana French Bayou accent.

I wondered, *Why in the hell does that matter?* My bullshit detector started beeping inside of my head.

"No, I haven't made any plans like that. I was thinking that I could get a room at a motel or something, that is, if I planned on staying more than a day or so. I was planning on just coming in for the day and leaving. Was there any particular reason why you ask?" I inquired, apprehensive about his answer. I just knew that my bullshit meter beeper would grow increasingly louder.

"I want you to do me a favor. I want you to get a room at dat dere Marriott Hotel," he said, with a voice sounding like a Cajun doctor who was giving a patient some medical news which they weren't gonna be pleased with.

"Why do you want me to get a hotel room?" I asked.

"Because I want to eat your pussy, and we gonna needs us a good room," he said with the same matter of fact Cajun voice as before.

Bingo! The bullshit meter was both flashing and beeping. He was yet another example of how I'd put my trust in another human because I was persuaded by flash and words and how that person had had an ulterior motive other than helping me.

"You want to eat my pussy? What does that have to do with my bad luck and spells or whatever? What does eating my pussy have to do with anything?" I asked, feeling both shocked and angry at the same time.

"Well, I had another client dat was going through problems, and, after I ate her pussy, she done came so hard, and she said dat the weight was lifted from on her. She told me dat she never com so hard in her life. So, I think I can cure you from dem evil spirits by making you com," he said with the same antiseptic, Cajun-influenced dialect which he had maintained during the entire conversation.

"I'll call you when I get to New Orleans, but I have to decline your other invitation," I said to him as the conversation ended.

I just could not believe that he would be so bold as to think that I was so vulnerable to fall for something like that. I knew I wasn't going to agree to something that foolish. I hadn't chosen my problems, but they were something that I had to deal with. No amount of oral sex, great, bad or otherwise, was going to magically convert problems into solutions. I had problems, and that was that. No magical tongue would change that fact. Not even the magical tongue of the so-called best oral sex practitioner in all of New Orleans could relieve me of my personal demons.

When I arrived in New Orleans, I managed to find a tour bus that took me to Marie Laveau's gravesite. Now, I could forgo both the fee of the priest and the uncomfortable feeling of being in his presence. I called him just to see if he would answer my call, and, as I had predicted, he did not.

The tour bus took me to the gravesite. My plan to draw my X's and leave my three pennies was thwarted by the fact that her grave was completely covered by X's and coins. *The trip wasn't completely for nothing*, I thought, as I still made my three wishes. The grave was covered with markings. I managed to mark three X's and leave three pennies. There were loose pieces of the grave scattered around. I took a pebble. I could clearly see that there were many people suffering and looking for answers, even from a myth and the remains of a person who was long gone.

"So, you think that your using voodoo may have led to your problems?" Karen asked, with a tone which made the answer seem more rhetorical than anything, but I knew that Karen was aware that the real problem was me. I had already confessed as much.

I responded, "I most certainly do, Karen. I placed my faith in voodoo. First, it was because of my frustration over my luck. The second time was because of the case against Thomas. I do believe that it opened the door for Satan to wreak havoc on my life and to try to get me to turn even further away from God. I professed to love God, and I claimed to have never stopped. The problem was that I was searching for anything that I thought would work, instead of believing more, praying more and being patient, and letting God work on my problems. I guess that I believed less since I turned to the occult. My faith was not as strong as I fooled myself into believing that it was. It had gotten weaker, and I was trying to rationalize using the occult by claiming that some of it was "white" and some of it was "black." The use of magic and spells is witchcraft regardless of how you try to spin doctor it. I have even had a priestess to bless my condo to rid it of demons."

"You had someone to do an exorcism on your condo! That's as wild as anything that you have said to this point," Karen laughed.

"Hey! That stuff is serious. I'll get to that in time. But one thing that I've learned is that you can't serve two masters. This situation is what I was talking about when I said that I would explain what I meant when you had asked me about serving two masters earlier. I was doing that by calling myself a God-fearing person and, at the same time, using the satanic principles of magic and witchcraft. I learned a lot from that. Now, let me get back to this story,"

I said.

"I just wanted to be sure about what that term meant, and you have proven that you are aware. 'You can't straddle the fence,' as the saying goes," Karen added with a soft smile.

Finally, I could see clearly as I mentally prepared for my ordeal in court. I clearly was a victim/ product/ purveyor of seduction on many levels. Using money, power, or words, these shysters had twisted them all, to coin a phrase. It was as if my life was flashing back in Cliff Notes. I went back thirty years to my affiliations with Dottie Mae and Nicole and my seduction of Sonya Littlefield and similar events. Then, I moved forward in time to Thomas. I saw how Satan had used my tendencies to be a willing participant in my own woes as a weapon against me.

I had probably seen signs in that church which suggested that they would treat me the way they did, but I ignored the signs and, ultimately, became disillusioned. I can't say that I was unaware of what was occurring in my life. In practically every case, I allowed myself to become a party to the events which have shaped my life, even though my better judgment was telling me to do otherwise. However, through my sheer gullibility and naiveté, I was, at once, the cause of and a victim of my circumstances.

"I will give you a bit of a break in some of your dealings. I think that all of those people are charlatans. You're just another one of their many victims," Karen said.

"Let me get back to the court scene," I said.

I met my co-workers a short distance from the courthouse. They seemed to be burdened with having to be there with me, but, still, they came.

I was very weak in both spirit and flesh, but I couldn't keep saying that to myself because I didn't want to make the situation worse. We had a quick lunch. Then, I had to leave to meet my so-called counsel. I tried to give them as accurate directions as I could since I didn't want them to be even a minute late. Once I arrived at the courtroom, I waited outside. I wasn't feeling comfortable with Katherine at all or her ability to represent me. I had a thousand thoughts circling throughout my mind at one time. I began to feel panicky, so I attempted to dial my previous attorney Jay's number.

As soon as I dialed the number, Katherine came up next to me, and I ended the call immediately. I knew that Jay was only ten minutes away, so I was going to try to make a last ditch attempt to secure him. Once again, I had

Meleisa Betts

gone against my instincts, and I was forced by circumstances that I had created to suffer for it. It was less than five minutes before court started. I was sitting on the front bench with Katherine. My co-workers were sitting behind us. The courtroom was beginning to fill up with lawyers and looky-loos. I kept looking around for Thomas and his attorney, but I didn't see them. This was a good sign. He only had five more minutes to get there, and, if he didn't show up, the judge would issue a warrant for his arrest.

The judge came into the courtroom. The roll call began, and Thomas was not in attendance. I was so damn happy! My name was called, and Katherine answered for me. To my surprise, Thomas's attorney stood up and answered for him. *Damn! Okay, he's still not here, so that's still good*, I thought. I was so nervous that I could barely sit still on the bench. The roll call was completed, and the judge called our case first. I went up before the judge with Katherine. Thomas's attorney, also, approached the bench.

"Your Honor, we are having subpoena problems," Katherine began. *What in the hell is she talking about? That's Thomas's and his attorney's problem, not ours. Whose side is she on anyway?* I wondered.

"Your Honor, my client is not here yet," Thomas's lawyer stated.

The judge said, "I'll give you a little time to step outside and try to resolve this."

At that point, I asked myself, "Why didn't Katherine ask for the warrant?" I sat back down in my seat while both attorneys went outside. After waiting for fifteen minutes, I went outside to see what the problem was. Thomas's attorney was on the phone, more than likely trying to reach him. Katherine was standing in the general area, not far away from Thomas's lawyer. He reminded me so much of my neighbor's little green-eyed monster boy from West Palm Beach. I stared at him for a minute.

I wonder if he's Jonas, the green-eyed boy, I thought. *If he is Jonas all grown up, then I am in trouble.* I was really in full conspiracy mode. That was one of the most outlandish of my making molehills into mountains, but anything was possible, I believed.

I asked Katherine about her actions or rather inactions. "Why didn't you ask for a bench warrant?"

She responded, "The judge is not going to issue a warrant."

"Katherine, how can you be so sure of what the judge

will decide?" I was upset, but I managed to keep a poker face.

She simply said, "I know." That was the end of that.

After forty-five minutes, Thomas still hadn't arrived at court. One of my co-workers, Mrs. Hall, had decided to leave. She said that the process was taking too long. Bonnie, my other co-worker that was in attendance, wanted to leave with her, but I managed to persuade her to stay. Finally, Thomas came strolling and rolling into the courtroom. He was fifty minutes late, and there was no consequence.

"It would seem to me that a bench warrant would have been automatically given," Karen said.

"Well, it wasn't, and I have no explanation as to why," I said.

"Your attorney should have pressed for one to be issued right away," Karen said.

Incredibly, Thomas's attorney, Jonas Burke, came over to Katherine with a settlement offer. He offered two thousand dollars and all the rights to my modeling agency.

I yelled, "NO!" The force of my no startled both Katherine and Jonas.

Jonas was a young guy who was probably in his early thirties. He was probably new to the legal profession, and he wanted some sort of win, but I was not budging. That settlement allowed Thomas to walk away a winner, and I was not going to consent to that! *Right is on my side*, I thought, *so I can't lose*. I would soon find out that, sometimes, right and wrong in the legal system is determined by who is the best or worst lawyer or the worst plaintiff or defendant.

After the discussion or lack thereof, we, then, went back into the courtroom. Most of the cases were over, so the courtroom was half empty.

"I don't blame you at all for your stance. I would have said no, too. How in the world can someone take seven thousand dollars and turn right around and say, 'I'll give you two thousand of your own money back'? That's pure nonsense!" Karen said.

"Karen, it was ALL bullshit," I lamented.

The judge asked all of us to approach the bench.

The judge said, "I looked over these papers. I'm trying to figure out how this is a criminal case."

I responded quickly, "Your Honor, can I give you the circumstances surrounding the case?"

As I began to speak, Katherine grabbed my left arm, pulled me close, and whispered in my ear, "Stick to the facts."

Meleisa Betts

After this action of arm grabbing and ear whispering, I lost my train of thought, and I couldn't finish what I had to say. I felt that the judge needed to hear, from the beginning, what had happened in order to fully understand. I knew that, when Thomas took the stand, he was going to be quite convincing. I was allowed to testify on my behalf, and, in the process, Katherine asked me two inconsequential questions. They were so inane that I can't even remember them. She entered a piece of paper as exhibit one to the judge and never even discussed or showed the paper to me.

Jonas Burke, then, asked me several probing questions. Based on the way he phrased the questions, it seemed as though I was in agreement with everything that Thomas had done, even using the monies to finance his business. In comparing the two attorneys, Katherine was clearly overmatched. There was not one objection raised by Katherine to anything that Burke asked or said. One of the questions was concerning the graphic designer, Rodney. He had been subpoenaed, but had failed to appear. I tried to speak to the facts of exhibit two, which was the email that he'd sent to me. Thomas had stated in the email that he was going to pay me out of his personal account. Burke objected, calling it no more than hearsay. The judge disagreed and denied his motion. My testimony lasted no longer than five minutes.

Now, it was Thomas's turn to testify. Thomas waddled up to the bench, struggling because of his weight, and he tried to look especially strained and sickly to garner sympathy points. More than likely, he was probably out of breath because he was running late. The judge asked him about exhibit two, the email. Thomas told the judge that when he wrote the email he was under duress. The judge asked him what kind of duress was he was alluding to. Thomas began to speak with his so soft voice and soothing tone. He should have been an actor. This man was so dramatic!

Thomas said, "Your Honor, Angiel was constantly calling me early in the morning. She wanted to bring nude pictures of herself over for me to see them. You see, she was trying to date me. Angiel, also, has underage females living with her. She prostitutes them out to older men. One of the men was killed by someone. She, also, has businessmen coming over for the girls. She's like a madam or a pimp, selling the girls for sex. Angiel called me last Friday, Your Honor. She said that she was coming over to Universal

Packaging, and she sounded like she was going to get me. I told her that it was Brandi's birthday and that I was thinking of her, even though she's no longer here. She refused to listen, and she came over anyway and was loud and threatening." He started to sniff, and he took a handkerchief out of his pocket and dabbed his eyes.

"Who is Brandi?" the judge asked.

"She was my wife, Your Honor. She passed away earlier this year."

At that point, he started to cry crocodile tears! The tears were just streaming down his face. I was mad as a dog with rabies, but I could only listen and slowly boil inside.

Thomas continued with the façade. "I kept telling Angiel it was Brandi's birthday. I asked her, 'Can't I just grieve?' Your Honor, Angiel said that she grieves every day because she had recently lost her mother, but she wouldn't give me that same consideration. Your Honor, Angiel, also, wanted to include sex acts with animals for the photo shoots with the models. It was just too much to bear," he said, crying.

I was standing there, looking at him in complete amazement. The people in the courtroom were, also, staring at him and alternately at me as if to say, "These people are crazy as hell." There's no way anyone can say anything like that and still be considered sane, but, without the benefit of rebuttal, they were predisposed to believe him. I was so upset upon hearing Thomas tell those horrendous lies, but I could do nothing but listen. My co-workers, who were there to testify on my behalf, said that I turned bloody red. It takes a truly sick mind to think of sex acts with animals, as well as to accuse someone of such things. I could never say that, think that, nor could I accuse my worst enemy of something so putrid. That was indicative of the extremes to which Thomas would go to gain his own end. This was the sickest shit I'd ever heard of in my life! It literally made me sick to my stomach, to hear him lie like that AND to include bestiality as something that I had discussed with him. I was livid!

The judge said, "That's enough! I don't want to hear anymore!"

I started to speak to those horrendous accusations, but I was cut off at "Your Honor." I was grabbed by the arm again by Katherine, who whispered in my ear, "That's okay."

It's not okay! What in the world am I paying her for? I thought.

The judge said to me, "I'm not saying that you are not going to get your money back, but I'm sending this over to civil court."

"Are you punishing me for the things that I did in my past?" I asked God.

"So, he told all of those nasty lies on you, and your lawyer didn't object even once?" Karen asked with the fervor of curiosity.

"Katherine didn't say a damn word," I sighed.

That son of a bitch could have won an Oscar for his performance as a frightened victim. The lies rolled off his tongue like honey. It was one lie after another, and each one was so seamless that, to the casual observer, they would have seemed plausible. In all my years on this earth, I had never seen anyone lie so well. I knew, right then and beyond a shadow of a doubt, that Thomas had killed Brandi, and that it was premeditated. I was ninety-five percent sure before this fiasco in court, but now I was one hundred percent sure.

I only imagined the torment poor Brandi had gone through. As far as the family goes, I knew they had gone through pure hell dealing with Thomas. No wonder they were hesitant about following through with the investigation. They knew what kind of hellion they would be facing. They would have been facing Satan himself. This man was totally consumed with and possessed by evil. I had met Beelzebub and didn't know it. Thomas was nothing but pure evil, nothing but deceit and lies and full of hurt. The only conclusion was that, maybe, something had happened back in his childhood that we may never know about. Perhaps, he was possessed, and the demon continued to rule him. There was no way a person could speak of all of these things and not have done or considered them, at some point in his past. Thomas most certainly had done many evil things and had gotten away with them. He was much too clever and too good at what he did, to have not made a practice of deception and manipulation. Maybe, his family was a band of drifters, gypsies, and con artists, and, maybe, this was how he had learned.

"Karen, Peggy did say that Thomas's mother wanted him to get rid of Brandi because she was too sickly," I said. "That tells me that this kind of unfeeling and lack of remorse had been taught to Thomas or he had inherited that trait. Whatever the case, it was like mother/like son."

Later that night, after court, I was visiting one of my co-workers, Mark, at his home. I received two phone calls on my cell phone. At the time, we were watching television and not really doing much else other than making small talk about work and keeping each other company. The calls were from Thomas, of all people! I couldn't believe that this bastard was still calling me. During the second call, he actually threatened to kill me and my dog.

"There's no way I'm gonna let you destroy what I worked so hard for," he said, trying to sound menacing.

On the first call, the television was up so loud that all I could hear was a male voice cursing, so I hung up. When he called back a second time, I turned the speakerphone on, so Mark could hear, too.

Mark said, "You need to call 911 right now!"

A police officer came out to Mark's home and took a report. We, then, took the report down to the judge who was on duty for night court. I asked for an application hearing on phone threats. The judge looked at the report, agreed that I had a case, and gave me a court date for the next week. That same day, I called Jay, my lawyer of choice before the horrible Katherine, and told him about what had happened. He told me that I should go and retrieve the application for phone threats because it would look like an act of retaliation toward Thomas. I, immediately, called the clerk's office. Luckily, the document had not gone out in the mail. I called Mark, and I asked him to meet me at the courthouse. Jay advised me to apply for a restraining order against Thomas. Mark met me at the courthouse. While we were in the hallway filling out the paper work for the restraining order, before we went before the judge, a sharply dressed Hispanic man walked up with a briefcase in his hands.

"Excuse me. Can I have one of your business cards?" I asked.

"Sure. My name is Arturo, but you can call me Art for short. Art Joseph."

"What would you charge to represent me in a civil case filed in state court?" I asked.

"What is the case about?"

"It's a difficult case dealing with a conniving con artist," I said. After hearing the most pertinent details, he said, "I'll charge you eleven hundred dollars."

I was shocked by his price because Jay had quoted me a price of five thousand to take my case to state court.

I asked, "Does the price include the whole process of going before the jury?"

"Yes, it does. It includes the entire process," he stated

politely.

"How much will you charge me to take care of filing a restraining order?" I asked.

"It will cost two hundred and fifty dollars," he said.

"I only have one hundred-fifty dollars," I said, trying to look sad.

"That's fine," he said as he smiled at me and nodded.

"Can you get the edict extended for more than ten days?"

"That won't be a problem," he responded very confidently.

The court attendant called us into the courtroom after about an hour's wait, and the judge asked questions. I told him about the application for a warrant that had been held on the day prior. The judge, then, set the hearing date for the following week.

I kept slightly bumping Art Joseph with my arm, and I guess that he was at a loss as to why. I was trying to get his attention, but he seemed to have read my mind and simply ignored me.

Art Joseph, finally, asked, "Your Honor, can we extend the date?"

The judge stated without hesitation, "No, we have to

hear these cases within ten days."

Hell! I could have saved myself one hundred and fifty dollars by not acting so impulsively. In looking back on that decision to hire Art Joseph, I can see that, once again, I was swayed by my assumptions based on the superficial. I had seen a well dressed man who looked the part, and I went with style, thinking as usual that looks equaled quality. As I am admitting to now, this tendency has not served me well with many of my decisions throughout my life.

Art Joseph set up the appointment for me to come by his office. Thomas's calling me while I was visiting Mark apparently wasn't enough harassment for him as he called me back two days later. I was at my doctor's office at the time. I purposefully had the speaker phone on, so the receptionist could be a witness.

"Britney is going to meet you to give you the money," he said.

"Thomas, don't you ever call me again!" I yelled for emphasis, getting the receptionist's attention.

I promptly hung up and dialed 911. The police came to the doctor's office and took a report. Although she was a material witness, the receptionist who overheard Thomas could not come to the hearing for the restraining order. She had to work for someone else who was out on sick leave, and there was no other option for her. I was out of luck yet again. Thomas had made the one call that I could have used to secure a harassment conviction on him, but I would have no way to prove it. It seemed to me as though Thomas had some kind of supernatural force protecting him. I felt that I needed answers to whatever it was that was helping him or hurting me.

As I look back on the situation, it was unbelievable but true. I headed back to New Orleans, once again, on the following day to seek out some supernatural help of my own. It was as though something or someone was making my decisions for me, but I went along with it. I had even decided to take yet another trip to voodoo priestess Marie Laveau's grave to make a wish for protection. In my mind, I could see no other way but to fight fire with occult flames, yet I still professed to be guided by God. Now, I realize that, while I continued to serve the wrong master, God stepped away to let me see what serving that master would accomplish.

I kept the report of the call that Thomas made, so I could give it to Art Joseph on the following week before the court appearance. I tried calling Art Joseph to let him know about the phone call, but he didn't answer my call. I thought nothing of it at the time when he didn't answer.

That night, before the trip, I had some strange things to occur, such as a flickering of my computer monitor even though the power was off. A vision of a tall and dark apparition had come to me three or four times in that night. I could only conclude that Brandi was trying to tell me something, if she was in fact the spirit who was making herself visible to me. I'm sure that it was because this particular entity started appearing shortly after the conflict with Thomas had begun. Needless to say, I had very little sleep that night. Maybe, Brandi was trying to keep me from making the trip.

Years ago, I had heard old people say things that you should and shouldn't do as far as superstitions of good or bad luck were concerned. They would talk about cooking certain foods on New Year's Day for good luck, breaking mirrors, or what certain weather signs meant among other signs. Most of these things were included in Jim Haskin's *Voodoo & Hoodoo*, which I again had with me during that flight to New Orleans. I had only read a small portion of the book on my previous trip to visit Marie Laveau's grave, so I finished it on the second flight.

As I had alluded to before, as a child and even until this very day, I can see visions of the departed. Sometimes, when I see an apparition, something would happen afterwards, as if the spirit was warning me about something. I was always too afraid to try and communicate with the spirit. I was literally scared out of my panties when they would appear. I was hoping that the spirit of Brandi or whoever it was, was not warning me of something.

I knew that the visions were happening, but I wasn't sure about what was really going on because I honestly did not understand WHY they were happening. Why was I burdened with this ability/curse of seeing spirits and the inconvenience of never sleeping with the lights off? I saw my Grandma Eliza's spirit two months after her burial as clearly as if she was standing in front of me alive. I'll never forget that night when it happened. I was lying in the bed, unable to sleep. I opened my eyes, and Grandma was sitting on my mother's bed, looking right at me.

"Mama, Mama, Mama!" I screamed.

"Baby, what's wrong?" Mama asked.

"I saw Grandma!"

"Baby, Grandma is dead. You were just having a bad

dream," Mama said. "You go back to sleep."

"No, Mama. I saw Grandma. She was sitting right there, looking at me!"

"Grandma is dead, baby."

"Mama, she had these little curls all over her head, and she had this white dress on, and it had a fluffy collar!"

My mother's eyes grew really wide because she knew that there was no way I could have known this. Mama never doubted that I had the gift/curse of seeing spirits from that day forward. My mother had the funeral home to curl my grandmother's hair into little Shirley Temple curls. Grandma's hair had never been in curls before her death. When I told my mother about the little curls in Grandma's hair, she knew that this was the only way I could have known.

"Baby, don't you be afraid. Maybe, she was trying to tell you something," she said, trying to comfort me.

"Mama, I don't want to hear what she has to say! I'm scared!" I was always terrified of them, whether they were trying to tell me something that I needed to know or not. Long ago, my mother revealed to me the nature of my power/curse.

"Baby, you were born with a veil over your face."

I asked her, "Mama, what is a veil? What does that mean?"

She went on to explain. "It's a very thin, wet, transparent layer of membrane covering the face. The doctor had to peel it off, but it came off easily. They say that, if you are born like that, then you can see spirits."

I started to cry. "Mama, please don't turn off the light. I'm scared!" The lights have been on every night since.

I never really understood what that meant as a child even with that simple explanation. However, she told me that story more than three or four times as I grew older. I can only guess that she didn't want me to ever forget that point. I didn't. I remembered telling this to a very spiritual lady at work by the name of Mrs. Tex, who was an evangelist in her other vocation outside of the Universal Packaging workplace.

"Mrs. Tex, my mama told me that I was born with a veil over my face. She said that I had a special gift, but I don't see it that way," I said, shaking my head as I gazed at the floor.

After I told her about my auspicious birth, Mrs. Tex looked at me with her wide eyes and said, "Why would your mother tell you that? It's a curse to be able to see the departed!"

I let that statement go into one ear and out of the other. I knew that my mother was a very spiritual lady, and her mere words did not bring the ability to me, but, rather, an act of God had. When I had problems, I would ask my mother for her opinion, and she would always say, "Baby, don't worry about it. The Lord will take care of it." It was always the Lord. If anyone in my life was speaking words with the power of God, it was my mother, but I had blatantly stepped away from His protection.

During my second flight to New Orleans, I had read the entire Haskins book more extensively. Even Haskins reiterated what I had been told in his writings about that long-standing supernatural belief of the veil. In his book, he wrote, when a person was born with a veil over her face, that that person is special on a psychic level. Those who are veiled are able to summon spirits and communicate with them. Unfortunately, wayward spirits often gravitated toward them.

My eyes got very big, and my heart began to beat rapidly as I thought, *Wow! Mama was right! I am a blessing!* Now, it was clear to me why Brandi was coming to me. She was trying to use me in order to tell her story. She, like me, wanted

Thomas to be prosecuted and for justice to be served.

Once again, I visited Marie Laveau's grave and asked her departed spirit for help. I, again, made my three wishes, drew three X's on her grave, and left three pennies, just as the ritual prescribed. I, also, took another piece of cement from her grave.

It's amazing that her grave is still standing. You can tell that many pieces had been taken. You would think that voodoo was predominantly a black person's belief, but that was far from the truth. In fact, I could barely get into these places because there were so many white people in front of me. There were so many whites in that graveyard. I couldn't believe what I was seeing. The Haskins book stated that white and other ethnicities feel comfortable visiting sites such as this, when they're in New Orleans.

"Angiel, it's sad but true that nothing unites the human race more than common suffering. During a crisis, Americans forget about their hatred and come together to help each other," Karen said.

"Yeah, you're right. The September 11th attacks was the scariest day for me, but it seemed that everyone in America was supporting each other, helping and donating money." I smiled at that thought.

"That shows how God works on the human condition," Karen said, smiling.

I had believed with all of my heart that the weekend trip was going to be successful and that a deceased voodoo priestess would grant my wishes and vanquish the evil which had tormented me for years. I was hoping that the good of so-called "white voodoo" was acceptable. I didn't feel as though I was seeking to place a spell on or wish ill on anyone, not even Thomas. Even though, he deserved it. I simply wanted some force of the universe, whether it was good or bad, to exact the justice that he deserved upon him.

Since I was already in New Orleans, I decided to seek out a voodoo priestess this time. Maybe, the perspective of a female would give me a different outcome, I rationalized. She was a huge black female with long dreadlocks tied back with a scarf and very colorful clothing. After explaining my situation briefly, she told me the procedure for preparing for the court appearance. She charged me fifty dollars for the advice, and I figured that amount was a bargain if I could finally defeat Thomas.

I returned home late that evening, so I would be well rested for the next day. It was the day of court, and I was about to put the effectiveness of my wish to Marie Laveau's grave to the test once again. One of my wishes was that the wrongs and injustices of my life be made right or avenged. It was a known fact that this particular county judge didn't stand for foolishness and histrionics. Thomas wasn't about to get in front of this judge and give another acting performance. I felt pretty good about going back to court. I arrived on time, and I had my representation, Art Joseph. I felt that I was fully armed and prepared for this court date. Thomas had a different attorney this time, instead of Jonas, the green-eyed attorney.

He involved poor Britney and Tracey in this fiasco once again by bringing them as witnesses for his defense. It was obvious that this man had brainwashed these young girls. Where were their families in the midst of all of this? Did the families of these young girls even know that he had told them to lie under oath, not to mention the fact that they were even in court? Britney didn't know about the lack of respect that Thomas had for her. He was literally using her as a lackey, a pawn, as he had used everyone in his life. I remembered asking Thomas what would happen to the business if something should ever happen to him.

"Tracey will take over the business," Thomas replied.

"Why wouldn't Britney be your first choice?" I asked.

"I like Tracey better than Britney. Besides, I think Britney is gullible and not too bright," he laughed. Not only was Thomas a liar and a con man, he had absolutely no loyalty to anyone. He was a perfect example of that old adage — "There is no honor among thieves." Britney had been with him from the outset of his business, yet he would screw her over because he found Tracey more attractive.

The court session had begun, and we had the no-nonsense judge. The first thing that Thomas's attorney did was hand the judge a piece of paper.

"This will help you with the pronunciation of my last name because everybody has problems saying it," he said.

In reality, he was trying to name drop with the judge in order to influence him. The piece of paper had the law firm's letterhead on it. He was Italian, and the judge appeared to be, also, being that his name was Enzio Lotta. This is an edge which may have played in the judgment as anyone might infer. He was smart to recognize that the judge probably didn't recognize his name from any random lawyer and to use the edge of a common ethnicity to his advantage. The law firm was one of the largest firms based in the entire state. He probably scored style points on both accounts. My attorney didn't catch on to his astute tactical thinking at all, but it probably wouldn't have mattered if he had.

My case was on the docket first. I took the stand, and my attorney began to ask me questions. I answered them to the best of my ability. However, his questions to me were strikingly vague and useless to my case. He was asking me things like how old I was and how long had I lived at certain places, such as the Devonshire. I did get the opportunity to go into some detail about the ordeal, and I recounted as much as I could.

Now, it was time for Thomas's attorney to have his turn at questions. His attorney cross-examined me, and this attorney seemed to ask relevant and compelling questions. Art Joseph didn't tell me to bring a copy of my phone records to show that Thomas had called and threatened me. As my counsel, he should have made sure that I was prepared. The opposing lawyer immediately pointed out that there was no evidence present of a call. The judge was in full agreement not to accept hearsay.

The judge said, "I'm not going to issue a restraining order because I'm not going to count the first phone call. She admitted that she really couldn't hear the call clearly. In order for it to be deemed as harassment, the filer had to have received more than one call. Since there was no tangible proof or a record of anyone other than the plaintiff alleging a call, then I see no grounds for granting the order."

Damn! I needed that receptionist here with me to testify, I thought.

"Your Honor, we are requesting attorney's fees," Thomas's lawyer said.

"No, I won't grant that determination because I'm not totally convinced that the calls weren't made. I am dismissing both cases," the judge stated with a firm voice.

I was glad for that decision, but the judge, also, said, "I don't want to see either of you in my courtroom again."

As we were leaving the courtroom, Thomas, once again, put on his victim's act, by making pitiful faces and crying. I overheard him say aloud, "She keeps bothering me. What can I do to stop her?"

The same crocodile tears were streaming down his greasy cheeks, but, this time, no one was listening.

Suddenly, the judge looked at Thomas and said, "Mr. Walters, you were lucky this time."

What exactly was the judge trying to say? It appeared as though he could see the guilt clearly, yet he was giving Thomas a break for some reason.

The voodoo priestess had instructed me to wear black and red to court and to leave candles burning at strategic points in my home. Even though I had followed all of the voodoo protocol, it'd had absolutely no effect whatsoever. If someone had to be declared a winner in the proceedings, it would have been Thomas. He escaped his terroristic threats, and he still had all of my damned money. After the court proceedings, Art and I stood outside for, at least, twenty minutes talking about the judge and what had been said. Thomas and his entourage were in the back of the hallway for about the same length of time. I couldn't hear what they were saying, but his facial gestures and the fake sobbing suggested that he was telling another of his endless lies.

I went to Art Joseph's office the following day to retain him and file the seemingly never ending lawsuit against Thomas. I mentioned that one of my previous lawyers, Mike, had taken six hundred dollars from me and didn't show up for court. He told me to write Mike a letter, and, if he didn't respond, I was going to contact the American Bar Association. This was the first time the bar association had crossed my mind. I retained Art Joseph for a fee of eleven hundred dollars, and he wasted no time in depositing it because the check was cashed the next day. He told me that he was going to type the lawsuit against Thomas. Art said that he would call me in a week, so I could look it over and sign it. After a week went by, I called him, and I called him yet again. Now, Art Joseph was not returning my calls. *What in the hell is going on with him?* I wondered.

In the meantime, Thomas's attorney sent me a list of the small amount of the so-called "work" that Thomas had done for so many hours. He wanted me to believe that all of my money had been spent on a pamphlet. I was so pissed off that I, once again, went to work doing my own investigating. This time, I uncovered new evidence over the internet against Thomas from a model named Marie. She was one of the models that Thomas had used in the four page pamphlet, which he called a "proposal package". Through a few choice correspondences, I persuaded Marie to send me all the emails she had received from Thomas. Marie said that she had tried to contact Thomas after she sent pictures to him, but she couldn't reach him.

I, then, called the Express Ink Company in Valeria, which was the company he had used to print the information. I discovered that, despite spending my seven thousand dollars and supposedly spending countless hours creating the so-called "proposal package," it had only cost Thomas a whopping twenty-eight dollars to make the four page pamphlet. I, also, found out that he had picked up the four page calendar/pamphlet on the day that he was fifty minutes late for court. He was late because Express Ink didn't have the calendar completed. He had done almost no work on the project prior to the court day, but he wasn't taking any chances on not having something, just in case the judge asked him to see the work that he had allegedly completed.

All of the models that he had allegedly contracted to appear on the proposal package for the investors were models that he had gotten off of the website MySpace. The damning evidence was that he had perpetrated an illegal act by using the women's pictures without their permission. I even contacted one of the "models" who turned out to be a plastic surgeon. Her name was Vanessa Grooves. She informed me that she had never spoken to Thomas and was extremely surprised to see her face plastered on the pamphlet. To make matters even more damning, he had, also, taken the names of their photographers off of their photographs, to make it appear as though the "modeling agency" had photographed the models. He copied editorial work from published articles. Everything was word for word plagiarism. He made it appear as though he had researched the information.

He had committed plagiarism, copyright infringement, and fraud to the ninth degree. I could not fathom how a man who had committed such blatant illegal acts was never caught or punished. He had lied and falsified documentation to get a higher level job, murdered his wife by overdosing her with painkillers, swindled me out of thousands of dollars and a business idea, committed slander on record at the court by accusing me of bestiality, and, now, he had stolen material from the internet and was attempting to profit from it. All the while, he acted as though he was some persecuted victim. It was just incredible!

I made an appointment with an attorney named Cathy Gerard. Cathy was one of the attorneys who I had spoken with during the time I was scurrying back and forth to find last minute representation. I met with Cathy on a Saturday at her home in Valeria. My plan was to persuade her to reapply for the application warrant for theft by deception against Thomas based on the new evidence that I had received. We sat down in our consultation, and I told her everything that was going on with the case. She told me things that should have shocked me, yet, at that point, I was jaded to almost everything.

She said "I'm not going to take your money, Angiel. I run my business out of my home as you can see. I represent drug dealers and other criminal types. So, morally, I can't afford to take someone's money and not represent them properly."

Once again, the sound or appearance of a person had caused me to form an opinion before actually knowing them. As was the case with other lawyers who I had encountered, she sounded the part. I had made the same mistake with Katherine, assuming that the aggressive nature of her voice meant that she would represent me better than Jay. I had solicited the counsel of Art Joseph because he was dressed in a nice suit and looked the part of a competent lawyer.

I learned a valuable lesson throughout all of this, that was not to make snap decisions. I had to allow myself the opportunity to find out who I was putting my trust in. This was something that I had failed to do on so many other occasions in my life, and it had cost me. Fortunately, Cathy was an exception to that rule.

"You should call Art Joseph on Monday. If he doesn't answer his phone, then you leave a message saying that you will be by his office to get your eleven hundred dollars back. Tell him, if he doesn't give it back that you'll be contacting the bar association to report him," Cathy said.

This was the second time that I had heard about the bar association, so this should be a great negotiating point. I did exactly what she said, and I waited for his response.

Monday morning came, and I, again, called Art Joseph, and he again neglected to answer his phone. I got dressed and went by his office. I parked my car and walked toward his building. Before I got to the steps, he came out of his building with his briefcase in hand. Art Joseph saw me standing there, motionless, waiting on him. I stared at him on purpose. I knew he could see anger in my eyes because I was mad as hell.

"I filed your lawsuit on Friday. I have not returned your calls because I was out of town," he said, making forced eye contact with me.

"I just left the courts, and they told me that the lawsuit was not filed. So, how could you have filed it if you were out of town?" I asked.

"I got someone else to do it for me," he said.

"Well, that someone else should have told you that he or she didn't file it because it's not filed," I said while my eyes were burning through him as though I was an X-ray machine.

"Okay. Then, I will go to the court to file it now." It was clear that I had caught him in a lie, and, now, he was trying to make amends. It was way too late for that now.

"Mr. Joseph, I'm not going through this kind of treatment with another attorney. I need for you to give me something in writing right now, saying that you will represent this case through the entire process in state court for the fee we agreed on of eleven hundred dollars," I said firmly.

Art Joseph did not hesitate. Right where we stood in his parking lot, he opened his briefcase and took out a pen and a note pad. He wrote all of the information that I had requested on the pad as a receipt and handed it to me. I didn't care what he wrote it on as long as he knew that I wasn't playing games. I just felt like fighting that morning when I saw him. At that point, I was tired of the shabby treatment that I had received from these lawyers. I had paid them my money to represent me, and they acted as if they were doing it pro bono. Art Joseph knew that I had been calling him repeatedly, and he purposefully didn't call me back. He was acting like a real arrogant son-of-a-bitch.

Art Joseph, finally, filed the paperwork on the next day after our altercation in his parking lot. He sent me an e-mail that stated that he had filed the papers.

"The young lady who filed the papers was new and accidentally filed them in superior court instead of state," he said.

I emailed him back with a thank you, and I ended the correspondence with the statement, "God knew which court He wanted it in." Maybe, he was not religious, but I wanted to let him know that I was putting my faith in God, despite my paradoxically using voodoo to try and solve my legal woes. In the meantime, I filed a grievance with the American Bar Association on the attorney named Mike for taking my six hundred dollars as a retainer and not showing up for court. Also, I, simultaneously, filed a report on Katherine for not properly representing me. I got a response from the state bar.

"You didn't waste any time, and I'm glad that you didn't. The only thing that I would say is that some might see you as somewhat litigious," Karen said.

"I don't have a problem filing a grievance against an attorney who doesn't properly represent me and who will intentionally take my money!" I said.

"That is a good point that more people need to stop walking away from cases after poor representation, and then complaining about how sorry their attorneys were without taking action against being neglected," Karen responded.

"In my opinion, if someone feels that they were shortchanged, then they should file a grievance against those unscrupulous shysters. If not, the hucksters will keep doing the same screw job to other unsuspecting rubes," I said without an ounce of remorse.

"Yes, this is exactly the reason why there are innocent people who are sitting in prison to this day. It's because of improper representation," Karen agreed.

"Karen, the bottom line is, some lawyers just don't give a shit about you. They see you as a car or boat payment, and that's it," I added.

"It's sad, but I have to agree with you wholeheartedly," Karen said.

I received two letters from the bar association denying both grievances. I wasn't at all surprised at the bar's decision since it is a fraternity of men and women of the same profession.

"So, they denied your grievance?" Karen asked while

simultaneously grimacing.

"Yeah, they sure did, but, as you have heard, that is the story of my life," I said with a sigh of resignation.

I decided to go back to the internet to find out what other things this monster, Thomas, had perpetrated. This time, I visited county courts. I managed to find all the civil cases in Georgia that involved Thomas. One case involved Thomas Walters vs. Brandi Walters. Thomas had taken out a protective order with the court against Brandi. It was granted for seven months. There were three witnesses to support him in the filing. The persons were Thomas's mother, a woman named Donna, and Peggy, my co-worker and my alleged friend. I decided to call Peggy to see how she could waffle about this new information.

After a few preliminary discussion topics about the job and life, I then sprung the question: "Peggy, did you ever write a letter for Thomas to help him get a protective order against Brandi?"

She paused for a count of three, which I inferred as her gathering the story that she would feed me. Then, she said, "I never wrote a letter for Thomas. Maybe, he put something in front of me without telling me the full nature of it, and I signed it without knowing what it was." She said this with the usual naïve tone to her voice.

"Peggy, would you really sign something that required a signature without reading it first? Who is that fucking ignorant?" I asked in a louder than normal voice.

"Angiel, I'm in my car, and I'm on the way home," she said. "I'll call you as soon as I get home."

Peggy didn't call me back that afternoon, as I had predicted, so I decided to call her back. When I managed to reach her, I gave her the information that I had gotten from the website which had revealed what she and Thomas had done to Brandi. I made sure that I had given her the evidence before she could say that she would call me back again. To be honest, she seemed reluctant and even somewhat combative about taking it.

"I'm not going to look at it today. I have to answer my EEOC case now, but I will look at it tomorrow, and, afterwards, I will give you a call," she said.

I knew that this was only a stall tactic, and she wasn't going to do what she promised, but I said okay, and we ended the conversation.

The next day arrived, and, of course, I never received a call from Peggy. At that point, after becoming frustrated with dealing with Peggy, I decided to speak with my co-workers, Bonnie Raye and Mrs. Hall, about Peggy. They were aware of the situation. We all agreed that this did not sound right. Why would Peggy side with Thomas against his wife? We were, also, in agreement on the fact that Peggy should have been more curious about something she wasn't aware of agreeing to and should have read it before signing.

Three days later, Peggy finally called me. Rather than discussing the information on Thomas, she began talking about her father's illness and every other issue in her life, as though, by talking about those things, I would forget about her involvement with Thomas. I quickly switched the conversation to the topic at hand, not because I wasn't sympathetic to her concerns over her father but because I wanted to get to the truth. I asked if she had visited the site, and she responded with a flat "no".

"Peggy, if you want, I'll go to the copy center and make a copy of the letter that I took from the website," I said.

She responded, "No, I don't want you to go out of your way. I'll get it later."

I didn't say anything because, at that point, I knew that she was lying. I decided that I needed to go and get a copy of the letter, before it mysteriously went missing from

Meleisa Betts

the website. In the meantime, I received an e-mail from Art Joseph, and it read:

Thomas Walters has agreed to pay you five thousand dollars and give you the rights to the Total Dimes Modeling Agency.

I didn't respond to the email right away. I allowed Thomas to fret a little and squirm over the prospect of my declining the offer. After having a weekend to think the situation through, I had a moment of revelation. I began to question myself, as well as the situation in general. I asked myself, "Why should I believe that Thomas is going to pay me any of my money? Hell! He has gone back on his word before."

At that point, I called Art Joseph, and, again, he didn't answer the phone. I sent him an email, and, in the correspondence, I asked him when I would get my money. Within a few minutes of the email, he returned my call.

"Hello, Angiel. How are you?" he began with his usual pleasantries.

"Mr. Joseph, why is it taking so long for me to get my money?" I asked defiantly.

"I gave Mr. Walters' attorney a week's extension," Art Joseph said.

"Why? Are we trying to win or help them win?" I asked with a raised tone.

"The reason that I granted the extension was because Mr. Burke has to type up the agreement," Art Joseph responded.

"It doesn't take a week to write up an agreement. Doesn't he have a receptionist?" I said in a tone which suggested that I was fed up with both him and all of the bullshit surrounding him.

"He asked for a week, so I didn't see a problem since they were settling," he muttered.

"Don't you remember that Thomas had agreed to pay me before, and he didn't?" I asked.

"I know that, but his attorney said that both he and Thomas are ready to get this thing over with."

"Okay, Mr. Joseph, but I'm telling you that Thomas is a tremendous liar, and he's gonna try to get out of this," I said angrily.

After we ended our conversation, I decided to call the superior court to find out the status of my case. After cutting through a lot of red tape, I finally found out that the extension had been granted for two weeks, instead of one week. I, immediately, sent Art Joseph an email asking him why he said that the extension was for one week, which was a lie. I got neither returned calls nor returned emails from him.

I kept calling him over and over until my fingers were nearly numb. Finally, I received a copy of an email from Art Joseph, with an attachment from Burke, which, in turn, had attached an email from Thomas, to me. Thomas had the audacity to request the following: "In addition to the agreement, I want a formal apology from Angiel because she said that I called her and threatened to kill her and her dog."

I was mad as hell! I quickly fired off an email to Joseph stating:

"Don't you ever send me a third or fourth party email from this man! You know what he's put me through. Yet, you forward emails to me from him? You should have known that this was a stall tactic from the beginning."

He did not respond to my email as was his usual way of ignoring the situation. It would have been the ultimate insult to apologize for something he did to ME! If I had apologized to him just to get my money and to put an end to the case, then Thomas could have called me a week later and threatened me again, and I couldn't expect anyone to believe me. If I had given him an apology for something that I hadn't done, I would have been admitting that I had harassed him, and that admission could have been used as evidence in any further court action. Anything that I said afterwards about him harassing me would have zero credibility. In actuality, if I had agreed to the apology, then Thomas could have done anything that he wanted to me at that point and gotten away with it. I probably would have ended up somewhere behind bars, having been manipulated by Thomas's lying ass. He knew exactly what he was doing, and I wasn't falling for it.

"Angiel, it was clear that was a scheme that Thomas used to buy time until he got his way. Your lawyer should have been a little sharper than that!" Karen said, raising her voice somewhat for emphasis.

"My lawyer didn't give a shit about me, Karen. Just like the others, he only cared about doing just enough to keep his license," I said.

A couple of days later, I received a letter in the mail from Thomas's attorney. It was just what I thought — yet another stunt to blur the truth once again. It was an answer filed to my lawsuit, instead of an agreement to settle the case. On that same day, I had called down to the court clerks. I called all day up until the court closed. They said that they had not received a response from Burke. I asked all three clerks of all three courts, if they had gotten anything concerning my case, and they kept saying that they had not.

Magically, at four P.M., the answer to the suit finally showed up. I questioned the improbable timing of its arrival, but they said that it could have been pushed deeply down into a basket of files. My suspicion was that they had back dated the answer to the lawsuit because of their negligence, but I couldn't prove it. It now seemed that Art Joseph never intended to take my case through the entire procedure. He was just looking for a way out. I emailed him yet again after calling and going by his office several times. Finally, I wrote him an email saying that I would be contacting the bar on Monday morning to file a complaint.

This was what Joseph was waiting to hear as that was his way out. He didn't waste any time filing a withdrawal from my case, and my complaint made doing so a moot point. My speculation was that he had done many clients this way. He knew that a lawyer could take his client's money and withdraw from the case at any point in time. A lawyer who sincerely cares for his clients wouldn't ever dream of this, but assholes like him would.

They had all heard my story. In the back of their minds, instead of listening to me, they were thinking, "How can I take advantage of her, too?"

Now, as I look back, I remembered sitting in Art Joseph's office. When I asked him a question, all his responses were either yes or no. He never spoke in paragraphs. I did all of the talking, and he would nod or, at best, say, "Uh huh." All the while, he must have known that he wasn't going to take my case all the way through to a jury trial for eleven hundred dollars.

Karen stated, "I truly believe now that Thomas had offered Burke a piece of profit share, and he felt obligated past the point of his being a client."

"He offered profit share to every damn body, didn't he?" I responded.

"Yeah, he did, but I imagine Peggy didn't get hers like he promised, obviously." We both chuckled.

I received a certified letter from Art Joseph along with all my documents saying he was, in fact, withdrawing from my case. I knew it was coming, of course, but this letter had its own finality. He formally made a request to the judge, and I had ten days to file a response. I sat down and wrote out the response along with my concerns, asking the judge to deny his request.

The next day, I took it down to the superior court to file it. I didn't have any idea of what I was doing, but it didn't stop me. I asked the clerk for help, but the clerk told me straight away that they couldn't give out any legal advice. I stood there wondering if I was filing the correct information. I met with yet another attorney named Alvin Whitten. I explained my situation and then asked him to take over my case. Whitten said that he would examine the facts that I had submitted to him, and then he would get back to me.

After six days of waiting for his response, he advised me that he couldn't discuss my case since Art Joseph was still my attorney on file. I had waited almost an entire week to hear him tell me that crock of shit. What he stated to me was a pure, unadulterated lie because I found out later, through the judge's law clerk, that an attorney can submit a 'substitute for an attorney' application at any point that the client or attorney severed their relationship.

"He didn't have to lie," Karen stated. "He should have said he wasn't interested in taking your case. There must have been a conversation with Joseph, or, possibly, he checked your record of complaints with the bar association."

"Am I just a magnet for these people? Are most lawyers this way? Is this karma for my past transgressions coming home to roost?" I asked. "At any rate, the wishes that I made at Marie Laveau's grave didn't change my situation one iota. All of that wasted time and money traveling to New Orleans!" I said.

"You had some terrible luck with those people!" Karen quipped. "You really did waste all of that money that you spent on that voodoo trip, which would have better served you by using it for therapy."

"You are right. I probably would have been better served by just putting that money into a church. I would have had the same results if I had just handed it to a bum on the street," I said, trying to make a joke of the situation, but, in reality, I knew what I had said was true.

"Next time, you can give that money to my practice. If all it takes is getting you to sign a check for six hundred or eleven hundred dollars and not showing up for court, and not do anything once I get there, I can do that. You were basically paying them for the title of 'attorney'," Karen joked.

"Yes, Karen. Once again, you're right," I sighed.

The sad thing about her snide joke was that she was telling the gospel truth. It was, also, the end of my session for the week.

{Chapter 9}

It was exactly two weeks later that I arrived for my third session with Karen. In addition to my legal woes, I had to be concerned about one of my rental properties. I'd had no luck finding a tenant for this single-family home. There was no way in hell that I could pay two mortgages. So, I saw this coming, and I decided to list it before I got behind on the payments. This had prevented me from making the previous therapy session.

The property was listed for ninety days. At least, that's what I thought. Adam Hamilton, my co-worker who was helping me to sell the property, was acting as my agent. He didn't reduce the price of the property in the multiple listing services (MLS) to the price that the mortgage company had agreed on. He wanted the property for himself at the reduced

Meleisa Betts

price. It was called a short sale, which drastically reduced the selling price of a property in order to induce a rapid transaction. I found out what Adam was trying to pull off, and I stopped him right in his tracks.

"Wait one second here. Let me stop you right there with a question. Why were you using a co-worker instead of a legitimate agent?" Karen asked. I could clearly see the skeptical frown that was on her face from behind her horn-rimmed glasses.

"He was a legitimate agent. He had a license," I said. "Plus, I didn't think he was as shabby and low-down as he turned out to be."

"Isn't Adam's primary vocation is with Universal Packaging?" Karen asked with obvious skepticism at my, again, using bad judgment.

"What's the point of that question?" I asked. I was getting a little agitated from the questioning for some reason but, deep inside of me, I could see the path that her response would take.

"The point is you got a real estate agent who was a Universal Packaging worker. Would you go to a dentist to get Botox shots or to a chef to fix your Lexus?" Karen asked. "Unless he could say that both jobs were equal in how qualified he was to do them, he's going to be doing one full time and the other part time. You could get a good result, but you could get a so-so result or even a terrible one as it seemed that you received," Karen said. Once again, she was speaking nothing but the truth.

"I can see what you're saying," I said in a resigned tone.

"The point is that if you need your car repaired, you don't get a hairstylist to do it," Karen said.

"Okay! I got it! Let me continue telling you my story. This is costing me."

"Yes, you have to pay me like every one of those one thousand others," Karen winked.

We have developed as much of a friendship as a therapist and client could, I thought to myself.

I had so much going on that I needed a staff of secretaries to handle it all. I cried out to God asking Him to please help me, although it seemed like my pleas were falling on deaf ears. Maybe God was upset with me for forsaking Him through using those occult practices. I was so confused. I asked God to please send me some answers. Maybe He had been all along, but, for some reason, I was deaf to His words. Had He heard my pleas? Maybe, it was me who was blocking the communication. I decided to begin a fast to open my mind and soul to an answer from God. I had no food for three days. Only liquids and my prayers were my sustenance. I was a total mess — fasting, crying, and praying.

I really wished I'd had either Cathy or Jay as my lawyers, but Cathy was only accepting criminal cases, and I was far too embarrassed, after dropping him so many times, to go back to Jay once more. If I had only done the sensible thing and kept Jay in the beginning, I could have spared myself a lot of time, trial, tribulation, and heartache. Again, if I had judged the situation by my head and intuition, rather than allowing flash and superficiality to rule me, then the outcomes in my cases would have been completely different. It was clear to me that I was my own worst enemy most of the time.

I set up an appointment with another attorney by the name of Harry Landenberg. When I arrived at his office, a man was standing outside drinking a cup of coffee. I struck up a conversation since we were both waiting on Mr. Landenberg. I found out that this man had been working with Landenberg for the past twelve years as a private detective. Harry Landenberg seemed to have all I needed.

This man is the real deal, I thought. When I met him, he was, also, quite a gentleman and so was the private investigator. I felt at home and comfortable, at last.

During our conversation, I wanted to be honest with Mr. Landenberg about everything. I told him about the grievances that I had filed on the other attorneys. I, also, told him exactly what happened with Art Joseph. After I had bared my soul to him, he said that he wasn't sure if he wanted the case. You should have seen the look on my face. It was as if I had fallen one number short of a winning lottery ticket. I wouldn't wish that level of sinking disappointment on anyone, short of Thomas. It was a horrible feeling. It was the same sensation one would feel if the love of his life left him for another.

As I left his office, I felt so down. I mustered up enough strength to make myself get on the internet. I spent twelve hours that day searching for another attorney. I was so tired. Landenberg had told me that he would think it over during the weekend, but I knew the answer. I had four thousand dollars to spend on representation, yet no attorney wanted to take my case, and that fact was, unfortunately, loud and clear.

{Chapter 10}

My friend Tatum had kept in touch with me while this debacle was going on. She wanted to spend some time with me, so I met her at a restaurant up the street from my home. After dinner, she followed me back to my house in her car. I was so glad to see her. I needed someone to talk to. I needed the stress released from my mind and body. Tatum could really relieve some of the pressure, particularly from a sexual aspect. There were a couple of things I didn't like about Tatum, though. She was a cocaine head, and she smoked weed and cigarettes. Tatum was pretty as hell, but she was so messed up. Tatum's beauty made up for most of the discomfort of being around her vices, though. We spent three days and nights together. We had sex off and on for nearly two days. We paused only to eat and sleep a little, and then we got right back into it. We were screwing all over my condo, from room to room, on the floor, or wherever the feeling moved us.

Now, as I'm thinking about her, I can remember how it felt to have her stimulate me from the back. Tatum's hands crept underneath my shirt and fondled my 34 D breasts. My nipples were as hard as rocks. She was good at circling my nipples with her fingertips as her soft lips touched my neck. When she pressed her hot breasts against my back, an electric impulse went up my spine.

"You are just full of different stories. They move from being swindled by people and lawyers to sex with all kinds of women and, occasionally, a man is thrown in for good measure. It's like there are two people living in your head," Karen laughed.

"Yeah, I'm a sex fiend among other things. You know my story now. I've been trying to flirt with you, but I know you won't give me any," I joked.

"No, Ms. Royal. Our relationship is strictly clinical. I am your therapist. Besides that, I only like guys," Karen said with mock disdain.

"Okay. We'll see about that. You may change your mind," I chuckled.

A couple of days passed, and I was still calling different attorneys. I just had to find someone who would represent me. Finally, I received a return call from Harry Landenberg. He said that he didn't sleep at all Saturday night because he was thinking about my case. He said that he had mentioned me to his wife over dinner and that he had asked her what she thought. Landenberg said his wife told him to go with his heart. He said that he kept having dreams of me and him in a courtroom. Landenberg said his wife asked him what was wrong because he kept waking up. He told her that he kept dreaming dreams, one after another, about my case and nothing else.

Landenberg, then, told me to make an appointment with his secretary. He had decided that he was going to take my case after all.

"So, what do you think about the dreams and my decision?" Landenberg asked.

"I think that God has answered my prayers, Mr. Landenberg," I responded.

I called his office, and his receptionist said that there was a cancellation. An appointment was now open, and there was just enough time for me to make it. I kissed Tatum goodbye, and headed for the highway. I made it to his office in less than an hour. Landenberg and I went over all of the parameters of the case, and I was pleased with his professionalism. Even though I was fourteen thousand dollars in the red over this case, at least, there was some light at the end of the tunnel. Mr. Landenberg was the answer to my prayers, I believed. I felt so comfortable in his office and with his staff.

He charged me thirty-seven hundred dollars. I had thirty days to answer the countersuit filed by Thomas and his attorney. Art Joseph had screwed my case up by giving them that freaking two week extension. Why did he get a verbal commitment of all things? He should have gotten all of it documented since that was the professional thing to do. If he had cared anything at all about me or my case, he would have taken the time to get all of the settlement parameters in writing.

It was crystal clear that Art Joseph only cared about getting that eleven hundred dollars out of me as a payment for filing the suit in Superior Court. He thought that this method would be a simple and effective scare tactic against the opposing attorney. He tried to force an agreement, since no attorney really wants to waste time in court. Art Joseph gambled everything that I had invested in him on that fact.

He would have been successful if he had simply gotten the agreement in writing.

A couple of weeks passed, and I received a notice from Mr. Landenberg, stating that I had to appear in court for mediation. I called him to inquire, and now he wasn't returning my calls. I received another notice from him a week later indicating that the mediation was postponed for two weeks. Weeks went by, and Landenberg still hadn't returned any of my calls. I continued to pray and hope that he hadn't gotten caught up in Thomas's and his attorney's lies. I wondered incessantly why Landenberg didn't return my calls.

{Chapter 11}

I had finally broken down, due to the pressure of my situation and my constant mistreatment by lawyers, and I went to see Mrs. Tex. I asked her to come over to my house and do an Absolution. An Absolution is a ritual of forgiveness. It purges evil from your life. Mrs. Tex came over and blessed my home. She sprinkled me with holy water and oils. I had gone to all extremes, from voodoo to the power of the Bible. Maybe, I was serving two masters in doing so, but that was not my intention. I was suffering, and I was seeking relief. I wanted to be free of the spirits that had been tormenting me for all these years.

"What is an Absolution again? How is that similar to or different from an exorcism?" Karen asked.

"The way that Ms. Tex explained an Absolution to me was that this is when the negative influences that are around a person and, possibly, in the home of a person are driven away by the strength of forgiveness. That makes it sort of like an exorcism, but the difference is that you are asking God to forgive you, rather than directing any prayers at removing demonic forces. It is then left up to God whether or not to forgive you of your transgressions," I explained.

"How long did this take?" Karen asked.

"The ritual lasted over five hours," I replied.

We burned oils, candles, parchment paper, and voodoo dolls, essentially anything affiliated with the practice of voodoo. All remnants of my trip to Marie Laveau's grave were thrown out. It was gone, never to return. I had turned from God by soliciting the help of occult practitioners, which was clearly something that was forbidden in Christianity.

My circumstances didn't improve immediately, but the severity was lessened somewhat. I should not have doubted God or questioned His methods. I was anxious, and I lacked faith and conviction. As a result, my turning to voodoo had cost me. I can't help but think about the thousands that I spent on voodoo. There were no effective or even tangible results other than sorrow and a lighter pocketbook. Why would I have doubted God, who had protected me and who had granted me the nine lives of a cat? I sat back and pondered my situation. I came to a valid conclusion and, once again, admitted to myself that, most of the time, I was a victim of my own circumstances. None of this was coincidental. It could have all been avoided if I had only followed my God-given instincts.

I finally mustered up the energy to begin writing up my complaint to the real estate commission against Adam. I found out that it was a six month process. In other words, the real estate commission was six months behind. Now, not only had I found out that there were unethical attorneys, but there were, also, unethical real estate agents and brokers, even if they were so-called friends.

"I am curious to know if the commissions are finding these agents accountable for their actions since this kind of situation seems to be pervasive in this economy," Karen stated.

"Hopefully, they're not like the bar association because, if they are, I might have to protest," I said. "I'm sick and tired of this garbage."

"I think the problem is that you have people in high positions who are elected officials, and they have friends

who they look out for. It's called the 'good ol' boy' system,"
Karen said softly while putting her hand to the side of her
mouth in a mock whisper.

"Yeah, many of them are making six and seven figure
salaries, and they aren't doing a thing to earn it," I replied.
"Nobody is holding these unscrupulous people accountable
for taking advantage of people. In many of these cases,
they're taking money under the table to get deals done that
never should have happened. That's one of the reasons
why I take legal action or report people; they have to realize
that not everyone will just take their bullshit treatment lying
down." I had stood to my feet in my fervor and had not
realized it. Karen simply smiled.

During the fiasco, which led to my property being
auctioned, I had yet another improbable event, which has
so marked my life. A "reverend" by the name of Yarbrook
had been trying to purchase the property, but he couldn't
secure financing. This song and dance between us had
gone on for three months. The worst part of it was that this
was also during the time that I had made the mistake of
trying to sell my property using Adam as the agent. It was
during the time of the foreclosure on the property, when
Adam had shown interest in it, that I inexplicably received

a call from Reverend Yarbrook.

"Angiel, I was just calling you about the property," he said. "I'm going to put in a bid for it because I know that it's in foreclosure."

"How do you know that the property is in foreclosure?" I asked.

"I know because the lawyer who is handling the proceedings called me yesterday and told me about it," he said sheepishly.

"Why in the world would he tell you anything about my property? What lawyer is stupid enough to violate the client confidentiality clause that opens him up to a lawsuit?" I asked defiantly. Something did not smell quite kosher.

"Well, when we were talking about me buying the property, I went down to the courthouse and attached a thirty-eight thousand dollar lien on it," he said rather matter-of-factly.

I was livid at this point. At this level of anger, I could have done anything.

"How in the hell can you go to the courthouse and put a lien on a property that you haven't put one damn dime into? Why would you even talk to a lawyer about my

Meleisa Betts

property? You ain't a damn reverend. You're a crook and a liar and a terrible liar on top of that!" I screamed.

"Well, I thought, at that time, that it was a done deal," he said in a hushed tone.

"Here I was thinking that I had to worry about Adam's cheating ass. Now, I have to worry about your crooked ass, too!" I shouted into the phone.

"I just put a lien on the property because we had an agreement that I would buy it." He kept the same demure tone as before.

"Yarbrook, that was like five fucking months ago! Your damn ass couldn't get financed. You got your fucking nerve, putting a lien on a property that you haven't put one cent of blood, sweat, and tears into. That shit you did was illegal, and I'm gonna get to the bottom of this!" I said as I slammed down the phone.

Reverend Yarbrook was nothing but a wolf dressed in sheep's clothing. How could anyone just go down to the courthouse and file a lien on someone's property without having done any type of work on it? This was bullshit! One thing was for sure, this wasn't the first time Yarbrook had done something like this.

"While we're on the subject of real estate, what

happened to your properties since I can infer that you have lost some of them based upon your statements?" Karen said.

"Oh, I never told you what happened with my condo and my other properties?" I asked. "Well, since you know the rest of my story to this point, then you may as well know it all. I once had six rooming houses altogether. I didn't have an escrow account on any of the mortgages, not even on my condo. The problem started when I forgot to pay twenty-two hundred dollars of property taxes on that condo. Vesta Holdings, the real estate company that I was using at the time, then swooped in and bid those twenty-two hundred dollars all the way up to one hundred and ten thousand!" I fumed.

"It's unbelievable that someone could do that!" Karen exclaimed.

"Hell, yeah! They did do that! It was the county's fault because they were very slow recording deeds after closing. It wasn't showing up on their records that I had a mortgage," I said.

"If that's how you lost your property, then that's pure swindling," Karen said.

"Well, I didn't want it to happen. True enough. I forgot

to pay the taxes, but those sorry bastards at the county contributed to it," I said.

"That was really unscrupulous, Angiel. That's the kind of thing that they do to elderly people all of the time, and they will, sometimes, end up losing the homes that they've owned for years," Karen remarked.

"Yes, ma'am. That was dirty, but I survived it, and I even prospered a little," I grinned.

"How did you manage to prosper when you were losing everything around you?" Karen asked.

"After everything was over, I ended up walking away with eighty-five thousand dollars free and clear. I surrendered my ownership of the condominium, but Vesta Holdings was stuck with an unknown mortgage of one hundred and thirty thousand dollars. It was one year later that Vesta found out that I had managed to get their eighty-five thousand out of the escrow account for the purchase that they were making on the condo due to the second mortgage that I had taken out," I said.

"So, in all of this, it seems like the angels were looking out for you, or maybe it was the devil, depending on your perspective," Karen quipped.

"Nope, those were my guardian angels looking out for

me. I was treated wrongly, and things were made right. I need to listen to God and see what He keeps trying to show me instead of doing the opposite things that cause me pain," I said.

"I will wager a bet that you have made God mad at you a thousand times during your lifetime," Karen said with a voice that was now strangely serious.

"I can't say that you are wrong about that. The only thing I can do from this day forward is to try to make Him smile instead of frown at me, I guess," I said with a smile on my face that Karen couldn't realize the meaning of. It was a smile to keep from crying.

{Chapter 12}

I called Harry Landenberg twice, and he didn't return my calls either time. I can only think back to the day that I was in his office. He was so nice. He asked his staff to come into his office to meet me. He told them that I was a special client. He made me feel good about myself and the case. I thought that he really and truly cared about me. As it turned out, he only cared about getting the thirty-seven hundred dollar fee from me, justifying it as being twenty-two billable hours. He said that, even if we had to do depositions, it wouldn't take twenty-two hours. When we got to mediation, Thomas's attorney told the mediator, Helen Carter-Weber, that they were not willing to mediate, yet they were prepared to do depositions.

Everything was preplanned. The reason that I firmly

believed this was the case was because I remembered what had transpired when I walked upstairs the day of mediation. Harry Landenberg was speaking with a deputy at that time. He stopped the conversation briefly to say to me with a stern look, "Go and sit in the mediation room, and I will be there in a minute."

One would think that, with Landenberg being my attorney and knowing that I had called him twice in a month without so much as a returned call, the minimum greeting that would have been a smile. His greeting to me was less cordial than one of those guards at Buckingham Palace.

I went to the mediation room to sit by myself, stew in my own emotions and just wait. After sitting in the room for about twenty minutes, in walked old green-eyes, Jonas Burke the attorney, Thomas, and his two trained puppets, Britney and Tracey.

I heard the clerk say, "The other party's attorney is not here."

Jonas Burke chimed up, "Yes, he is. He's in the hallway. I just saw him. I'll go get him."

With that statement, Burke leapt into action and out of the room in a nanosecond.

Suddenly, it all dawned on me. Burke knew

Landenberg, and they had pre-arranged every damn aspect of this hearing. I was all alone in a fight with evil once again. I was about to be bamboozled out of a rightful decision for what seemed like the thousandth time. They had met and conversed over my situation and case, and it was painfully obvious. We were now in the review phase of the mediation. Landenberg's speech made it seem as though he was making an offer to settle for twenty percent of the value of the modeling agency. He stated that, in his opinion, it was valued at around ten thousand dollars. Once I was allotted an opportunity to speak, I briefly explained to the mediator what was going on. I tried to warn her about Thomas and how he lied so well.

Once Jonas Burke and the sniveling Thomas Walters were allowed to present their frivolous case to the mediator, Mrs. Weber, then, went into an adjacent room, where the hearing was held. She apparently had heard enough to make a proper judgment. While we had a break in the proceedings, Landenberg asked me if I had the money to pay for the mediation, which was two hundred fifty dollars.

I said to him, "I thought that it was coming out of the thirty- seven hundred."

"No, Ms. Royal. The agreement was for services

rendered, not for filing fees or ancillary court costs," he stated as though he was reading from a contract.

I said, "Well, if that's the case, then I will have to mail you a check."

I could have probably paid him right there, but I decided not to make things that simple for him to drain me.

He was visibly upset, but he happened to have a blank check in his wallet. He took it out and then endorsed it for the amount of the arbitration. He had taken thirty-seven hundred dollars from me just to go to mediation. This was an unheard of fee for something as simple as that. Even Georgia's top attorneys would not have charged that much for something as minor as attending mediation. I had been advised by both Landenberg and Mrs. Weber, prior to the mediation, that the outcome that would be rendered would probably have been the same if I had gone to trial or come to a mutual agreement. I was advised that going to trial would cost me even more money and that it would be best if both parties mutually agreed to dismiss, yet I persisted.

The resulting decision of the arbitrator would be that neither I nor the defendant would have rights to the modeling agency. When we were leaving the proceeding, Landenberg stopped Burke by grabbing his arm, and he told him, "You can just come by the office and pick up an original copy of the agreement."

This was the body language and camaraderie of two buddies, not two warring parties. Once Landenberg and I walked out the court room, we were surrounded by, at least, three potential clients. Each looked at me closely, gauging my level of satisfaction with Landenberg as their eyes said that they needed an attorney. I tried to convey to them with my eyes darting left to right that they should keep looking. As I got ready to leave, I turned to Landenberg, and I looked at him with a stare of resignation and disappointment.

He asked me, "When is your birthday?" This was an odd question given the circumstances.

"It is on August the 23rd," I responded without looking at him.

"Don't worry about sending me a check. I'll let that be your birthday gift," he said as if that were a grand gesture. The fact was that he was coming away from my situation thirty-five hundred dollars richer for doing virtually nothing.

I smiled and walked away. For some reason, I felt that he was not going to get away with my money scott-free.

"Based on that interaction, he doesn't seem to be the

most confident of attorneys," Karen said.

"Karen, he seemed so different until he got my money. In fact, they all acted differently before and after the money. Customer service in the legal industry is lacking as far as I'm concerned. I went through more lawyers with that Thomas bullshit than most people see in a lifetime, and what did it get me?" I said.

"Angiel, I have known you for a little more than a month, but I have a suggestion; maybe, you should stop judging a book by its cover, and, maybe, you should read a few pages before you buy the book. When you go to a bookstore, do you just pick up a book that looks good and buy it? You read ten to twelve pages or maybe even a chapter, if you have the time. That's the way we should judge people, but most of us go by the pretty cover and we end up buying an uneventful book. By that time, it's too late, and you have a lousy book as a coffee table piece," Karen stated.

"That point is well taken. Preach on, sister!" I joked.

{Chapter 13}

Even though Thomas Walters had screwed me out of money and taken my dream, I was not defeated. He was going to pay if it took every ounce of energy that I had. I immediately went back to my investigation. I managed to get a copy of the court documents concerning statements from Peggy in Thomas's order against Brandi. After months of fighting the spirit of depression and thanks to the prayers and the Absolution by Ms. Tex the spiritualist, I had enough strength to go down to the county court house and look through Thomas's entire file, which was in the public domain.

I sat down at the counter and read the entire thing. Afterwards, I made copies of all his files. Twenty-five cents a copy was not a problem, but it was difficult to sit there and read all of the lies that this man had gotten away with.

It was like reading a novel by the world's greatest con artist. Thomas had beat the system by appearing to be the victim in all of his claims, and they were all basically the same. He claimed in each case that he felt frightened for his life and for that of his family's. He claimed to be afraid of Brandi. He said that he had felt that she would kill him. That so-called fear was the basis of the protective order against Brandi and the reason why she was put in jail. He even accused Brandi of trying to molest his "son" Barry. What did he have to gain by saying that this child was the victim of a sexual assault? I wanted to cry when I read that evil charge, but I held back my tears. I began to feel flush in the face, but I had managed to hold on until I got into my car where the floodgates opened. I truly felt deeply for these people who Thomas had hurt both physically and emotionally. Now, I had to confront Peggy over her involvement in the wrongs that were done. I went to the job and waited on Peggy until it was time for her shift to begin. She arrived within an hour. I showed her the letter that she had previously said she knew nothing of.

"This is my signature, but I didn't write the letter," she said, claiming that she had never seen the letter.

"Peggy, this letter has your original signature on

it, and it's on record. Surely, you would not have signed a blank document without even looking at it. That is the most idiotic thing that I have ever heard! Did you know that this letter had Brandi locked up and taken away from her son for seven months?" I shouted.

Peggy didn't utter a sound. The look on her face was that of a person who had seen someone from her past who had come back to hunt her down.

"Well, if you didn't write the letter, are you willing to go down to the court house and tell them that?" I asked.

"I—I have too much on my plate, right now," Peggy stammered. "Why are you so damned obsessed with this anyway?"

"That bastard has screwed over my life, stolen my money, and probably killed his wife. Somebody needs to stop him or, at least, make him pay for all the people he has hurt. That's why I am obsessed!" I said with my voice remaining at a high volume.

I am so glad that my co-workers Bonnie, Mrs. Hall, and Mrs. Moldon, knew about the situation. They had all heard Peggy say that Thomas had given Brandi a massive overdose of ibuprofen to the tune of 12,000 milligrams in a twenty-four hour period. Now, it would not be my word against hers if there was a trial.

"I'll give a sworn statement if Brandi's family gets an attorney and subpoenas me to appear in court as a witness," Peggy offered as her proof of being on the side of right. I wasn't sold.

I was beginning to think that Peggy may have, in some way, assisted Thomas. I didn't want to think that, but everything led me to believe that possibility, especially after reading that horrible letter that she had written for Thomas to corroborate his lies against Brandi. Maybe, they had a business arrangement, or, maybe, there was a sexual aspect because no one is involved in someone's life to that degree without a reason.

As it turned out, Brandi's case was never re-examined. The family gradually stopped communicating with me. I had left a message on the answering service of the original brother who I had contacted in the beginning. He never returned the call, and the only other number that I had was now disconnected. I stopped researching the Thomas Walters paper trail as I had done all that I could do to bring him to justice.

I have always believed that anyone who does wrong gets away without punishment. Call it karma or reaping what you sow or whatever. I have certainly suffered a lot for my sins and my arrogance, to the tune of thousands of dollars and lost relationships. It's funny that I never felt that I was doing wrong, although a part of me knew that I was not quite right. As I said before, it is as if I have an angel on one shoulder and a devil on the other. The difference is that I will make every attempt to tune into the angel.

Maybe I have lived my life as a character in a sad and twisted screenplay, a good thought in the mind of an unknown writer which never materialized into the movie or play that it should have been.

"Thomas will pay," I told myself, and the only thing I wanted was to leave this chapter of my life and move to the next.

"So, nothing was ever solved in the Thomas case?" Karen asked.

"Nothing ever happened to him as far as the courts go, but he did get a sort of payback. About six months after I had resigned myself to Thomas not being punished, his business was over. Someone supposedly had left an iron used to dispense glue plugged up, and his business caught fire. He, apparently, did not have the proper level of insurance to cover the losses and the expensive items, so he is out of the upholstery business. The word is that he skipped town because of debts to loan sharks, but he has not been seen or heard from since." I looked up and smiled as I saw that the clock revealed that our weekly session was over.

{Chapter 14}

Karen sat back in her oversized mahogany chair and exhaled a grand, "Whew! That was one heck of a story, with all of its twists, turns, and intrigue. I feel like I've lived some of your life in a small part. Anyone can clearly see that you have lived an oversized, surreal kind of life, Angiel. You could serve as an example to a lot of patients as to the methodology of dealing with hardships. You've done a lot in your lifetime," Karen said.

"I have done a lot of stuff, mostly to myself, been with a lot of men and women and seen a lot of things. I'm like the cat who has lived eight of its nine lives," I sighed.

It was now four in the afternoon. Karen and I had been talking for the customary fifty minutes, but it seemed like five hours. I had given Karen the bullet points version of a complicated life, and it felt refreshing, as though I had purged my soul of some bile or venom that was making me spiritually sick.

"You know what, Karen. There's something else that I didn't say, so since I've been baring my soul to you, I might as well tell it all. Now, I don't think it has anything to do with my losing blocks of time in my life, but I really want to discuss this, " I said.

"You might as well since you have told me everything else about you. Your time is technically exhausted for this session, but, since you are my last appointment, we can continue for a little while longer," Karen said.

"Okay, this one is hard, but, hell, it shouldn't be. It's kind of silly that I am hesitant about telling you this, but here goes. With all of the men and women that I've been with, I have never once had an orgasm," I said.

"I find that difficult to fathom," Karen said, with a tone that was laced with total shock. "How many people have you been with?" she asked.

"When Mrs. Tex did the Absolution on me in my condo, she asked me to write down the names of all of the people I'd had sex with on a piece of paper to be torn up and stomped on. Before it could even reach the tearing phase, it had taken forever. I had written the names of over two-hundred men and women and some of them I couldn't even remember. Mrs. Tex looked at me as if to say, 'How many damn names could you have for it to take this fucking long?'"

At first, Karen laughed for about a minute. After she finished, she asked, "So, with over two-hundred men and women, not one of them even came close to giving you an orgasm?"

"It's true, strange as it may seem. To give you an example, with the men, it would be exciting to do everything, the kissing and fondling. I would be aroused right up until they penetrated me, and then there would be nothing at all in terms of gratification. It was much better with women as I loved the softness and everything that made a female a female. Even though I loved women, I still could not climax with them. The only thing that I could really say about it was that the sex itself was still enjoyable, just without the stars and fireworks," I said.

"So, you have NEVER had an orgasm is what you are telling me?" Karen asked.

"I never said that," I stated flatly.

"Okay. Now, you're using semantics and being evasive.

Have you or haven't you ever had an orgasm?" Karen said with a tone that suggested that she was annoyed.

"Yes. I have, but it wasn't until this year that it happened. A friend was having one of those parties that are really meant for you to buy something from the hostess. This was not a Tupperware party, but a sex toy party where you buy dildos, vibrators, edible panties or anything that you wanted. I was told that if I wanted to experience an out of this world orgasm that I should try this egg-shaped vibrator.

I bought it, and I used it that night. I had my first orgasm, and it was so fantastic! It was as if I was falling off of the earth. I felt the vibrations inside of me. They were like waves of pleasure and explosions. The orgasms felt so wonderful that I started crying. I think that maybe my whole life has been my pursuing this little bit of heaven on Earth. Now that I have the vibrator, I don't feel the need to have female, or, for that matter, male companionship. If it comes, fine. If not, then I know how to get off on my own now!" I joked.

"That's a rather blunt way of putting it. However, I see where your perspective is coming from," Karen said. "No, a lack of orgasm is a clinical diagnosis for, say, a sex therapist, but that is not my field of expertise."

"Dr. Oppenheim, it's been good talking with you about this shit that I have been dealing with. I feel like the weight of the world has been lifted from my shoulders. Sometimes, you just need to talk with another person, instead of keeping stuff bottled up. A talk is good medicine sometimes."

"Most of the time, I listen to patients talk and then nothing much is revealed. I feel as though we are making headway. Now, if you would kindly write a check for three thousand dollars, I will pretend to be your attorney. I can't do any worse than your previous ones," Karen joked.

"Don't you hold your freaking breath waiting for that check because it ain't showing up. In fact, there's a 100% probability that hell will freeze over first," I said.

Karen and I laughed for two minutes before anyone had the energy to speak again.

"See, that comment probably made your guardian angel laugh," Karen said.

"It's about time that I gave him or her something to laugh at," I quipped.

At that moment, Karen received a page from her receptionist, and she excused herself in order to go and speak with her. I stood and went over to the window to the left of her desk to look at the view. Sitting in full view was my file, so I decided to glance at it. I quickly shuffled through the pages until I arrived at this statement:

It is my considered opinion based upon a diverse series of experiences and interactions from her childhood to the present that the patient, Angiel Royal, suffers from Narcissistic Personality Disorder. My diagnosis stems from the clinical symptoms of grandiose opinions of her own self-worth, her belief that everyone and everything centers their actions on her life, as well as a general view of entitlement. Her relationships can be described as egocentric, with a concern of self over others. This syndrome may have its causation from overindulgence by her parents, which is a general catalyst for this condition as well as is alienation from or a distant relationship with a parental figure. In addition, the patient may suffer, to a lesser degree, from Disassociate Personality Disorder, the clinical diagnosis of dual personality. I will attempt to explore this diagnosis in future appointments.

Karen's assessment was stunning to a degree in that she said that I was both an egomaniac and someone who may have a split personality! I had never thought seriously about what my problems may have been, yet anything was possible.

I quickly placed the file back on the desk mere seconds

before Karen returned. I made up an excuse to leave and quickly exited. I winked at the receptionist, as usual, as I left the office.

{Chapter 15}

On my drive home, I started to take stock of everything that I had revealed to Karen. I couldn't be upset with anything that I had read while scanning through my file. I have lived a convoluted and abnormal life. Life to me is not like a box of chocolates. Life is a Pandora's Box filled with what ifs. Ultimately, it doesn't matter how rich you are or how poor you are, you're going to go through hell in some form or fashion, unless you are just plain lucky. Most of the time, in my case, I have been fortunate, yet the author of most of my bad breaks seems to be me. As much as I can find fault with people using me, I can, also, say that I have used others. That's probably where the narcissistic diagnosis originated. I could not admit to me being the problem in my life; I was a perfect angel who was always wronged. The reality was

Meleisa Betts

that I was not the perfect angel that I had imagined myself to be.

I have to say "Thank you, God" on the days when I am sitting here, and I notice how peaceful my surroundings are. My bills are paid, and I have money in my pocket. I should have been saying those thank yous to God before I met Thomas, but I had let Satan and my want of material items enter into my life to create doubt, chaos, and depression.

Some people believe that life is predetermined from birth. I don't believe that in the least. I believe that we ARE our choices and we live our decisions. Why would God predestine me to such an uneven life or decide before I was born that I would suffer assaults to my physical and mental well being? Did God make the decision for me while I was in the womb to have sex with over two hundred men and women? The directions that we take are not forced upon us, but they are paths that we choose on our own and whatever the result, good or bad, right or wrong are directly related to those choices.

All of my life, it has seemed as though it has been one thing after another to torment me. I know that, sometimes, I have brought things on myself by not thinking before acting. Other times, the storm just came blowing my way, and I was swept up as an innocent bystander. I could have eliminated so much stress in my life, if I had heeded my instincts. As I look back, if I had only remembered the times before when I was rescued right in the nick of time, then I would have realized that the angels were there to protect me. If I just would have thought about my actions before I proceeded! With careful consideration, I could have foreseen the ramifications of what I had planned to do before I moved forward with that plan. If I had simply kept to the road less traveled that God had laid out for me, then I most assuredly would have escaped the horrors that I have suffered over the years.

Always, there are days that I forget to say my prayers and thank God for His mercy on my harried soul. There are nights when I get into the bed without kneeling and thanking Him for putting my one foot before the other and bringing me home safely. One thing I now know is that, I was watched over throughout my life more than I knew at the time that He was protecting me.

Some might ask how I can speak about my life while in the same breath speaking of God. The simplest answer is the honest one. I didn't make me; God did, and it was for a specific reason. I didn't choose my sexuality and personality any more than I chose the color of my eyes. It was an act of nature, the universe, or anything else other than an unborn combination of my mother's egg and my father's sperm fertillized and implanted in my mother's womb. I am not trying to think of my life and mistakes in a negative or positive sense, but in a factual way. I am what and who I am. I believe that God loves us for our hearts and not because of something that one has absolutely no choice over. My sexuality and my mental makeup ARE me, and no amount of prayers or interventions can change that unless there is a deep-seated desire in me to be something else altogether.

For instance, if I had hidden my sexuality and forced myself to live a lie based upon society's social codes, I would be married with a house filled with kids. Then, having become a housewife, who stayed home to cook and clean, would I still have tried to sneak and be with a woman? Would I have become a "Housewife Lesbian," as was the case with many of the hundred or so women I've slept with, who openly denied any homosexual feelings toward another female, yet who were more than willing to have sex with me in private? No, to do so would mean that I was living a lie. The worst person in the world that you can ever lie to is yourself. I can say this with all conviction, even though I was married twice. I was living a lie, and that lie not only hurt others, it also affected my soul.

With all of this suffering, we, sometimes, forget the most important thing. We've forgotten how to love each other, but, most importantly, we've forgotten how to love ourselves. I have to find the way to learn to love Angiel, unconditionally. The problem is clear to me now that I've realized that I never really knew myself while I was growing up. It has taken me years to discover this, and I see that I am a serious work-in-progress. I was too busy trying to get more and then more of whatever it was, be it money, women, men or whatever the case, to really discover who I am.

I had to learn the hard way what the consequences of being greedy were by being struck repeatedly across my ass with a mop or by being drained financially by bad deals. All I had to do was listen to my inner self. I could have spared myself so many hard lessons. I have learned and lost so much from my mistakes that I honestly cannot afford to make any of them ever again. I could keep on making the same thoughtless choices as before and ultimately end up on a trash heap. To a degree, I have learned to listen to my guardian angels, to laugh with them over the happiness of a sensible venture with good intentions, rather than sharing tearful moments lamenting yet another bad decision. Thank you, God, for keeping me alive through all of the turmoil! Committing suicide was surely not the answer to my problems, and, though I tried, I now realize that act would have been one of cowardice. I may be a lot of things, but I am no coward.

If I had a chance to live my life over, what would I do differently? I would have never gone to that dance club that night, for sure. I would have never had either abortion. I probably wouldn't have had so many sex partners. I most certainly would have never tried to kill myself. I would have transferred to Neverwills instead of Valeria. I would have never put so much blind trust in people without taking the time to really know them. I would have never gotten married so fast and so many times. The most important change is that, I would have never doubted God! I did and I can see clearly where my doubts left me— on Satan's doorstep filled with grief. "Tell the truth and shame the Devil" is an old saying that I have put into action by openly baring of my soul.

What will be the outcome of my revelations to Karen?

Who really knows the future? I do know that karma will eventually exact its perfect revenge on Thomas, if his losing his business and his abrupt disappearance is any evidence. It may have already occurred. I can only hope that exposing my life in such a bare and explicit way that Karen or whomever will understand the value of honesty, honor, and truth in dealing with others, something I didn't understand until recently. I've had many years to recall and reflect. I honestly can say that I put the material before the spiritual most of the time in my life, and I had brought tears to myself and my family.

As I traveled down the busy highway, I freely shed tears. They were tears from a place that I couldn't determine. I wasn't sure if they were tears of sadness, joy, or just downright relief from revealing a huge part of my life's story to Karen Oppenheim and most importantly being honest with the most important person — me. One way or another, my Absolution was coming soon. I could feel it. Could my problem be that I was the one who was unforgiving? To find out, I had to completely bare my soul and come from a place of total honesty in my next therapy session.

It was time for my weekly appointment with Dr. Oppenheim. I had decided the week before that I would tell her everything that I had held back. I had left some important things out because I didn't want to be judged, but if I wanted to forgive myself completely and cleanse my soul, I had to be forthcoming with everything, regardless of how it made me seem. For some reason, I was nervous for the first time since I had begun therapy nearly two months before.

As I walked into the usual room that my sessions were held in for the eighth time, it seemed like it was the first. I was uncommonly uneasy this time, so much so that I felt like leaving. Despite that feeling, I gave a deep sigh and sat down in the mahogany chair, which had become my familiar friend.

"Well, Ms. Royal, I can sense that you are tense this session. Is there something specifically that you would like to discuss? It doesn't have to be on topic, it can be whatever you want," Karen said in a soft and reassuring tone.

"Karen, I've been holding back some important things. Sure I have told you a lot of intimate information, but there are a few more things that I have kept to myself because I felt that they would be too much. I didn't want to be judged, and these things are a little harsh," I said.

"Now, after discussing rape, your sexuality, and the other things too numerous to mention that were hard-core, it surprises me that you would think that I would start judging you now, after eight weeks of sessions," Karen said in a tone which sounded like she was talking to one of her children that had broken a lamp or something.

"The thing is that I need to say a lot more about how I made money. I know that you know that working at Universal Packaging does not add up to driving luxury cars and living in high rise condominiums. Plus, I never told the complete story of why Paula decided to leave. I need to discuss that aspect of my life and a few other issues if I am going to really cleanse my soul and clear my mind. Maybe, if I come clean, then I can piece together the blocks of time that I can't mentally account for."

"Alright, Angiel. I'm listening," Karen opened my file, thumbed through to her previous ending point, and placed her pen there. I looked up at the roof for ten seconds, sighed again, and then I sat there, not speaking but rather looking at Karen. She was making piercing eye contact as though she was waiting for the story of the century, and, because of that, she didn't want to miss a word.

"Okay. Here it goes. This is the 'bad angel' stuff, the things that I do that I seem to be powerless to control. I know that it's wrong, but it's like I was watching myself on television, like there was another Angiel that was living through those things while I watched, powerless to stop her. Do you understand what I'm trying to say, Karen?" I pleaded.

"I think that I do, Angiel. Go ahead with your story. I'm sure that once you get this out into the open, it will move you even closer to a good mental place," Karen said in a truly reassuring way.

I had seen how Dottie Mae, my ex-friend from Tuscaloosa who was now in prison, had become so rich and powerful; it was because of drugs, and I wanted to get in on that racket. I decided to deal in marijuana to get my feet wet before moving on to harder things. I bought two ounces of weed from a dealer and sold them in dime bags. I nearly tripled my money and that hooked me into the drug world. Back then, you could get a lot of weed for ten dollars or a "dime bag" in drug terms, so there were a lot of customers to make money from.

My frequent visits to West Palm, eventually, led to my

decision of permanently moving there. Of course, meeting Andrew Bollinger, the older guy with the Silver Shadow Rolls Royce, made the decision easier because of my access to the car. Andrew had trusted me to drive it back and forth to Alabama, but what he didn't know was that I was bringing two pounds of weed back with me on each trip home. I was essentially dealing in interstate drug trafficking. Back then, a pound of weed cost four hundred dollars, so I was profiting eight hundred to one thousand dollars per haul.

I had made an agreement with my female friend Nicole's nephew who lived in Neverwills that he would sell the weed for me. His name was Jeb, and he was a long-time drug dealer in his own rite. When I would make my buys, I would stash the weed in my room in my parents' home. I had discussed the weed with my mother, and, once, I even showed a pound bag to her. As usual, I didn't keep any secrets from her, and she didn't keep any from me. She wasn't just my mother; she was, also, my best friend.

When I had made the decision to sell marijuana, I said to her, "Mama, I have a way of making some extra money," and she never asked a question or even commented on that statement. This silence to whatever I did or told her about was a constant after Daddy had beat the living shit out of me after cashing his checks and stealing from him every week. I had convinced myself that I didn't know why he had beat me, and I had even tried to convince my mother, yet she kept her tongue.

To soften her up for springing my marijuana business on her, I first whined to her that my father had started off buying me stuff all of the time, buying me whatever I asked for and spoiling the living shit out of me. Then, all of a sudden, he had decided to stop. I said that I needed to make up for what he had taken away from me; I talked about gas and car payments as justification. She knowingly looked at me and just nodded.

The first time that I showed the weed to Mama, it seemed like she stopped breathing for a second. Then, her eyes got really big, and she said, "Baby, you gonna have to get this out of this house. If Daddy found this stuff in his house, he would kill you."

I said. "Okay, Mama. Don't worry. I'm taking it to a dealer tonight. He's gonna sell it and give me eight hundred, which is double what I paid for it, and he keeps the profit."

She said, "Baby, you shouldn't be doing this. This is wrong."

I told her that everything was alright and not to worry. That night I took the pound of marijuana to Jeb. I thought that everything was going so smooth and that I had planned for everything. Hell! I had taken the time to drive all the way to West Palm to get Andrew's Rolls Royce to transport the drugs. I had believed in that plan because _What cop was gonna stop a pretty lady in a Rolls Royce?_ I had done all of this ground work, and all Jeb had to do was sell the weed. The marijuana in Florida was the best grade going at that time, and that was why I went so far away to West Palm to buy it. The weed in Neverwills apparently sucked big time. Even though I wasn't a smoker per se, I had plenty of reliable sources that told me what was going on with the weed quality of mine versus what other deals sold. I had a great market in Neverwills because there were plenty of unhappy weed smokers in the city.

Jeb had originally told me that he could have the weed sold in one week, but I decided to take a ride by his house on the next night. I decided to do the unannounced visit because my instincts were telling me that Jeb wasn't being honest. I had felt something about him when I first met him, but I hadn't trusted my gut. Instead, I just knew that I could trust Jeb.

Jeb wasn't expecting me until the end of the week, so I caught him off guard. He was just standing there on a dimly lit corner. I drove up and asked him to get into my car, and he did.

I asked, "Well, how's it going? Did you sell anything today?"

He responded, "Well, last night, I was playing dice, and I played for both pounds of weed and lost."

I looked at him and said, "You lost my fucking weed in a dice game? Both damn pounds?"

He responded, "Yeah," like it wasn't anything.

I said, "Okay. Get out."

He got out, and I burned rubber out of that alley. I was as hot as a flamethrower!

I went to my oldest brother's house and asked him if I could borrow his pickup truck for an hour. After he said yes, I took his keys without so much as a thank you. I was too furious to think about my lack of manners. His truck was black; I was dressed in black with a black sweater cap on my head. It was cool outside, and this was in the late fall going into winter, so this would not be suspicious. It would have been perfectly cool enough for Jeb to stand outside and be comfortable enough to sell my weed if he hadn't fucked it up.

I went back to my parents home to get my .380 caliber pistol. After retrieving it, I loaded it, and off to Jeb's apartment I went. Before I left, I could hear the police scanner playing in my parent's bedroom. This was the entertainment that my father liked to listen to, the crimes in Neverwills, but I didn't think anything of it at the time. Right before I opened the door to leave, Mama asked, "Baby, where are you going this late?"

It was around ten P.M., so it wasn't late, but her motherly instincts were on alert.

I said, "I'll be right back, Mama."

I stormed over to Jeb's apartment. When I arrived, I saw that his car, an old blue colored Camaro, was parked right where I expected. I sat parked for about ten minutes as I looked around, and it was quiet. Once I saw that everybody was inside of their apartments, I pulled up close to Jeb's car, which was about twenty-five feet away. I took out my gun and started shooting at his car, trying to blow out his tires. I shot ten bullets at his piece of shit car. It seemed like the more I shot at it, the more the bullets failed to hit the target at all. I unloaded the clip, but I didn't see one bullet hole.

There was an emergency gas can in the bed of the truck that had some gas left in it, so I poured what was left on that piece of junk, and I put a match to it. When it started smoldering like a barbeque, I jumped back in the truck and fled home. I parked my brother's truck behind my parents' home and decided to take it back the next day. When I walked into the house, I could hear the police being called on the scanner to Jeb's apartment. I went to bed and prayed that nobody had seen me or the tag on the truck.

The next day, the first question that Mama asked me was "Angiel, do you know anything about the shooting in uptown last night?"

I responded, "Yes, Mama. The dealer who was supposed to sell my weed lost it in a dice game, and I shot his car up, but nobody saw me."

I didn't say a word about the burn job. She shook her head and started singing a prayer song. I felt really bad. I knew that Mama was worried about me. I told her that I wasn't buying any more weed, and I could see some relief on her face. At that moment, I decided to permanently move to West Palm and only come home to visit occasionally. I still had five thousand dollars and a sugar daddy, so I was fine. It was time for me to grow up and start looking for a career and stop worrying my mama.

Andrew and I were on bad terms, and he had kicked me out. That was when I had moved in with my aunt. Even though I was not friends with any rich people, I, somehow, started to meet successful people and get invited to nice parties. One night, I was invited to a pool party at a huge mansion. I was invited back to this private room by the host and shown a bowl full of white powder which turned out to be cocaine. Despite not being a drug user, I tried it, and I was feeling pretty good. I went back to the pool area, wearing regular clothes, while most of the women were in bikinis.

For some reason, I was thrown into the pool with the other women. I couldn't swim, but, somehow, I held my breath. It seemed like an angel had dragged me to the top of the pool when a guy grabbed me and pulled me out of the pool and off to the side. They all were laughing like it was funny when I kept asking, "Why did you do that? I told you guys I couldn't swim!"

They kept laughing because they were high as hell. I left the party soaking wet and high as a cloud.

After that experience, I decided to chase the dollar again. Since most of my friends were snorting cocaine and so many high society people were doing it, the light bulbs went off in my head as to how to make money off of their asses. I decided to buy a kilogram and start my cocaine business. After I found a dealer (which was easy), he taught me what to do as a dealer.

For instance, the first thing you do is taste the cocaine and make sure that it numbs your tongue. You, then, snort a line of it to see if you get high. If you are satisfied with the quality, you make the buy, and then take it home and wrap up grams.

I used my memory when it came to the weight. I honestly think that they got more than they bargained for since I didn't have a scale. I was so high and mighty that I had decided to get a one bedroom apartment just to sell my cocaine. I was paying three hundred and fifty dollars a month, a lot of money at the time, for a nice apartment in a nice area. The problem was that I had started snorting cocaine myself. I was making money, but I was snorting the profits. I was committing the number one sin of being a dealer: Never get high on your own supply!

My biggest problem with cocaine, besides using it, was that I had snorted it so much until I couldn't get high from it anymore. It started to become more of a need than an upper. It wasn't the quality of the drug because my buyers were happy; it was me. I was becoming just like the common addict in that I had adjusted to cocaine, so it turned into a crutch rather than a high. Before I ended up as a junkie in rehab, I decided to just stop selling cocaine.

I was involved with selling and using it for three months and had not profited one thin dime. I moved out of the apartment and back with my aunt once again. I stopped hanging around with my coke fiend friends. One lesson that I learned was that I was surprised to see how many professional people were snorting cocaine. It goes to show how much or how little that you know about the realities of living. These people were making decisions about people's lives while as high as a mountain.

When I first transferred to Georgia from the Universal Packaging job that I held in West Palm Beach, Florida, Paula Pierce was the first person that I saw once I had arrived in Valeria. She was just standing there, looking so incredibly beautiful. I knew, right then, that I had to have her. I worked my way over to her and asked her about places to go, to hang out, and whatever form of small talk that I could think of. She seemed to know the city quite well, and she was very approachable and outgoing. I found out, later, that, maybe, she was a little too outgoing. I asked her if she would show me a couple of places. It was my way of asking her to go out with me in a roundabout way. She was a people person, so she quickly said, "Yes!"

When I went to pick her up, I drove up in my two seat Mercedes convertible, and she came out of her house looking amazing. I happened to notice this guy mowing her lawn, but I thought nothing of him since he appeared to be just a landscaper.

We went out and had a wonderful time. This led to our spending more time together, and it never seemed to be enough. Around the third week of us hanging out, I couldn't stand being in her presence anymore as just friends. Paula had to know how I felt about her, so I told her. She said that she had never been with another female, but she was a bit curious. That was all that I needed to hear.

We couldn't make it back my condo fast enough for me. I pulled over to the side of the Interstate and began to kiss her lips, her breasts, her neck, and every place on her body that was reachable. We, finally, had to stop once this eighteen wheeler passed by, and the driver nearly crashed from looking.

Once we made it back to my place, I rushed to undress

her as I did myself. She was more into me making love to her with a dildo than me performing oral sex on her. It didn't matter since I just wanted her, and I wanted to please her. I had already fallen in love on that first day that I met her.

This was like a dream finally coming true. I couldn't have asked for anything more in a woman. From that day on, it was love making every day between us. We spoke, at least, ten times a day over the phone. At the time, I was working the afternoon shift, and she was working the day shift, so our calls were back and forth. She was as in love with me as I was with her. The problem was that the man who I thought was just the gardener was actually a lover of hers. Despite knowing that he was in the picture, I kept seeing Paula.

The first two years of our relationship were great. She had supposedly broken up with the guy companion, but he managed to still hang around her. By this, I mean that I found out that she was having lunch with him still, and, when she went on company trips, he went, also. Even though he was supposedly staying in a different room, as she had claimed, I found out that she was attending banquets with him. He was her date for all of her business affairs.

During the football season, she was always going to tailgate parties with him and her friends. I would question her about why was he at every tailgate party. She always responded by saying, "He is friends with my friends, so I cannot stop him from showing up." After questioning her about the lunch dates with him, the tailgate parties and banquet dates, I started to become very frustrated. I felt as though she was lying to me. There was one morning in particular where I just happened to look out of the window. It was four in the morning, freezing cold outside, and he was parked by a tree waiting on her to leave my house. I freaked out so badly over that incident that I had to apply for a restraining order against him in order for him to stop calling Paula at my house and for him to stop sitting out in front of my home.

This was when the arguing started between us. I was already catching hell at work from the female supervisor who I, eventually, filed the EEOC suit against. It was both frustrating at work and frustrating at home.

When we decided to buy a home together around the third year of our relationship, I rented my condo out, and she sold her home. We bought one of the most beautiful condominiums in midtown Valeria. It was a high rise complex located right on Peachtree Street. Things had started getting back to normal, but, after another year of being together, she started the same old shit with the so-called ex-lover.

The difference was that, this time, I wasn't having it. When we would argue, I felt as though my words were not coming across strong enough, so it was at that time that I decided to beat some understanding into her, with all five feet zero inches of me. Paula would never fight back, and, even if she had, it wouldn't have made me stop abusing her. I was determined to make her respect me by physical force. I know that insecurity played a very important role in my actions in hitting her.

What I didn't realize at the time (but I did much later) was this: I never gave Paula a Christmas card, birthday card, flowers for Valentine's Day, not anything. We went 50/50 with the bills, and I would tell her that I loved her almost every day, but I didn't show her. I realized how important this was much later in life. Paula was good to me. She cooked meals during the week despite working. We ate out on weekends, and she would treat me. She washed and folded my clothes. She cleaned. Hell, I never knew what it was to wash anything.

She would buy me clothes to wear. She gave me Christmas gifts and birthday gifts. One Christmas, she told me that I was a selfish lady. I asked her why she would think that. She responded by saying, "You never buy me anything, but I'm always doing things for you." I laughed at that comment and went on about my business. I now wish that I could go back to that day and listen instead of laughing. Maybe, things would be very different. I would buy her flowers everyday if I could go back to that time.

One day, as I was coming in from work, she was leaving with a vase of roses in her hand. I asked her, "Whose flowers are those?"

She looked at me with a smile and said, "Mine."

I asked her, "Who gave you flowers?"

She answered, "My guy friend."

I looked her straight in the eyes and said, "Put them in the trash right now!"

With no questions asked, she did. When I got home that night, I asked her, "Why were you in such a hurry today? So where were you going to put the flowers? Wouldn't that have been just too damned disrespectful to me?" She just sat there as I said to her, "Do you hear me?"

She didn't look at me or say one word.

At that point, I started to beat her so badly that it was a crime. I never hit her in the face because I knew, if I had, she could have had me arrested because of the physical evidence. I had started to abuse her so regularly that she was calling 911 once a week. Before the police arrived, I would always talk her into telling them that it was a misunderstanding and to tell them with a smile that she was okay and that I had left. The beatings had become a regular routine in our lives. It had gotten to point that it was the only way we could make love.

I would intentionally start a fight with Paula, and then I would apologize for hitting her. I would begin kissing her and telling her how much I needed her and how much I loved her. Then, we made such wonderful love. The next day, I would start all over again. My routine was that I kicked her or hit her anywhere but the face, and I pulled her hair. All she could do was cry, but I didn't care. I was tired of her and this dude. I was asking myself what it was going to take for her to completely cut it off with him. My solution was to whip her ass.

It was in the sixth year of our relationship that Paula sat me down and told me that she wanted to leave me. I went berserk and got my pistol from the drawer. I put the gun to her head and, through tears, threatened to kill her if she even thought about it. I was in love with this lady even if I was destroying her spirit.

I couldn't imagine living without her. My family loved her. During Christmas time, Paula would always buy my family Christmas cards, and, on Mother's day, she would send my mother a card. We would visit my family on the week before Christmas because, on Christmas Day, Paula would cook a feast for her entire family. They all came over to celebrate, but they didn't know that we were living together. We put all of the pictures of us together in the closet. Anything that was mine was hidden, so it looked as if she lived alone. I would leave before they arrived, and then come back. I would get the concierge to call her as if I was arriving for Christmas dinner. I was always the last one to arrive, so they never knew.

Somehow, we managed to stay together for two more horrible years. On the eight year, I knew it was time to let go. Sex had completely stopped between us. Before I made that decision, I noticed that she was gone a lot on the weekends, and she had started arriving home late. Also, when I called her job, she was never there. I knew that

Paula didn't talk on the cell phone unless it was an emergency.

When I managed to get to the mailbox before her that following month, I got her phone bill. I opened it, and I found that there was over four hundred dollars in calls. I was in total disbelief. I called the numbers, and they were not to the guy that I had known, but to a man that I would not have ever guessed she was running around with. I knew him, and he was a complete dog— and a married one to boot.

I couldn't wait until she got home! When I confronted her about the man, she didn't say a word. I called the number right in front of her face. The dog's wife answered his phone, and I told her that Paula had placed calls to her husbands' number to the tune of four hundred dollars.

She had him take the phone, which was now on speaker. Paula was still quiet during all of this. When I questioned him about the calls, he acted as if he had no clue. After five minutes of his lying to his wife, we hung up. I had gotten my point across though. The minute I ended that phone conversation was the minute that I began to beat Paula like she had stolen something from me. This time, she fought back, but I was so mad that it meant nothing. She was twice my size, but that didn't matter. I beat her ass for the final time, and I wanted to make it last in her mind forever.

Mission accomplished. Years later, Paula married the guy who she cheated with after his wife divorced him. Even though we were no longer involved, we kept in touch. She would often tell me how she would have nightmares that I was hitting her. I felt bad whenever I would hear that because now I see that I ran her away by being selfish. I wish that I could reverse what I did to her, but I can't. I've told her several times how sorry I am, and how wrong I was. There was and still is a monster in me that I struggle with every day.

After Paula and I broke up, it seemed like my whole world fell apart. Before Paula, I was always attracted to older women, but, after we broke up, I decided to visit this lesbian bar, located one block from my Midtown home. I had always noticed crowds of young women every Friday night. The line into the club wrapped around the building and all of the way to the corner. All that I could see were girls, beautiful girls, trying to get in. I had never wanted to visit a lesbian club until after the breakup.

I had to do something to get my mind off of Paula. I was still in love with her. At times, even to this day, I feel that I still am. I keep searching and searching for someone like her, but there isn't anyone even close. Six months after the breakup, I worked up enough nerve to visit the lesbian spot. Ironically, that was the nickname of the club used by most of the regulars since the club was rented out just on Friday nights to lesbians.

I walked into the club, and all eyes were on me as if I was new candy. I sat at the bar, and, within minutes, this fine, young girl walked up to me and asked me to dance. I said sure since she was so hot. After we danced several songs, I invited her back to my condo.

We walked back to the condo, and, within minutes of walking through the doorway, we were making hot love. She was a real freak. She taught me things that I didn't know could feel so good, such as licking my ass. Even though I was self conscious about it, it felt good.

We hung out for a couple of months afterwards, but, because she was much younger than me and we had nothing in common other than sex, I couldn't develop any true feelings for her. A year passed by, and I had gone through, at least, ten different young women. There were no emotional attachments. I asked myself if I had forgotten how to love or if Paula had actually broken my heart beyond repair. What was wrong with me? What I had done to Paula had turned me into a cold-hearted monster.

The girls wanted to be in my company. Why not? Here I was, living in a popular Midtown high rise, owning a two seat Cadillac convertible, a Range Rover, a convertible Corvette, and a smooth S-class Jaguar with twenty inch chrome rims. I looked like what they were attracted to: money.

These cars later became my pimping tools.

I started hanging at the strip clubs in order to keep meeting girls. These were my favorite spots because I could always find a troubled, abused, or addicted stripper who I could turn. Turning is what it sounds like; I would find a willing girl and turn her into a friend or lover. Since these girls wanted to hang with me, I had no problem getting to them. Most of these young girls needed money, which I didn't want to give. Instead, I thought of my straight male friends who were always begging me for pussy. That was when I made the connection. I would make these women my friends, and, later, I would pimp them out. This was my next dollar-making scheme: I became a female pimp!

This was my pimping game: After I met the young ladies, I treated them to lunch, some dinners, and rides in my luxury cars. I would hook them by treating them well and having fun. Once I had managed to get them into bed, I would tell them during lovemaking that I loved them. They would, to a woman, tell me that they loved me back. They wanted to hang out with me, and, if it took doing anything that I wanted, then they would do it.

When they hinted around (which I always knew was coming) that they needed money to pay a bill, I would tell them that I had a friend coming into town that weekend. Sometimes, I would say that I had a co-worker or that I had this good friend that I wanted them to meet. I would make sure to include that he was a professional and that he was rich. They would always ask why I was introducing them to guys, and I would say something like, "I'm just trying to help you out because I love you. I want you to have dinner with my friend and laugh with him like you do with me. He's going through some heavy shit right now, and, in return, he's gonna give you three hundred dollars."

They would virtually always respond with the same question, "So, that's all? Have dinner with your friend, and he's just gonna just hand me three hundred dollars?"

I would always say, "Well if he wants to fuck you, what's wrong with that? That's three hundred dollars. He's only gonna fuck you for five minutes. And you'll make three hundred dollars in five minutes. Some people work all week for three hundred dollars, but you can make it in five minutes." I knew the next question that was coming was "Well, why don't you fuck him?" I would always say, "Didn't you hear me say he's like my brother or best friend. He doesn't even look at me like that!" I would scream to the top of my voice.

Then, there would always be silence. That method never failed, not even once. I knew the routine with the girls, and it would play out in the same way pretty much every time that I turned a girl. I would, then, break the silence. I would say, "Look, you need the money. Don't think that I will look at you any differently or treat you differently. I love you and that will never change. In fact, I will love you even more if you did this for me! I will take you there and pick you up, so nothing is gonna happen to you, nothing!"

They would always say something like, "Okay, just know I'm only doing this for you. I wouldn't do this otherwise but only because you asked me to." I would be thinking in the back of my mind, "Yeah, right. Sure. It's about me and not the cash," but I would always respond, "Thank you, baby. This is why I love you so much. Now, I know you love me for real, for real. You're my girl for real, for real!" Sometimes, for emphasis, I would clap or jump up and down. You know, make a show of it.

Then, as a present to seal the deal, I would ask something like, "How much did you say that you needed for your electric bill?" or whatever bill that they had. Whatever the amount of the bill was, I would always charge my male friends two hundred more because I knew it was going in my pocket. So, in essence, I would, sometimes, charge the men five hundred dollars and the bill was paid from the extra two hundred. I was trying to make money, not help friends save on sex.

If the girl said that she needed a hundred dollars, then I would flatly tell them, "Well, since I'm helping you and everything, I'm gonna get five hundred from the guy, and I'll keep the two hundred, okay?"

She would scream, "Oh, hell no!" as they always did. I knew this was coming, so I always said, "Look. You need your damn electric bill paid now, and this guy comes into town every week. Do you think a bank just gives you loans for free? They charge you interest! The bottom line is that I can either get someone else I know to get his money or you can get some of it. What you want?"

They always responded, "Okay."

I made sure the girls got to the destination, which was always a hotel room. It was never a dinner like I had told them. I couldn't have my friends buying dinner for the whores. I walked them into the hotel room and introduced them to the "customer." I always made up fake names for the guys, which my male friends had pre-selected. I always told my male friends that this was best for them because they didn't need any stalkers. They didn't need to get attached to any one girl because I had more in my collection that were always more beautiful than the one that I had brought.

This was my salesmanship. I made my friends feel like the next time they would be getting a beauty queen or supermodel. This was my way of keeping customer loyalty between me and my friends, by making them happy and satisfied. I was keeping the girls happy by keeping their bills paid and some cash in their purses. What I didn't want to happen was for them to get together behind my back, so I made sure that no personal information was given to either party. I would tell them this before I got to the hotel. I would say, "Don't give them real names or phone numbers, or I will cut you loose." This threat kept them in line without fail.

Once we got into the room, the male client, without hesitation, would give me the money that I always asked for. I would always sell the girl with questions like, "Look at that ass. You like that? Look at those titties and that pretty face. Ain't she fine?"

The guy would always respond with a grin and a "YES!" I would wait in the lobby of the hotel for an hour at the most, and the timing never failed.

Once the girl would come down from her "appointment", we would get into my car, and I would hand her one hundred dollars. I would kiss her on the lips and say, "I love you, baby. Thank you for doing this for me. This means everything to me."

I would drive the girl home, and not one of them ever questioned the fact that I was making two to three times as much as them without doing much more than overseeing them.

I had gotten my list of girls up to seven, and they were all pretty women with nice figures. They were the very definition of the term "head turner". They all did what I asked without putting up any resistance. Even if a man requested two women, he got them. He just had to pay twice as much. The girls wouldn't talk to each other behind my back because they generally were trying to please me and that made them jealous of each other.

My clientele list began to build through referrals from satisfied customers. I had gotten doctors, pilots, co-workers, and their friends and friends of their friends — basically, men from all walks of life. Money was getting to be pretty damned good. All of the girls had regular clients for either the weekend or during the week. We were making money hand over fist, and it was our secret.

After the girls started selling themselves, I actually stopped performing oral sex on them and only used the dildo. I guess they had gotten emotionally attached to me, so it didn't matter what I did, but, in reality, they wanted dick instead of licking. That is the reason why they were so upfront about being escorts. They could, then, have their cake and eat it, too. I wasn't a fool by any means.

This "escort service" went on from 2000 until 2007. Sometimes, one of my girls would bring in a friend that they could trust, and they would have two on one sex for one thousand dollars. The other side of the coin was that there were a couple of times where some girls would try and set up those situations on their own, which was against my rules. Once they betrayed me, I would always take them for a long ride to a particular lily-white upper crust neighborhood and make them get out of my car, stranding them there, while taking their cell phones.

Leaving them standing there in the middle of the street was my way of punishing them like the betraying dogs that they were. To me, this was the same thought process of someone taking an animal that they didn't want any more, out into the countryside and letting it go. In my mind, they were unfaithful bitches who could no longer live in my house. In my mind, I felt like I had been good to them. It was obvious that they were not going to work out since they had been so underhanded. It was obvious that they loved the screw-for-pay game. It was, also, obvious that they needed money to pay their bills. The loyalty factor was the thing that I just couldn't get past.

I had met Deborah in the spring of 2007. She was very hot and very young. She told me that she was a massage therapist as well as a dancer in the strip clubs. I became fixated on her, but the business side of me was scheming on how to bring her into my "service." I tried my usual methods on her, and they worked, but only to a point. With Deborah, I could not move her past the sex with me phase into the sex with my clientele part. I couldn't get her to do so much as give a client a massage, even though it was her so-called second profession.

Finally, I just stopped asking her. I don't know if it was the fact that she had the backbone to resist me or if it was just pure attraction, but I was beginning to like Deborah a whole lot more than just being a potential trick. We were hanging out all day every day. We were making love all day and night. Because of Deborah, I completely forgot about my clients and the girls. In effect, Deborah made me forget one of the most important things in my life: the almighty dollar.

For a little while, the most loyal girls would bring money by my home from their jobs because I had even stopped taking them to the hotels like I had done in the beginning. I would just set up the appointment from home via the phone. Eventually, they all broke my code and started exchanging numbers and seeing each other behind my back. I couldn't really blame them because I had become a sorry-ass, lazy pimp.

I had allowed my business to go to shit because of one

girl. I had gotten completely sidetracked, but I didn't care. Deborah was giving me the best love I'd had in a while, yet I still didn't love her. I loved the lovemaking, and nothing else. Finally, I was getting fewer calls, the girls started their own separate client lists, and everything fizzled away. Eventually, I was out of the pimping game, and Deborah was, also, a distant memory.

I didn't realize it, but I had been speaking about the newest revelations with my eyes closed. When I finally opened them, Karen was looking at me over her intertwined fingers. Her hands were supporting her chin. She had taken off her glasses, and I could see a hint of tears welling up in her deep-set eyes.

Karen cleared her throat and began speaking. "You were right; those stories were more revealing than the previous stories to a degree. I don't judge anyone on their lives or transgressions because that is not my right or my place. I am here to help you find clarity, and those parts of your life have to be examined, not by me but by you. Tell me, what would you say about yourself? Pretend that you are speaking to you. What would you tell yourself about your actions?"

I sat, arms crossed, in the mahogany chair for what

seemed like two minutes, gathering my thoughts before speaking.

"Angiel, you are a selfish person. No, you are not an evil person or someone who openly tries to hurt people, but you do. Why do you do it? I am not sure. Maybe, you think that you are the center of the universe. Maybe, you think that the rules of life don't apply to you. It could be that you were spoiled from birth, and you are a spoiled brat now. You have used people, taken advantage of others, and, in some ways, karma has come back to you as people took advantage of you.

Of course, you couldn't see it because you were never the problem. It was always someone doing this or that to you, not acknowledging that you have done as much to or more to others. In looking back at your life, Angiel, the only person who mattered, besides your mother, was you. You would do or say, sleep with or marry whomever…whatever it took to get what you needed or wanted, and you had no conscience. I don't like you very much right now, Angiel, and I would like you to be someone else!"

At that point, I burst into tears, looking up at that same familiar spot in the ceiling, but, this time, thinking and feeling much more unburdened.

Karen offered me a tissue from her box, and I dabbed my eyes and cheeks, which quickly disintegrated the tissue. She, then, stood up and came over to me and patted my right shoulder.

"Angiel, that was good what you just experienced. It is what we call in the world of psychology — 'self-actualization'. What this means is when an individual can step outside of his or her own ego and be honest about who, what, why and where they are in life. Some people go an entire lifetime deluding themselves, and they never come to terms with their reality. When you self-actualize, you really know yourself, you cease to lie to yourself, and, most importantly, you become accustomed to being who you are, and you own it.

It takes a lot of courage to speak about yourself in ways that shatter your personal myths and reveal you to be someone other than the superwoman that your ego tells you that you are. The question is whether or not you decide to change, to be a more compassionate person or to revert to the narcissistic, selfish version of yourself. As the saying goes, 'if you talk the talk, you have to walk the walk'. Anyone can talk about changing, but how many can actually do it?"

By this time, I had dried my tears, and I was more composed. "There is one more thing that I didn't cover, and that's this."

At that point, I opened my pocketbook and took out a box of matches, and I, then, placed them on Karen's desk.

"I didn't think much of it until our last meeting and I thought that it was some childish act, like keeping a lucky charm or something. The truth is that, since as far back as I can remember, I have kept a box of matches at all times. Sometimes, I would strike a few, and they would relax me, calm me for some reason. After thinking about it, I wonder if this fixation has anything to do with why I am the way that I am or even why I have those blocks of time where I can't remember things," I said this while making unbroken eye contact with Karen, as if I was looking for an answer in her eyes.

Karen sat back in her chair and said, "Angiel, I had considered recommending hypnosis as a means to uncover some of your lost memories, and, now that you have revealed the matchbox fetish, I am all the more convinced. I would like to schedule a time to proceed. As it stands, I am available this Wednesday."

"I didn't know that you were a hypnotherapist. Sure, if

it can get to the bottom of why I am this way and why I have behaved the way that I have, then let's do it!" I perked up. I was excited about what was to come.

"Fine. If you will make an appointment with the receptionist then, I will see you on Wednesday," Karen said.

I was in anticipation, and I could not sleep for two nights. My appointment was scheduled for ten A.M. that Wednesday, and I arrived nearly thirty minutes early. On this occasion, I was directed to a different room, which was like a lounge as it had a couch with a pillow, a music system, and refreshments. Along the side of the couch was a chair and a table. On the top of the table was what looked to be a digital recorder. I stood in the room, not knowing exactly what to do when Karen entered with my file in her left hand. She ushered me over to the couch.

"Angiel, I want you to relax. Make yourself comfortable. This hypnosis session is not dangerous. You are in control of what you do and say, and no one can influence you. Contrary to movies and television, you cannot be hypnotized into jumping off of a building or doing anything that will harm you. Your subconscious mind guards against you doing anything of that nature. So don't worry. We are just going to try to regress you into your childhood in order to get a few answers. Okay?" Karen said with a soothing, if not motherly tone. "Would you like a cup of chamomile tea? It is very relaxing."

I nodded, and Karen poured a cup of the tea and handed me the cup along with a bottle of sugar. I sweetened the tea and drank it. It was warm and comforting.

"I'm not afraid of anything. In fact, I'm excited to possibly understand the matchbox fixation and what may have caused my loss of time. Any time that you are ready, we can get started," I said with anticipation.

After I finished my tea, she took the cup and placed it on the table where the teapot stood.

"Let's begin," Karen said as she dimmed the lights of the room to a point where I could see stars and planets on the ceiling. They were florescent, and it looked as though it was a view of outer space. The only other light was a small light that Karen was using in order to write and operate the recorder.

"Angiel, I want you to breathe slowly. Inhale through your nose, and exhale through your mouth. When you exhale, imagine that you are blowing your troubles away. I want you to count to ten. Now, I want you to empty your mind. Imagine that you are filling with blue water starting from your feet and ending with your head. Imagine that the water is you and you are the water. Keep breathing in through your nose, out through your mouth slowly. You are doing very well. Now, I want you to go back, back in time, back to when you were five or six, back before you started loving the matches…"

I-I can hear somebody outside in the woods next to the house where we kept the tools and the tractor. I know Mama had told me never to go outside by myself, but there is something going on. I can see a light through the trees and bushes. It sounds like somebody is crying, it sounds like "please" or "I'm sorry". I am so curious; I have to see what it is. I put on my shoes, but I still have my pajamas on. The house is dark, and everyone else is sleeping, I think. I tiptoe out of the back door, and I walk along the fence and slip behind the car parked there. It is dark, so I don't think anyone can see me.

I move closer and closer to the lights and sound, and I get close enough to see through the grapevines that grow in the fields. Now, I can see who the people are. It's my brothers Blaine and Carlton, and they have a man tied up. He looks dirty, and he has a grey beard, and long, greasy brown hair, and he wears overalls and a red flannel shirt. The man is on his knees, and I watch as my brother Blaine hits him in his chest. Then, he lands a hard punch to the mouth. My brother Carlton, then, hits him in the back of the head with the back of an ax. Then, the man falls, face first into the mud that was on the ground. I can hear him plead, "I'm sorry! I'm sorry! Please give me another chance! I'll turn myself in! I swear!"

My brother Blaine yells at him, "You should have thought about that when you were raping my sister, you piece of dog shit! You don't get forgiveness where you are headed!"

Blaine takes the ax from Carlton, and, in one swing of the blade, the man's head is hacked halfway off of his neck, and blood gushes from the top of his torso like a fire hydrant. I put my hands over my mouth to keep from screaming. It seems like I have been in these bushes for two hours, watching as my brothers hack the man into pieces. They dig a hole in the ground, and then they throw everything — the bloody clothes, the ax and the body of the man — into the hole. They douse it with gasoline and then light the pile of flesh and clothes into a bonfire. It burns so high, so high that it lights the night.

"Burning, burning, AAHH! Fire! AHHH! I'm scared!"

"Angiel, I want you to calm down. It's time to wake up now. I'm going to count to five, and then you will wake up, refreshed, and you will feel happy. One, two, three, four, five..."

Epilogue

It has been nearly two years since my therapy sessions with Karen Oppenheim. I have made great strides, and the periods of lost time have diminished to the point that I only have the occasional need to talk to a professional. The cases in which I was a person of interest are still pending. However, I am now free to travel at will since there was only circumstantial evidence linking me to the events.

No one has seen Thomas since the fire that put him out of the furniture upholstery profession, and he is now considered a "missing person." Britney, his favorite assistant, has turned his place of business into a thriving modeling agency, albeit the fact that the "models" are more of the exotic dancer variety.

Adam, the so-called friend, has lost all of his properties, and two were alleged victims of arson, though the insurance company is investigating the claim since an informant called them to implicate Adam in insurance fraud. The informant supposedly told them that Adam had paid him one thousand dollars to set fire to the two duplexes.

The reverend who had tried to buy my property from under me succeeded in doing so, but the property became infested with mold and rats, causing him to lose thousands in repairs. Because of this and not being able to rent the property to a paying tenant because of the danger of the mold, he, too, lost the property to foreclosure.

As of the moment, I am doing as well as can be expected, considering the underlying issues that I have lived with for my entire existence. The hypnosis, as described by Dr. Oppenheim, revealed the trauma, which led to many of the obsessions that I manifested. I am now socially functional, and I have good and bad days just as anyone. I have tried to view things through my perspective of how I want to be treated — the "Golden Rule" way. I am not perfect, and I still, to this day, find myself having to resist a self-centered view of any situation. I struggle with this like it was an addiction, and, in a way, it is. It is the addiction of egocentrism.

One Thursday afternoon, I happened to be watching the show *Mind Talk* with Dr. Sara James. Dr. James is a renowned psychiatrist who deals in topics of the mind and spirit. On this particular show, the topic was "Unusual Personality Disorders." I was only half-listening, while I was cleaning my condominium, until I heard Dr. James say, "Joining me now is a psychologist who has written a book on deviant personality disorders. Her book, titled *No One is Forgiven,* tells the story of her work with an extreme patient who, not only suffered from a narcissistic disorder, but who exhibited signs of dual personality syndrome. Please welcome Dr. Karen Oppenheim."

The audience applauded while I stood in front of the television appalled.

I could not focus on the screen as I was in a daze. Karen Oppenheim was now an author, and she was on a nationally syndicated talk show! Whose story was she revealing? Who was suffering from a dual personality? Could that person be me? If the person was me, then who or what was the other personality? Had Karen learned things about me that she had kept hidden?

At that moment, I had to do something. My head was spinning, and my thoughts were going in all directions. I grabbed my keys and rushed to my car. It took what seemed like two hours to drive to the bookstore as this trip was at the height of rush hour. I jerked the car into park, slammed my door, and rushed into the bookstore. I made a beeline to the psychology/self help section of the bookstore, and I found Karen's book sitting prominently in the section as a featured book. The words of the book were in crimson red and in bold print on a silver toned background. The title shouted, "NO ONE IS FORGIVEN" by Dr. Karen Oppenheim.

I snatched a copy of the book from the shelf. I didn't even bother to read the blurb on the back of the book nor one single page. I simply stood in line and paid the $24.95 retail price, and I went home to read what Karen had revealed. I needed to know who was the subject of her book, what the subject person of her book did or said or if she was or wasn't using me and my story for profit. Was I being used once again by someone who I had trusted? Was I being used once again by a person who was sworn by the oath of her profession to secrecy? If that was the case, then I have had more than enough, and there would be hell for someone to pay.

Before going home, I had one more purchase to make on that day. I stopped at the local convenience store for a box of wooden matches, the childhood obsession that I had weaned myself of two years ago. I sat in my car for a while as I laughed and I cried simultaneously, the mixed emotions being perfectly appropriate for the circumstance. I looked with smoldering anger at the book sitting on my passenger seat, which I felt seemed to be both ironic and, at the same time, mock my entire existence. I opened the book to the first page, and, with trepidation, I began reading.

No One is Forgiven

By
Karen Oppenheim

CHAPTER ONE

Who really knows who we are? As a clinical psychologist, I am exposed to a myriad of different personality types, which range from the simply deviant to the highly psychotic. Each case is different; yet, they share basic similarities: childhood trauma, shock, chemical imbalances, and other such reasons for the behavior. Typically, I am nonplussed by the nature of what the patient reveals. Yet, on certain rare occasions, there have been patients of extreme note, even ones who merit study and documentation as a paradigm.

One such case is the subject of my dissertation, a woman who I will refer to during the course of the book as "Eve" for the sake of anonymity. To use the name of a subject would be in violation of the client/doctor confidentiality clause, so I will not give any description of the patient. I will only discuss the extreme manifestation of her psychosis.

To the original question of who we are, the answer to this is an enigmatic one in many ways. Are we what we appear to be to others or are we what we appear to be to ourselves? Is a man or woman good or bad, or is this simply a subjective concept that varies from one person's consciousness to another? Can we be good people and do bad things, or is the concept of what is bad or wrong merely a human construct? The question remains: Are we what we think, and do we become what we believe ourselves to be? This is a paradox of existence which is as much of an argument as is the chicken/egg question.

Eve was a relatively innocuous client on the surface; yet, underneath, in the recesses of her mind laid the most convoluted series of personality combinations, rationale, and a blatantly egocentric view of life. She was apparently indulged and coddled by her parents to a ridiculous degree, which bordered on fantasy. This treatment led to actions which necessitated a diagnosis of "Narcissistic Personality Disorder" or in layman's terms an egomaniac. In her perception, it is literally a case of the proverbial "world revolving around her." Although there are many instances of extreme ego in everyday life, in my opinion her disorder symptoms were the cause of a subset of schizophrenia called "Dissociative Personality Disorder."

The accepted, non-clinical term for this disorder is "multiple personalities." Eve was a chaotic pool of emotion and pseudo-logic, and she exhibited paranoia, in addition to her other maladies. Frequently, while in counsel with Eve, she would seemingly morph into a series of personalities: A ruthless female who was filled with hate, venom and revenge, a male figure who was manipulative and dominant, and then to a childlike, innocent girl who was always good and never hurt anyone.

It appeared that Eve was, at times, vicariously aware of the other personalities as she spoke of them, at times, being "a spectator in my own life." These personalities may have been involved in shady activities that would implicate Eve in criminal investigations. Yet, these entities seemed to operate in a state of law created by the need of each entity. For instance, if one sought revenge, then there were few boundaries. If the other wanted material trappings, then the only rule was the objective. These entities seemed to possess a "take no prisoners" aspect of their existence, and no one was immune to their objectives.

I did not stop until I had read Karen's entire book, which took me a little more than eleven hours. I started pacing around my condo like a caged animal looking for a way out. My head was spinning, and I felt a sense of betrayal. The story was about me and supposedly due to the "Eve" pseudonym, not about me. What more had Karen learned about me during our hypnotherapy sessions and withheld from me? Could it be possible that she was simply embellishing the book to make it sell? Even if that were the case, it seemed that far too much of it was based on my life. If "Eve" was not exactly me, then what percentage of her was? What was the story of the multiple entities? Was there a man who resides in my subconscious?

The book was an amalgamation of so many things both monstrous and sublime that it made me furious whenever I thought about it. I started feeling emotions that I had never felt in such a way before— feelings of malice and a desire to hurt. I began to frantically rip pages from the book as I laughed and cried like a madwoman. After I finished trashing the book, I threw the pages into the garbage can next to my coffee table. I took the bottle of bourbon that I had kept, unopened for years, out of my kitchen closet. I opened it and took a huge swig from the bottle. I soaked what was left of Karen's book, and it joined the ripped pages, which were also drenched.

I opened the box of matches, lit a match, and placed it to the cover. It took a while, but, eventually, the book was

Meleisa Betts

awash in flames. I, then, blew the match out, and I watched the ceiling intently as the cascading blue smoke formed an "O" before disappearing into nothingness. That journal of untold truths had been tossed into the waste where I felt it belonged. I watched as it became equal parts binder, torn pages, and ashes. I struck yet another match, and I gazed at the flame, seeing nothing but the yellow of heat and the burning stalk that gave it sustenance. I thought to myself, *Karen chose the perfect title... absolutely no one, not a one of them, will ever be forgiven. Someone, somewhere, somehow, or even something will certainly make sure of it.*